A DECEPTIVE HOMECOMING

Center Point
Large Print

Also by Anna Loan-Wilsey and available from Center Point Large Print:

A Lack of Temperance

**This Large Print Book carries the
Seal of Approval of N.A.V.H.**

A DECEPTIVE HOMECOMING

Anna Loan-Wilsey

CENTER POINT LARGE PRINT
THORNDIKE, MAINE

This Center Point Large Print edition is published
in the year 2015 by arrangement with
Kensington Publishing Corp.

The text of this Large Print edition is unabridged.
In other aspects, this book may vary
from the original edition.
Printed in the United States of America
on permanent paper.
Set in 16-point Times New Roman type.

ISBN: 978-1-62899-698-2

Library of Congress Cataloging-in-Publication Data

Loan-Wilsey, Anna.
A deceptive homecoming : a Hattie Davish mystery / Anna Loan-
Wilsey. — Center Point Large Print edition.
pages cm
ISBN 978-1-62899-698-2 (library binding : alk. paper)
1. Large type books. I. Title.
PS3612.O23D43 2015
813′.6—dc23

2015023866

To Maya

Acknowledgments

I would like to thank Sarah Elder, Curator of Collections at the St. Joseph Museums, for her time, her expertise, and her willingness to guide me through tunnels below what is now the Galore Psychiatric Museum and was once part of the State Lunatic Asylum #2. Her insights into the history of St. Joseph were invaluable, and any errors are mine alone.

I would also like to thank the St. Joseph Convention & Visitors Bureau, especially Mary Supple, for going out of their way to be helpful and welcoming. I left their office loaded with historical research materials, a contact list of local experts, and the address for the best tearoom in town. A true Midwestern welcome!

To the art duo of Kristine Mills and Judy York at Kensington, I want to express my gratitude and awe for re-creating the very scene I imagined as Hattie returned to her childhood home.

Finally, I'd be more than remiss if I didn't thank my husband, Brian, for his inspired suggestions. This would've been a very different book without them!

It is more shameful to distrust our friends than to be deceived by them.

—CONFUCIUS, 551–479 B.C.

A DECEPTIVE HOMECOMING

Chapter 1

And then it was my turn to view the body.

So, why was I hesitating?

Was it the whispers I heard as the girls spoke to each other behind their hands? Did they think I hadn't noticed their stares? Was it the surprise and dismay that flashed across Ginny's face when I arrived? Was it the unpleasant transformation of a room I'd laughed in, played in, felt at home in? Or was it the memory of other dead bodies I've seen in less familiar settings?

"Ahem . . ."

I turned to the buxom woman waiting behind me in line at the casket. The plumes of gray egret feathers on her hat dangled down, tickling her cheek. She ineffectively tried to blow them away.

"Are you going to pay your respects, miss?" She blew at the feathers again.

"Yes, of course." I took a deep breath and took a step forward. I glanced across the room at Ginny once more, now deep in conversation with a woman I faintly recognized, before turning toward the body.

Poor Ginny, I thought as I gazed down at the dead man. And then I froze, breathless. Despite seeing my share of dead bodies, nothing had prepared me for this. I'd known Mr. Hayward in life. Besides being my friend's father, Frank Hayward had taught me everything I knew about bookkeeping.

Oh my God, what happened to him?

"I heard he was disfigured," the woman behind me said, leering over my shoulder, "but I had no idea." I could feel her breath on my neck as she blew at her feathers again.

Frank Hayward had aged considerably since I'd last seen him: His hair was completely gray, deep wrinkles stretched out about his eyes and mouth and across his forehead, and the skin beneath his throat sagged. I couldn't resist the urge to gently touch his cheek. His skin felt waxy as I expected but was dotted with strange indentations, as if someone had periodically poked him with a pencil. And then there was his nose, or at least what the undertakers had made of it.

"Trampled by a horse, they say," the woman, her breath reeking of onions, said against my ear. I jerked my hand away.

Why must she stand so close? I glanced behind me hoping she would take a step back, but her eyes were focused on the body in the casket in front of me. She blew at her feathers again.

"*Un, deux, trois . . .*" I began counting in French to calm down. The woman wasn't going anywhere, so I took a deep breath and turned toward the body once again.

The animal had smashed the left side of the

dead man's face, crushing his left cheek and completely disfiguring his nose. The undertaker had attempted to reconstruct his face, painting his face with a tan cosmetic, filling his cheek with something to try to puff it out again and adding painted clay to his nose. Whether he was working from a poor memory or a bad photograph, the undertaker had failed in his effort to make the deceased appear as he had in life.

Something's not right, I thought.

Crash! "Aaaah!"

We all turned at the sound of glass breaking and startled shrieks. Marigolds, periwinkle, rosemary, and branches of cypress, mixed with small shards of glass that twinkled in the candlelight, littered the floor. A wreath stand, one of its three legs broken, lay sprawled on top of the flower heap. In its descent, it had knocked down several glass vases set on a table beside it. Two middle-aged women, both with red faces and hands held to their chests, stood a few feet away. One took a deep breath and giggled in embarrassment.

"How silly to be startled by flowers," she said to no one in particular, "though the stand did nearly hit us." The other woman nodded as she continued to stare at the jumble of glass, ribbon, wood, and flowers near her feet.

A young girl appeared almost immediately with broom in hand. A stout woman with dimples rushed in to help. I glanced over at Ginny. She, like the rest of us, stood watching, transfixed by the unfortunate scene. When she looked up, our eyes met. She immediately turned to the portly man beside her. I turned my back and stared down once again at the corpse. I instantly felt the overwhelming sense of anxiety again.

"Please move along." The woman behind me nudged me with her elbow. I ignored her and stood my ground as I searched the dead man's face, hands, and body for a clue to explain my misgivings. The woman behind me, in danger of herself being replaced at the casket's side by an elderly man with a cane, not so gently bumped me with her ample, plump hip. "You've had more than your share of time."

"I'm sorry." I stumbled a few steps away from the casket, not so much from the woman's push but from the growing apprehension that I was missing something vital.

"What's wrong with me?" I mumbled to myself. The face of the dead man had been disfigured and then reconstructed almost beyond recognition. What was it I expected to find? And then it hit me!

I glanced in horror at the tableau before me. The white casket, the flickering candlelight, and the bouquets of brightly colored flowers struck a sharp contrast to the lifeless figure lying prostrate, the line of grieving well-wishers, and the distraught daughter receiving more friends and family all dressed in black. It was wrong, all wrong.

Suddenly I felt a hand on my shoulder. I nearly jumped.

"Miss Davish, are you all right?" Miss Clary, a slender young woman, stood before me with concern in her large blue eyes. "You look like a specter tapped you on the shoulder."

I'd met her when I'd first arrived and had to wait to speak with Ginny. She was the secretary to the president of Mrs. Chaplin's school. I stared at her, unable to respond.

"Are you all right?" she repeated. I nodded but allowed her to guide me to a nearby chair. I sat, staring at Ginny. Did Ginny know? How could she? How could she not?

"How could who know what, Miss Davish?" Miss Clary was standing beside me. I'd no idea she was still there. I'd no idea that I had said anything out loud.

"It's not there," I whispered, barely audible to myself let alone the young woman beside me.

"Did you say something, Miss Davish?" Miss Clary bent down to hear me. I shook my head. What could I say? I couldn't tell her the truth. But I knew whom I should tell. I rose from my chair, aware of Miss Clary's hand on my arm. "Feeling better?"

"If you'll excuse me, I need to speak with Miss Hayward."

"Of course. Poor Virginia."

I merely nodded in response, still in shock

and baffled as to how I was going to tell Ginny what I discovered. Her father wasn't the man in the casket.

What am I doing here?
Ginny had asked me the same question when I arrived earlier.

I had traveled hundreds of miles across the country to be here and had come straight from the depot. Thinking only of her, I'd immediately scanned the Haywards' parlor for Ginny. Little groups of people, dressed in black and speaking in hushed voices, had mingled about, and the room was bursting with bouquets, wreaths, and colorful, fragrant flowers. The fireplace was lit to warm the crisp morning air, but the room was dimmed by the thick, drawn curtains. I dabbed my eyes with my handkerchief as I stared at the mantel. A portrait I knew to be of Mr. Frank Hayward was draped in black crape above it; the end of the fabric had been singed by the fire. I then glanced at the white coffin against the far wall, its lid raised like a flag and glowing in the reflection of a dozen candles lit nearby.

I spotted Miss Gilbert, the longtime typing instructor, a tall, thin woman with pursed lips and gray hair with a few lasting black streaks, who must now be in her late fifties. She chewed on the nails of her long fingers as she watched over the proceedings. I caught her eye and gestured to her in recognition. She nodded slightly before focusing her attention on a group of young girls, students most likely, who were whispering behind their hands as I passed by. Each stole a glance at me and then giggled.

What's that all about? I thought.

"That is her," I heard one whisper before they all openly stared at me.

"Girls!" Miss Gilbert hissed, appropriately chastising the girls into silence.

And then I spied Ginny and forgot about the girls. She was standing near the piano, the instrument barely visible beneath dozens of garlands of marigolds. She was flanked by a portly, middle-aged man, with a profusion of white curls and long, thick burnsides, who held her hand in both of his, on one side, and a stout woman of similar age, with wispy, fawn-colored hair, deep creases about her eyes, and dimples, pronounced despite her clouded countenance, on the other. Both were dressed in the highest fashions and wore black mourning jewelry, embellished with diamonds.

With porcelain skin, silky, perfectly coiffured yellow hair, Ginny stood out, as she always did in any crowd. It didn't matter whether it was a ball, an etiquette class, or a stroll in the park; she always drew everyone's attention. So I wasn't surprised that even at her father's funeral, dressed in a black Henrietta, embellished with black ribbon and crape, and a simple bonnet with a long crape veil, she was stunning. I pulled a stray strand of hair behind my ear, brushed my skirt for soot (a useless task as I was wearing black as well), and straightened my hat before making my way across the room.

"Hattie?" Ginny said when she saw me approach. She was fiddling with the gold heart-shaped locket her father had given her on her eighteenth birthday. I was one of only a few people who knew it contained a lock of her mother's hair.

"Oh, Ginny. I'm truly sorry." I leaned in to give her a hug. She barely returned my embrace.

"What are you doing here?" It wasn't the response I'd anticipated.

"What do you mean? As soon as I learned what happened, I had to come. How are you doing? Is there anything I can do?"

"How did you find out?"

"Someone sent me the funeral notice from the newspaper." *Why does that matter?*

"It was nice of you, Hattie, but you really didn't need to come all this way."

And with that she turned to the man who'd been standing beside her since the moment I walked in. He put his arm around her and whispered something in her ear. I stood still for a moment, half expecting her to turn back to me, half waiting for her to introduce me to her companions. When she didn't, I glanced behind me at the line of callers waiting to speak to Ginny and slowly

18

stepped aside. When an elderly lady in a half-mourning hat of black and brown stepped in front of me to catch Ginny's attention, I took the moment to study my long-time friend. Her deep-set frown was understandable, but not at all the expression I expected. I'd seen my share of sorrow, especially of late, but Ginny didn't show any visible signs that I recognized: red-rimmed, puffy sad eyes, and bowed, trembling shoulders. Her countenance bore deep-seated dismay or displeasure, and not grief. She hadn't even been holding a handkerchief. The Ginny I knew would've been inconsolable, not simply put out.

Has she changed that much in the time that I was gone?

At Mrs. Chaplin's School for Women, Ginny, Myra, and I had been close, the Three Musketeers, Mrs. Chaplin had called us. We'd taken every class together, attended every lecture, picnic, and concert together, and shared with each other the dreams only young girls dare to have. When my father died, I'd been so shaken, so despondent, I'd thought of leaving school. Ginny and Myra had convinced me to stay. After we graduated, we corresponded regularly. Myra had taken a post as a stenographer in the mail order department at Jordan Marsh in Boston while Ginny stayed in St. Joseph to run her father's household. Like me, Ginny's mother had died when she was young and her father had never remarried.

Tragically, Myra died of influenza a little over a year ago. Ginny had been my last true friend, until I met Walter. Ginny and I had continued to write. In fact, she'd written me less than a month ago voicing concerns about the school. She hadn't confided any details and I'd been left to wonder. When I'd learned of her father's sudden death, I didn't hesitate to attend the funeral and do whatever I could to ease her pain.

Yet now, after seeing the wrong body in the coffin, I wished I had never come.

Chapter 2

"May I have a moment, Ginny?"

"Of course, Hattie. What is it?" She glanced around the room instead of looking at me. I followed her gaze and noticed the gentleman with the muttonchops who had comforted her earlier now preoccupied by several women in a corner of the room.

Who is he? I wondered as I watched him nod his head in earnest agreement to something one of the ladies had said. He then embraced the woman. When I returned to Ginny, she was still watching him.

"It's very important, Ginny." I needed to pull her attention back to me. I touched her lightly on the arm. She flinched at my touch.

"Well, what is it?"

Her impatience took me aback and I hesitated. What had happened to the girl I knew? Grief alone couldn't possibly explain her coldness, her altered behavior. I hadn't been sure how to broach the subject, but now it took all I had to tell her the truth.

"You might want to sit down."

"Thank you for your concern, but I'm fine."

"What I have to say may come as a shock."

"My father's dead, Hattie. What could be more of a shock than that?" She still refused to meet my glance. She began twiddling with the locket again. I leaned in closely even as she shied away from me.

"The man in the casket isn't your father, Ginny," I whispered. My friend's head snapped around and her eyes flared open.

That got her attention. Was that hope, shock, or fear I saw flash across her face? In an instant, the look was gone, replaced by a very distinct snarl of anger.

"How dare you?" she seethed under her breath, grabbing my arm and pulling me to the side.

"I know it sounds inconceivable, but it's true."

"Hush, Hattie. You hush up!"

"Ouch, Ginny, you're hurting me." She released the pinching grip she held on my arm and took a step back.

"I'm sorry," she said, unable to meet my gaze.

21

"I'm sorry too. I didn't know I'd upset you this much. I actually thought you'd be relieved." If someone had given me hope that my dear father had been alive, I would've been grateful, not livid. "I thought it would bring you hope."

"What are you talking about, Hattie?"

"The man in the casket doesn't bear your father's eyebrow scar." It was the one distinguishing mark I knew Mr. Hayward to have, a prominent scar above his right eye, across his eyebrow. I remember staring at it as a student wondering what had created the wound. Being that close, it must've been a relief when his eye wasn't damaged. I'd asked Ginny once, I'd been so curious, but she didn't know.

Ginny's shoulders sagged as she took a deep breath. With her eyes still averted, she shook her head. Finally, she looked at me. "I'd heard you'd been mixed up with the police and murders and other ghastly business, but I never thought it would affect your judgment. You've always been a very rational, practical girl, Hattie Davish."

"I still am. Your father had a scar above his right eye, across his eyebrow." I motioned to the exact placement of the scar with my finger above my own eye. "The man in the casket doesn't bear that scar."

"It was above his left eye, Hattie. His left." His left side was the side damaged by the horse. Any

22

trace of the scar would've been destroyed by the trauma done to the poor man's face.

Oh my God, what have I done?

As realization of the mistake I'd made dawned on my face, Ginny surprised me again. Instead of railing against me for my ghastly mistake, for the false hope I'd placed in her, for the spectacle I'd made at this most solemn of occasions, her countenance softened and she patted me on the cheek.

"I'm his daughter, Hattie. Do you think I wouldn't have noticed?"

"I'm sorry, Ginny." I placed my hand on hers. "I don't know how I could've made such a dreadful mistake." Truly, I'd no idea. All of my memories of Mr. Frank Hayward had the scar cutting across his right eyebrow. Could time have tainted all my memories of home? "Can you forgive me?"

"Of course, Hattie. You meant well. Coming all this way after all these years. I remember how difficult it was when your father died. You were trying to spare me the same grief."

She was right. If my memories of anything or anyone in St. Joseph were tainted it was because they were clouded by the loss of my father and the memory of his horrible end.

"Thank you for coming, Hattie." She gently pulled her hand away. I nodded, still shocked by what I'd done. I was suddenly eager to put distance between me and the friend whom I'd traveled hundreds of miles to see. I'd come to comfort her, not to cause her more pain. "Be safe returning home."

Home. She'd said it gently, but the irony wasn't lost on me, even in my present state. Where was home? Newport? Where Walter waited for me? Richmond, where Sir Arthur lived? Any of the countless cities and towns I'd visited in my travels? No. Wasn't St. Joe supposed to be my home? I'd been born and raised here. I was baptized here. My parents and baby brother were buried here. Yet clearly Ginny knew, whether I wanted to believe it or not, that St. Joseph wasn't my home anymore.

"We will begin." A broad man wearing the clerical collar of a minister took his place near the casket.

As I made my way toward my seat, I heard Ginny call out, "Mr. Upchurch," a slight pleading in her voice. I glanced back to see Ginny reaching out to the man in the muttonchops. He immediately left his companions, crossed the room in a few long strides, and took her hands in his.

"Are you not well, my darling girl?" Tears began to stream down her face as she shook her head. He gently guided her into his comforting embrace. He then led her to her seat.

I turned away before the tears welled up in my own eyes. I nodded greetings to a few girls who inappropriately waved and giggled as my gaze fell upon them. Before I had time to ponder why they were acting silly, the minister began the service. I put my head down, unable to look at Ginny or the casket, while the minister's voice rose and fell in accordance to the sentiment he was trying to convey. I heard little of his actual words. Instead, I prayed: for Mr. Hayward's soul, for Ginny's peace, and for forgiveness for my unconscionable mistake. When I finished, I glanced up and wished I hadn't. Ginny sat stiff in her chair, a handkerchief clenched in her hand in her lap. Her face was frightfully pale, even her normally rosy lips were pale. She looked straight ahead, her clear eyes unblinking. For an instant she glanced my way and our eyes met. Mortified, I dropped my gaze once more. When I finally glanced about again, a small bouquet of flowers caught my eye. In a vase, set between a large wreath of intertwining cypress and weeping willow, and a bouquet of marigold, heliotrope, and forget-me-nots, was an arrangement of zinnia and mullein with sprigs of agrimony tucked in.

How odd, I thought.

If I'd been anywhere else but a funeral, I would've dismissed the message the flowers conveyed as accidental or ill-conceived. But here, I couldn't fathom how anyone could make such a blunder. Or maybe I could, immediately recalling what I'd just done.

How could I've made such a horrible mistake?

I glanced at Ginny. Her posture and gaze hadn't changed. With a tightening growing in my chest, I focused again on the flowers. The sprigs of agrimony must've been added as an afterthought, for surely the florist would've corrected the error. Obviously someone hadn't realized the message they conveyed by adding the tiny yellow flowers. Agrimony means "gratitude" or "thankfulness." What an unfortunate sentiment to make at some-one's funeral.

With the service finally over and one last glance at the bouquet, I rose from my seat as quickly as decorum allowed. I slipped past the mirror and the paintings draped in black crape in the hall, and was one of the first out the door. The warmth of the sun on my face was cold comfort knowing that I wasn't the only one who'd made a dreadful mistake today.

Chapter 3

"I can't believe I'm talking to Miss Hattie Davish," the girl squealed. She, and several of the girls around her, giggled.

"Hush, girls. This is a place of mourning. You will pay more respect to the occasion, and that includes not pestering Miss Davish."

"Yes, Miss Gilbert," the girls answered in unison.

"Thank you, Miss Gilbert. It was very nice to meet you all, though." I was still taken aback by the attention I'd received from the students.

After the funeral, I'd taken a place toward the back of the procession that walked to the cemetery. After the interment of the body, many of us walked back to the Hayward house for a light meal. The moment I stepped in the door, I'd found myself surrounded by starry-eyed, giggling students from my alma mater, Mrs. Chaplin's School for Women, who bombarded me with questions.

"What was it like to find your employer in a trunk?"

"Is it true that you saw a dead Santa Claus?"

"Were you really poisoned by a traitorous copperhead?"

"Wasn't it glamorous to work for Mrs. Mayhew?"

Other than Mrs. Trevelyan's death, which, due to her political prominence, had made several national newspapers, I'd no idea that word of my misadventures had preceded me. From their smiles and giggles, these silly girls had no idea how horrible it was to find a dead body. Their enthusiasm was ghoulish and particularly inappropriate. My friend's father had been brutally killed and these girls wanted to know about how many times the Newport socialite changed dresses during the day. I was quite relieved when Miss Malinda Gilbert, the school's typing instructor, stepped in.

"Besides, you'd think Miss Davish was a celebrity for all the hullabaloo."

"But she is, Miss Gilbert," one of the students, a round-faced, chubby girl, said. "She's worked with Mrs. Charlotte Mayhew, Mrs. Edwina Trevelyan, and countless other rich and famous people. And she's solved murders that the police couldn't! Geez, Miss Gilbert, Miss Davish is probably the most famous person to ever attend our school."

"Fiddlesticks! Now go, all of you. Go help with refreshments."

"Thank you, Miss Gilbert," I said, watching the girls race away. I was still taking in the idea that these naïve girls thought I was someone to idolize. "Can you believe that we were that young once?"

"I wouldn't encourage them," she snapped. "I wouldn't want you to be responsible for having those impressionable young minds see you as a role model, given the path you took."

"Pardon me? The path I took? I'm well-respected because I took advantage of my education at Mrs. Chaplin's, and I strive to be the best at what I do. I'd never discourage another girl from emulating me." I'd never had to defend myself so blatantly, but then again I'd done all kinds of things in the past year I'd never done before.

"No one denies you've been very successful in

your professional life. But to involve yourself with the darkest side of our society calls into question your personal judgment."

"The darkest side of our society? I've encountered a great deal of unseemly behavior of late. Which are you referring to: saloon smashing, poisoning, smuggling, slogan shouting, extravagant spending, rotten vegetable throwing, or character assassinating?"

"Murder, Miss Davish," Miss Gilbert said coldly. "No woman can soil herself with the stench of murder and think she is clean."

"I didn't kill anyone."

"You didn't have to."

She bit the nail on her little finger. I remembered her habit from my student days. "To type, one must keep one's nails very short," she'd explained. I preferred to use a trimmer and file.

"Hattie!" Mrs. Chaplin shouted as she approached, trailed by several faculty members I recognized from my days at her school. I smiled as I recalled how often that same booming voice had sent shivers of fear down my spine. Now she was coming to my aid.

Unusually tall with thick white hair piled on top of her head, she'd barely changed since the last time I saw her. She had a few more wrinkles about her shrewd blue eyes, perhaps, and a slight stoop in her right shoulder, but she was the same dynamic woman I remembered. She stopped before me and patted me briskly on the back, almost causing me to take a forward step. She'd lost no strength in her hands, but I could see now why she'd decided to give up her post as president of the school; her fingers were knobbed with arthritis.

"I see you've been reacquainted with our capable Miss Gilbert." That wasn't the word I would've used to describe her, but I held my tongue and simply nodded. "And, of course, you remember these ladies?"

"Of course." I was glad to see their smiling, friendly faces.

Madame Maisonet, the French teacher, a tiny, white-haired woman in her late sixties, took my hand and patted it. *"Bienvenue, ma chère!* Welcome!"

"Merci, Madame."

Every student of Mrs. Chaplin's school was required to take Madame Maisonet's rudimentary French language class. "Every educated person in this world knows some French," Mrs. Chaplin had said. She'd been right. My lessons had allowed me to read menus at several high-society dinners, as well as communicate with Mrs. Mayhew's French chef more easily. But in addition to adding a touch of sophistication to my résumé, I owed much of my sanity to this little French lady. Without her trick of counting in French to calm down, I probably would've let my impatience and frustration get the best of me more than once.

"We're very proud of you, Miss Davish," a middle-aged woman with spectacles that kept slipping down her thin nose said. I couldn't recall her maiden name but remembered she'd taught the shorthand classes before she left the school to marry.

"Yes, we all are." Mrs. Chaplin's voice boomed as she nodded vigorously. "Especially since we can take credit for some of your success!" The ladies shared in a subdued laugh. "You wouldn't have broken out of that shell of yours if we hadn't pushed you. 'Don't sell yourself short,' I said. 'Don't drown in a typing pool,' I said. 'Be a secretary, Hattie,' I said. 'A stenographer or a typist is paid to do, but a secretary is paid to think,' I said. Do you remember, Hattie?"

"Of course, I owe you all so much."

"Well, then, when you have time, if you get a chance, perhaps you could share some of your secrets for success with my students?" Miss Corcoran, who taught English and penmanship, said. A few years older than me, she'd been teaching only two years when I took her class. I remembered her as a small, meek woman with stubby fingers. She differed little from my memory, except now a few strands of gray streaked through her dark flaxen hair.

"Of course, if you think it appropriate." I purposely avoided Miss Gilbert's glare.

"Always the humble one," Mrs. Chaplin said. "Ah, Hattie, you haven't changed a bit. Of course you will speak to the students. I've already spoken to Mr. Upchurch and it's all arranged."

There was that name again—Upchurch, the man with the muttonchops who was comforting Ginny. I wanted to inquire as to who he was, but first I had to know what Mrs. Chaplin was talking about.

"All arranged? What's all arranged?"

"As soon as we found out that you were coming, we arranged for a lake party. You'll be the guest of honor," Mrs. Chaplin explained. "You can speak to the girls then. The girls will be inspired and the faculty will get a much-needed morale boost."

"A lake party?"

I needn't ask which lake. When someone in the area said "lake," there was no doubt that they referred to Lake Contrary, thus called because its source, Contrary Creek, flowed north, contrary to all other creeks and rivers in the area, including the Missouri. A large oxbow, created when the Missouri River changed course, it was once nearly eight miles long and one half to a mile wide. And I needn't ask why host a party there. It's what everyone did in St. Joseph in the summertime. One could easily find an announcement for a lake party every single day, May through September, in the *Social and Personal* of any area newspaper. But why now?

"I'd be glad to help distract everyone from the shock and grief of losing Mr. Hayward," I said, "but do you really think a lake party appropriate this soon after—"

Mrs. Chaplin cut me off. "Yes, yes, it's tragic what happened to Frank Hayward, but I think even Virginia would agree that your arrival couldn't have come at a better time."

I knew for certain Virginia wouldn't agree. She'd have been happier if I hadn't arrived at all. And I certainly could think of a better time to arrive than for a funeral.

"I myself won't be attending, so I expect a visit from you before you leave town, young lady." As I opened my mouth to protest the lake party again, she said, "I won't hear a 'no' from Mrs. Chaplin's School for Women's star alumna. You must think of the school, Hattie."

"Very well, Mrs. Chaplin," I said. "If you think it will help."

Chapter 4

Even at this early hour, pedestrians crossing the street had to step carefully to avoid the pungent dung piles. Horses and buggies already had to compete for space on the street with men in caps, pushed back high on their foreheads, pulling carts covered with heavy, stained canvas and with electric streetcars, attached to the air by wires, clanging down tracks in the middle of the road. Despite the warm air, smoke from chimneys curled up from all parts of the city—the power plants, the forges, and the mills had begun the workday. I'd forgotten why I'd always risen early, not because my profession demanded it of me, but because I was accustomed to it. The city awakened before dawn. And this morning had been no different.

After promising Mrs. Chaplin I'd be ready when the carriage arrived to take me to the lake, I'd returned to my hotel. The St. Charles Hotel was an unassuming three-story brick building with two wings, a central second-story balcony, red-and-white-striped awnings, and a corner entrance, a few steps away from the streetcar tracks on Fifth Street. It was nothing like the Pacific House over on Third and Francis or the Arcadia Hotel in Eureka Springs, but it was respectable, reasonably-priced, and far better than I was once used to.

With the events of the day catching up to me, I'd avoided the dining room and had gone straight to bed. I'd fallen almost immediately to sleep, but after a few hours I tossed and turned as images of rearing horses, caskets, and the scowl on Ginny's gentle face filled my head. Eventually I gave up on getting any more rest. I splashed water on my face, pulled my hair into a bun, and changed into my golden brown bias skirt and my new tan-and-white-striped shirtwaist with excessive sleeves. I pinned my braid straw with the yellow silk bow on my head and went for a stroll to reacquaint myself with the city of my birth.

But things had changed. As I strolled up and down the busy city blocks, the sunrise was often blocked by the towering rows of three-, four-, and even five-story buildings. The changes clashed with memories that I held dear. Some were expected: Some of the streetlamps had been converted from gas to electricity (St. Joseph being one of the earliest adopters of electricity), many of the streets were paved black with asphaltum, unsightly wires and telephone poles forty or fifty feet high were prominent, and the streetcars no longer relied on horses or mules to pull them along the rails laid in the middle of the streets. But there were other, more startling changes as well. City Greenhouse, where my mother bought a bouquet of flowers for every occasion, had occupied the block that was now Smith Park. Not a hint of the massive greenhouses remained. The slopes of the hills east of town were completely covered with houses, both large and small, as far as the eye could see. The ridge north of town, where I once played in overgrown empty lots on Hall Street, was occupied by mansions, smaller but similar to those in Newport, with elaborate stonework, stained-glass windows, expansive lawns, and carriage houses.

No wonder they need so many streetcars, I thought, as the fifth streetcar in twenty minutes clanged by.

Thousands more people now lived here, many of them rich and prospering, and the city was sprawling in every direction but west. Only the expanse of the Missouri River had kept St. Joseph from spreading in that direction. That it had continued to grow ever since didn't surprise me. When my father arrived just before the War broke out, St. Joseph was one of the most important cities in the country. Serving as the western terminus of the country's railroads, operating as the eastern terminus for the Pony Express mail service, and offering telegraph service to the east, St. Joe was a major staging point for the Oregon-California Trails, a major steamboat hub, and one of the major connections to California and its huge gold reserve.

But it was also growing up: Single-story buildings, though not common in my youth, were now almost nonexistent. Businesses had expanded, been rebuilt, or been forced to move away. For every shop I recognized, there were three others that had different establishments operating or were completely gone. Where a livery once stood, there now towered a four-story dry goods warehouse. Where there was once an undertaker's, there was now an insurance company. Every other shop was a dressmaker, grocer, or saloon. I'd seen drastic change in my youth; in the year I turned eight alone, I saw the demolition of the market house, the start of construction on City Hall, and the end to river ferries when the iron bridge was completed. And yet it was still disorienting to see such change.

Therefore I was thrilled and relieved when I saw HAMLIN MILLINERY in bold white letters on a square sign jutting out from a strip of buildings on a once well-known corner. I'd purchased my first hat from Mrs. Hamlin. I'd used my own money, earned from reading every Sunday afternoon to the blind butcher's widow who smelled like cabbage and stale tobacco. The millinery shop wasn't open yet, so I admired a currant red straw with exquisite white egret tips and a decidedly continental military air about it in the window. And then I caught sight of my reflection.

There were dark circles under my eyes, pronounced freckles across my nose, and my long neck was a bit saggy and thin. At the back of my head, a long curl, as usual, had escaped the pins and was trailing down my neck.

It's not just the city that's changed, I thought.

I shouldn't be surprised that no one treated me the same as before, not Ginny, not even Mrs. Chaplin. I'd changed. I was now either the infamous Hattie Davish, tainted forever by the unfortunate events of the past year, or the woman who worked for Mrs. Charlotte Mayhew. I'd hoped to be recognized for who I was, but that was foolish of me. What I'd seen and done in the past ten years had molded me into a person even I wouldn't recognize if I'd passed myself on the street.

What would my parents think? I wondered.

I tucked the loose strand of hair under my hat before adjusting my head below the hat in the display, blurring its image with that of the hat on my head. I smiled at my reflection and liked the woman who smiled back. A shopkeeper emerged to rearrange the window display, catching me admiring my image. She smiled, but I stepped back, feeling silly, and hastily turned away. But the moment of confidence and self-approval hadn't completely dissipated.

They would be proud, I thought, as I spied the new models of Remington typewriters in Wyckoff, Seamans & Benedict's window a few doors down. EVERYTHING FOR THE TYPE-WRITER, a sign in their window declared.

Yes, my parents would be pleased to know how successful I'd become. But what of my less agree-able traits: my impatience, my newly acquired readiness to lie or hide the truth, and my curiosity bordering on nosiness? Would they overlook those and recognize my need to do whatever was required to keep my position? Would they recognize me if they saw me on the street? To my shock and delight, I got an immediate answer.

"Hattie? Little Hattie Davish?" a voice called, interrupting my speculation. I turned to see that I'd passed Boone & Bro. grocers. Unlike many of the businesses I'd passed this morning, it hadn't changed a bit. And neither had the man smiling broadly at me from the shop doorway, wiping his hands on a white apron.

"Could that possibly be Mary Margaret McAnich's daughter before me?"

"Good morning, Mr. Boone," I said, returning his smile.

Mr. Boone had owned and operated Boone & Bro. grocers since before I was born. He'd opened the store with his brother, Jacob, hence the name, but soon after Jacob Boone joined the Pony Express. When that ended, he headed west. As long as I could remember Mr. Boone had a full head of white hair, even in his youth. Now in his middle fifties, it was more appropriate but gave to my eye the sense of agelessness.

"You're looking well," I said, approaching him.

"It is you! I barely recognized you!"

"I visited your store every other day for almost seventeen years, Mr. Boone. How could you say such a thing?"

In fact, not only had I been a loyal customer, it was well-known that Mr. Boone had been my mother's suitor before my father arrived in St. Joseph. There had been an unspoken agreement between them to marry. "Poor Rufus Boone," my mother used to say. "From the moment I met your father, he didn't have a chance."

But oddly, Mr. Boone, as far as I could tell, harbored no ill feelings toward anyone in my family, though he insisted on using my mother's maiden name. Instead, he treated my mother and then me as special customers, always finding us the freshest blackberries (my mother's favorite) or holding aside a pound of hazelnuts when a shipment came in. Granted my father never once stepped foot in the store, out of courtesy or out of fear of what Mr. Boone might do, I never knew. But either way, I'd always regarded Mr. Boone as a friend of the family.

"But that's when you were a little girl. Now look at you—a grown woman!"

"I was seventeen the last time you saw me." I laughed. "Hardly a little girl."

"A fine lady, I should say." He nodded his head with approval. "Your mother would be proud."

"Thank you, Mr. Boone. I'd like to think so."

"Oh, she would. She would." He reached out his long, broad arms. "Not too old or too fine to give your old friend a hug, are you?" I shook my head and happily let him wrap his strong arms around me. He pulled me close and tight, almost choking the breath out of me before holding me out at arm's length. "Still as skinny as a rail, I see. But you look good. Something must agree with you. Is it working for the rich ladies or finding them dead in their trunks?"

I cringed as yet again someone mentioned a piece of my past I'd rather forget. He, on the other hand, laughed wholeheartedly at his tactless jest, letting go of me and holding on to his belly trying to contain himself. Finally, he noticed the expression on my face.

"I'm sorry, Hattie. I couldn't resist. I've followed your escapades in the paper. You're quite famous around here, did you know?"

"Yes, I'm beginning to realize that." First the mourners' reaction at the funeral and then the students from the school and now Mr. Boone. I'd misjudged how my misadventures would be perceived by those who knew me.

"What's it to be, then? Mrs.?" I cringed again. "Who's the lucky man that benefited from the biggest mistake my boy ever made?"

"I'm still Miss Davish, Mr. Boone." I smiled, trying to take the sting out of admitting I was in danger of becoming an old maid.

"What? How can that be?"

"How is Mrs. Boone?" I asked, changing the subject. Despite his unrequited love for my mother, Mr. Boone did eventually marry.

"Mrs. Boone is well. And . . . since you're both still unattached, you might be interested to know . . ."

His hesitation could only mean one thing. He

41

was about to relate some news of his son, Nathan, someone else I knew well as a child. Nathan was a well-known Christian name in Daniel Boone's family. The irony was that Mr. Rufus Boone wasn't related in any way to the famous frontiersman. Mr. Boone had named his son Nathan because it would "be good for business."

"That Nate performed for Queen Victoria last week?" My reply was slightly more sarcastic than I intended, but then again Mr. Boone's jest at my expense still stung.

"No, actually he played at the World's Fair last week. Nate hasn't played for Her Majesty yet, but he has played for several presidents. Did you know he played at President Harrison's inaugural ball?"

"No, I didn't." *And I don't care,* I wanted to add but didn't.

"Yes, he's been to the White House many times, but that's not what I was going to say. No, what I wanted to tell you was that you've timed your visit right. Nate's due home any day. We haven't seen him since he started that tour of Europe. Now isn't that a coincidence?" He winked at me. And then he frowned. "Are you all right, Hattie? You've suddenly gone quite pale."

I was speechless. What was the likelihood that Nate Boone and I would both be in St. Joe at the same time? Could it be a lamentable coincidence or was there more to it? I'd wrongly assumed Ginny had sent me the funeral announcement for her father in the mail. Then who did? Could Nate have lured me all this way because he knew he'd be here as well? Would he stoop to playing such a nasty trick? But to what purpose: to gloat, to try to win me back, to apologize? None of it made sense. I hadn't heard one word from him in almost ten years. Why now?

Un, deux, trois, quatre, cinq, six . . . I counted in my head as I unclenched my fists.

"Hattie?" Mr. Boone's face was full of concern.

"I'm sorry, Mr. Boone. I'm fine. I was marveling at the amazing coincidence."

"Yes, it is amazing. We'll have to have you over for dinner once Nate gets home. You don't still eat like a bird, do you?"

"I appreciate the invitation, but I came for a funeral and I don't anticipate being in town long. My employer expects me back in Newport by the end of the week." It was a complete lie and yet I hadn't hesitated.

Definitely one of the ways I'd changed that neither of my parents would approve of, I thought. And yet I didn't regret saying it. I'd no intention of crossing paths with Mr. Nathan Boone and yet I didn't want to hurt the feelings of his dear father.

"Well, maybe next time then. Did you come for the Hayward funeral?"

"Yes, Virginia Hayward was my closest friend at Mrs. Chaplin's school."

"I don't know the family, but it was in the *Gazette.* Terrible way to die." He scrunched his nose and grimaced. "To be trampled by a horse. A customer came in this morning saying he was disfigured."

"Yes, I wouldn't have known him."

Mr. Boone held open the door for a woman with two empty baskets in her hands. "I must get back to my work, Hattie, but it was great to see you."

"And you, Mr. Boone."

Wouldn't have known him, I'd said without thinking. As I returned Mr. Boone's wave before he disappeared inside his store, I immediately recalled my thoughts yesterday at the funeral. *Could there be any doubt?*

Chapter 5

After my encounter with Mr. Boone, I strolled down Edmond Street, passed the elaborate limestone City Hall and its market, dodging vendors and customers bargaining with each other over the colorful fruit and vegetables in stalls lining the sidewalks, passed the new electric powerhouse, with its assortment of poles and wires, and headed toward the river. I lifted my skirts and carefully navigated the railroad tracks that ran alongside. After a bit of looking, I found a grassy spot on the muddy embankment and sat down. The riverside, completely deforested and eroded with only weeds to hold back the mud, was nothing like the idyllic Cliff Walk I'd hiked in Newport. And the water was dirty brown.

There was nothing aesthetically pleasing about it, but it was the river of my childhood. I lingered there, watching as a steamboat pushed back from the dock, its twin chimneys spewing black soot into the air. A dozen ring-billed gulls squawked, squealed, and flapped furiously high above the churning water. I pulled up some Kentucky blue-grass and tossed it, hoping, in vain, that it would catch in the wind and fall into the river. Instead, it blew back toward me.

I gazed downriver to the iron bridge. Spanning hundreds of feet across, it was St. Joseph's only connection to Kansas. I'll never forget the day the bridge opened. To commemorate the occasion, there had been a parade that stretched for six miles, the longest parade in the city's history. After growing tired and sore from waving my flag and craning my neck to see all the wagons, dignitaries, and marching bands, my father let me sit on his shoulders. That night everyone in the city poured back into the streets where the parade had passed, and danced beneath the light of Japanese lanterns. Now it was just an ordinary day on the river.

After several minutes, a train entered the center of the span from the Kansas side. Within seconds, it rumbled across the bridge, blocking my view of the foot and horse traffic crossing on the side lanes. The ground trembled beneath me as another train approached from the north. I held on to my hat as it whisked by. I read CB&Q as it passed, heading toward the depot.

What am I waiting for? I wondered.

I stood, brushing soot from my shirt and grass from my skirt, and headed back across the tracks. I strolled by the Tootle Opera House, a large, imposing square building that covered a quarter of the city block on the corner of Fifth and Francis streets. The five-story building was constructed of red brick, ornamented with fine-cut limestone in front, and embellished with ornamental cornices. I'd never been inside, but I'd heard it described as "truly magnificent." When I was small, I'd accompany my mother on her errands. Regardless of where our shopping would take us, we would inevitably walk past the Opera House, my mother hoping to catch a bit of music reaching the street as the musicians practiced inside. It was quiet now.

What was that? I thought.

I headed toward Felix Street when a sudden chill ran down my spine. I glanced over my shoulder, expecting to find someone walking too close behind me. No one was there. But hadn't I heard footsteps? Directly across the street, a man in denim overalls and a navy blue cap stood in front of a tailor's shop, his back to me. With one hand holding a pail of soapy water and a rubber scraper in the other, he was obviously preoccupied with washing the windows. A young woman walked toward me with a jilting gait that sent her fluted brimmed straw hat flopping down over her brow with every other step. A group of talkative nuns carried woven baskets full of produce halfway down the block. I'd been completely at ease by the river a few minutes ago. Why was I suddenly jittery?

"What's the matter with you?" I said, berating myself out loud.

I brushed some more soot off my sleeve, straightened my hat, and continued down Fourth to Felix. *The White Way*, as it was known, was, even in my youth, one of the busiest commercial streets in all of St. Joseph. My father had chosen well when he bought his shop there. I turned the corner and stopped. A man, with the broad brim of his Panama hat pulled down over his eyes, muttered something as he barely avoided walking into the back of me. I didn't care. I ignored his grumbles as he stepped around me.

From where I stood, the triangular State Savings Bank towered over the traffic of pedestrians, while buggies and wagons with their numerous horses all vied for a space to hitch. One team and wagon was parked in the middle of the street. Being without a driver, it forced others to drive down the wrong side of the street. On the north side, a row of attached limestone and brick buildings, individualized with awnings or lack thereof, differed in cornice ornamentation, glass storefronts, and signs. All but one building was three stories; I headed straight for the two-story building at 405 Felix Street.

I hesitated outside, gazing up at the second-story windows, trying to picture the parlor they belonged to. I imagined my mother in her rocking chair next to the window, darning socks, shucking peas for dinner, or playing her fiddle, while I did my schoolwork sprawled out on the carpet floor. My father smoked his pipe and read his newspapers across the room in his armchair.

Home, I thought.

And then I stared at the shop door. The store-front was as much home as the rooms above it. This was where my father reigned as one of the most profitable hat merchants in St. Joseph. This was where, after my mother died, we'd sit together at a little table in the back room and pick at whatever the housekeeper had cooked for us. This was where, hiding behind the counter pretending to do my homework, I'd learned the values my father cherished: quality of service, quality of product, loyalty and friendship. This was where I'd listen to my father debate with fellow fanatics the various abilities of baseball players or the decisions of the ball clubs' managers and owners. I didn't know until I was twelve years old that there were other sports besides baseball.

Everything about our life together was embodied in this two-story building. And it looked exactly the same as I remembered it: the green-and-white-striped awnings, the white-washed pilasters around the recessed doorway, the metal step with the maker's mark, HOERMAN BROS. MANUFACTURING CO. WASHINGTON, KS, slightly worn down from thousands of feet treading on it, and even the sign, DAVISH'S FINE HATS FOR MEN, painted in bright gold letters across the top of the storefront window. And wasn't that Mr. Minier coming out of the shop? One of my father's most loyal customers had aged considerably since I'd seen him last, but he was sporting the latest in men's haberdashery.

I took a deep breath, straightened my hat, and reached for the door handle. The same familiar bell rang as I entered. I was immediately brought back to my youth by the smell of silk, felt, and furniture polish.

And then I stopped, frozen in the doorway. Like the exterior, the interior of the store hadn't changed either, except for the hats displayed on the various stands throughout the room. The oak hat stands, the glass counters, the brass lamps, and the chandelier were all as my father had left them. The same Persian rug my father bought from a wholesaler months before he died lay in the middle of the room. Tears filled my eyes when I discovered that even the hash marks my father had used to measure my growth on the back of the tall mirror hadn't been painted over. It was as if my father had stepped out of the room for a moment. I was overwhelmed with memories of my life with him and my loss.

"And how did your husband like the straw derby, Mrs. Ames?"

"Mr. Davish, I don't know how you do it, but my Henry actually liked the hat and Henry never likes hats, always taking them off as soon as he can and even sometimes when he shouldn't. But the hat that you suggested for him fits him like a glove! And he doesn't perspire in it like he usually does. Mr. Davish, my Henry doesn't even grumble when he has to put it on. You're a wonder, sir!"

"At your service, madam." The old woman beamed as my father bent at the waist, flourishing a hat he'd grabbed from a nearby stand.

"Needless to say, I would like to order two more," she said.

"In fur felt for autumn?"

"Yes, just so. What colors would you suggest?"

"Every man can use a black and a gray."

"Yes, and maybe a brown as well?"

"Excellent choice, madam. Shall we say Thursday for delivery?"

"Oh, yes, that would do nicely. Please put them on my tab, will you, Mr. Davish? I thank you and my Henry thanks you." The lady waved to my father before heading out the door.

"How do you do it?" Frans Van Beek, my father's assistant, said. He was a tall man, standing several inches above my father, with spectacles and a perpetually stiff neck, who never showed his teeth when he smiled. "Even I know Mr. Ames is a notoriously difficult customer. According to Joe over at Lockwood's he's been to every haberdashery in town but once. Now you have a standing account with his wife. How, George? How do you do it?"

"Well, my good man, it's simple. The customer gets what the customer wants. Our hats are superior in quality, of course," Father said, winking at me when he caught me watching over the counter, "but when it comes down to it, the quality of the hat can get you only so far. Service, my friend, is the thing. Mrs. Ames wants her hats delivered, we deliver."

"But we don't deliver. No one does," Mr. Van Beek said.

"Exactly, except we do delivery to Mrs. Ames because that's what she wants. She also expects our full attention, our flattery, and seemingly"—he grabbed my hand and pulled me around the counter, twirling me around three times—"a little bit of showmanship."

He twirled me around the room as we laughed. Mr. Van Beek shook his head. From the moment he had arrived, Mr. Van Beek disapproved of my presence in the store. He couldn't understand why my father allowed me to sit on the floor behind the counter every day after school, with my books and my piece of peach cake meant for my father's customers, while they conducted the day's business. My place was at home upstairs, he once said. Father's reply was, "What home upstairs? This is our home." Realizing the truth in that, Mr. Van Beek never said another word about it. But that didn't mean he liked it.

"I cringed when you bowed like that. I can't imagine doing that in front of Mr. Minier or Mr. Heath." Father stopped and I, not anticipating his sudden lack of movement, collided into his chest; as always, he smelled of shaving soap.

"Nor would I," Father said. "That's what I mean about the customer gets what the customer wants. You have to be able to look at every customer that walks through that door and know what kind of service he or she wants. Mr. Minier wants to pick out a hat without any extraneous chitchat, Mr. Heath has to try on each new style while you praise the comely shape of his head, Mr. Ames prefers to have Mrs. Ames buy his hats, and Mrs. Ames wants to be flattered and entertained."

"But I can barely remember returning customers' names, let alone remember how they like to be served."

"But it's essential, Frans. You'll never do well in any business if you can't remember a person's name and face. And if you can recall their children's names, their dressmaker or tailor, their favorite food, their wife's birthday or their anniversary, all the better."

"But how do you do it?"

I smiled at my father, knowing full well he wouldn't be able to answer that. For him it was instinctual. As I suspected, Father shrugged.

"I don't know, son. Lots of practice, perhaps."

"And you have to like people, not hats," I added. Father and Mr. Van Beek both stared at me. Mr. Van Beek furrowed his brows in annoyance, thinking perhaps that I'd somehow insulted him, but Father burst out in laughter. He grabbed me and twirled me around again.

"That's my clever girl!" He danced me across the showroom floor until the bell over the door rang again. I dodged through his arms and dashed to my hiding place behind the counter. My father straightened his tie and turned toward the door.

"Ah, Mr. Skinner, I'm pleased to see you've returned safely from your trip to Omaha. I set aside the latest top hat styles in your size, in case you should stop by. Would you care to see them?"

And with Mr. Skinner's curt nod of his head, my father's charm had worked again.

"Can I help you find something, madam?" A young, clean-shaven man in a well-tailored blue single-breasted suit stood before me. He had a slight chip in his front tooth that added charm to his wide smile.

Embarrassed to be caught up in a myriad of emotions, I quickly wiped away my tears, smoothed the lines on my skirt, and straightened my hat. "No, thank you. I was simply admiring your shop."

Instead of glancing away and allowing me a moment, the man did the opposite. He stepped closer and leaned in to see my face. I leaned back, my grief and sadness replaced by irritation.

"You aren't any relation to George Davish, the previous proprietor of the store, are you? I'm sorry to be rude, but you look a lot like him."

I immediately glanced at my face in the nearest mirror. Except for his green eyes, I'd always thought I resembled my mother. I still didn't see it and the thought made me want to start weeping again. Instead, I squared my shoulders and took a step back. Mistaking my need to compose myself for annoyance, the young man's cheeks flushed as he bobbed his head.

"I'm sorry. That was impertinent of me."

"It's all right. I'm his daughter."

"You're Hattie?" The man's face darkened even more. "I mean Miss Davish, I . . . I mean Mrs. . . . I mean . . . Mr. Van Beek didn't tell me you were in town."

Mr. Frans Van Beek didn't know I was in town and I'd no intention of telling him. After years as my father's assistant, and then as his partner, Mr. Van Beek took over the running of the store when my father fell ill. When Father died, Mr. Van Beek paid me $1000 to "buy my father's share in the store," and gave me two weeks' notice to evacuate my childhood home. It was a fraction of what my father's share was worth, but being a girl of seventeen and having no family to help me, I could do nothing but thank him and look for somewhere else to live.

At least it paid for the funeral and my last year's tuition at Mrs. Chaplin's, I thought. Obviously Mr. Van Beek hadn't changed a single thing since he took over.

"No, I'm in town for a short while, for a funeral."

"Oh, sorry to hear that. Still wanted to stop in

and see the old place then, huh?" I ignored his question.

"Are you Mr. Van Beek's assistant?" The man straightened up to his full height and wiggled his tie.

"I am. I'm following in his footsteps. This will be my shop someday."

"May that be many years to come." The boy frowned, not sure how to take my comment. I headed for the door. I didn't need to see any more. Despite nothing having changed, everything had —my father wasn't here. "Please give my regards to Mr. Van Beek," I said only out of common courtesy.

"Of course. But before you go, wouldn't you like to look at a hat? For your husband perhaps? We recently put out the latest styles for autumn. A chic new fedora, maybe?"

I shook my head. "No, thank you." I pulled open the door and heard the shop bell ring one last time.

In my haste to be out in the open air again, I crashed right into a man entering at the same time. The brim of my hat bent on the thick knot of his tie before I was able to take a quick step backward. It was the same man who had almost walked into me a few minutes ago on the corner.

"Excuse me," I said, trying to dodge around the man blocking my way.

"Of course, excuse me." The man stepped out

of the path of the door. He tilted his head and hat in an apologetic nod, preventing me from getting a glimpse of his face.

"Thank you." I gained the doorway and hurried out into the street.

Before the door closed completely behind me, I heard the man say, "Was that Hattie Davish?"

I was halfway to the streetcar stop before I had the sense to wonder: *How did he know that and why did he want to know?*

Chapter 6

"In the name of the Father, and the Son, and the Holy Ghost, amen," I said, kneeling before a granite obelisk that read:

BELOVED WIFE
AND MOTHER
MARY MARGARET DAVISH
1840–1874

BELOVED HUSBAND
AND FATHER
GEORGE STUART DAVISH
1835–1882

BELOVED SON
EDWARD PADRAIG DAVISH
1867–1870

After visiting all the places of my childhood, before I could leave town, I had to make the pilgrimage to the site of my father's one true transgression. He had not respected my mother's dying wish. I took the streetcar via the Frederick Avenue Line and then walked the two blocks to Mount Mora Cemetery, the oldest cemetery in the city. As I'd walked through the gates and followed the winding roads, under trees that had grown tall since I'd been here last, I sensed that none of my family was truly here, but it was the closest I could get.

They were such different people I often wondered how my parents ever fell in love, let alone stayed happy together. My mother was a foot shorter than my father with her boots on. She often wore an old-fashioned woolen scarf over her curly dark brown hair while my father sported the latest styles in men's hats. My mother attended Mass every day and always carried her rosary. The only time I saw my father enter the cathedral was for my mother's funeral. My mother had big blue eyes, tiny teeth, and coarse hands that she used to cup my cheek with. My father had freckles across his nose and soft hands that he used to shake everyone's hand. She whistled or hummed constantly but often went hours without speaking. He made his living by talking. She was firm with me while my father indulged my every whim. How different they were and yet all of my memories of them together were of laughter, smiles, and music.

Until she died, I thought.

She'd wanted to be buried in the Catholic Cemetery, south of town, alongside my baby brother, Edward, but my father had always fancied himself being buried among St. Joseph's economic and social elite, including the governor of Missouri Robert Stewart, M. Jeff Thompson, a one-time mayor of St. Joseph and Civil War general, and James Benjamin "Bean" Hamilton, a Pony Express rider. Father would often remark on the growing number of grand mausoleums entombing members of St. Joseph's wealthy and influential families and how they dominated the entrance to the cemetery.

"I like the idea that one has to pass all these great names to find mine," he once said. And, of course, my father hated having my brother interred all the way on the other side of town. Thus he purchased a plot that would accommodate them all, in Mount Mora. I learned later that it wasn't a coincidence that it was then that Mr. Van Beek became a partner in Father's business. It was the reason my father could afford the plot.

"You'll be buried with your husband, Hattie," Father had said, "or else I'd have bought a bigger plot. It pains me to know that you will spend eternity away from me, but that's how it must be."

I was a child at the time and had no idea how soon we would be parted.

I'd visited every Sunday after Mass while I attended Mrs. Chaplin's school but hadn't been back since the day I left. I glanced at the stones around me and could tell by the dates on the stones that most were far older than my parents'. Mostly modest rectangular monuments, the words etched into the stones were barely readable and they were covered with streaks of black dirt or lichen. Why would my father have chosen one of the older sections? Was it all he could afford or was there some other reason? I examined the stones nearby. Before I could get my answer, I suddenly had the same presentiment as earlier. Someone was watching me.

I crawled closer to my father's tombstone and huddled there. I held my breath as I heard footsteps approaching. I unpinned my hat, carefully setting it next to me. I held the pins out in front of me for defense. A long-legged cellar spider crept over the top of the stone and across my brother Edward's name. By the time its legs hovered above my father's name, my racing heart couldn't take much more. I brushed the spider into the grass and peeked around the edge of the tombstone. Approaching me were two men who, except for the color of their hair, from a distance looked like twins, both tall, broad-shouldered, and wearing identical navy blue uniforms and caps.

Their uniforms seemed familiar, but I couldn't place them. With the deportment of policemen, despite looking more like train conductors, they made their unhurried way toward me. They stopped often to circumnavigate the larger mausoleums, or to glance behind every large obelisk and headstone. If they had seen me, they gave no impression of doing so. But why would they be coming for me? Why was I hiding?

"It's your jitters again," I chided myself. "What's wrong with you?"

I snatched up my hat and pinned it back on while I watched their progress. When they were a few yards away, I stood up from my hiding place.

"Aaahhh!" one of the men shouted, both leaping back a few steps.

"Oh, madam," the man with the ginger hair said, his hand over his heart, "you certainly gave us a fright!"

"What are you doing here?" the other one asked. Both the first man and I looked askance at this ridiculous question. I glanced around me at the tombstones and mausoleums.

"Obviously she's visiting someone's grave," the ginger-haired man said.

"I'm sorry. That came out wrong. What I meant is that you should take care being here, especially alone."

"And why should I take care?"

There were always those who say that ghosts

haunt graveyards at night but even if I believed in such nonsense, it wasn't even midday as yet. The only shadows here were caused by the speckling of light on the stones as the sun shone down through the trees. I'd actually found it very calming and comforting to be among the silent stones warmed by the late-summer sunlight. At least I had until they arrived.

Then why had I hid at the slightest of noises?

"Because there's an unpredictable, dangerous man about," the ginger-haired man said, as if hearing my thought.

"Is that whom you were searching for among the graves?"

"Yes, it would be easy to hide in a place like this."

Could this be whom I'd sensed watching me? It would explain the unease I felt. Or after all I've been through lately I could just be getting jumpy.

No, that isn't it, I thought. Maybe the man they're searching for was here.

"Who is this man?"

"A patient from the asylum who escaped a few days ago," the fair-haired one said. "We've got men all over town searching for him."

"The State Lunatic Asylum?" I realized now why their uniforms seemed familiar. The two nodded their heads.

"I'd keep your wits about you, if I were you."

"I'd recommend not going about alone,

especially in a deserted place like this," the other added. But I was barely listening to what they said.

The State Lunatic Asylum, I repeated in my head, a shiver running down my spine. I hadn't heard that name for many years now. The palms of my hands felt damp upon hearing it. And I'd prefer never hearing it again. I shook off the dread, fought the nausea slowly rising in my throat to hear the orderly say, "He's a pale-skinned man, five feet ten inches tall with broad shoulders, weighing one hundred eighty pounds."

But he couldn't possibly be talking about my father, I thought.

"Excuse me. Did you say the man was in his fifties, with mostly gray wavy hair, broad shoulders, and very prominent cheekbones?"

"Yes, he also wears a mustache and beard and has brown eyes. If you see him, don't approach him. Please contact the asylum or notify the police."

I nodded my head absently as the two men continued their search of the cemetery grounds. The events of the funeral and interment returned to my thoughts again. I had found a semblance of peace in the presence of my parents' graves, but it was now completely gone. For if I hadn't known better, the two orderlies described, with the exception of his scar, the now-dead and buried Frank Hayward.

• • •

With the peace of the cemetery shattered and my mind racing with thoughts about Frank Hayward and the missing asylum patient, I was at a loss.

Now what do I do? I wondered.

I stood staring at my parents' grave, and finding no answers there, I began walking. I'd reached a newly built limestone mausoleum for the prominent Crowther family, which included foundry owners, lawyers, and politicians, when I realized I'd no idea where I was going. I sat on one of the spiral-shaped stones flanking the mausoleum. Should I pack and take the next train back to Newport? No, I couldn't disappoint Mrs. Chaplin. She was expecting me at the lake. Should I write to Walter about my muddled impressions of Frank Hayward's funeral, the odd reception I'd received from Ginny, and the memories both joyous and sad I'd relived this morning? I longed to talk to Walter, but writing it all down now would force me to relive it again. I watched as several winged seeds of the nearest maple tree spiraled through the air. I could go hiking again. I sighed.

If only I had some work to do, I thought. I'd finished all of the tasks set to me by Sir Arthur before I'd left Newport.

So, with the sun high and nothing productive to do, I brushed myself off, straightened my hat, and retraced a hike I used to take frequently with

64

my father. Little did we know that the dirt country road would be immortalized by Eugene Field, the famous poet and one-time city editor of the *St. Joseph Gazette*, with his popular poem, "Lover's Lane, St. Jo." Being a secluded lane, Mr. Field had courted his wife there, and after living in London to recover from illness, wrote fondly of those days. I remember when the poem came out, years after I'd left home. I'd memorized it immediately, relating to his longing for that peaceful place. It was the promise from my favorite line that drew me there now.

But I'd give it all, and gladly,
If for an hour or so
I could feel the grace of a distant place—
Of Lover's Lane, Saint Jo.

Rochester Road, as it was officially known, was still lovely, with large trees shading the lane, sections of rail fence and stands of willow and alder. I knew it as a remote spot popular with young lovers for that very reason. But no longer. I wasn't alone in strolling along the shady lane, and several carriages passed me as I went. As always on my hikes, I was aware of the plants that I passed. After my father died, I'd often sought solace and solitude here and it was here that I collected some of the first specimens in my plant collection. My collection had grown considerably since and I wasn't expecting to find anything new, but I looked about nonetheless. After an hour, I decided to stop. I leaned against a fence post. I was thirsty and tired. Although welcomed, the quiet and serenity weren't enough to overcome the melancholy that plagued me since I'd arrived.

Had it only been yesterday? I'd found little peace thinking about Ginny and our lamentable reunion. I'd thought over and over about my mistaking which side her father's scar was on. Without work to preoccupy my hands and mind, without Walter's reassurances, I hadn't felt this alone since the day my father died.

Why did I come back here?

And then I saw a small, toothy-leafed mustard plant I didn't recognize. It smelled oddly like garlic. I readily collected a specimen, folding it several times and then pressing it between layers of my handkerchief. Thrilled with the unexpected pleasure of finding a new specimen for my collection, I felt ashamed of my self-pity moments before.

"Buck up, Davish," I told myself. I stood up, brushed the dirt and litter off my gloves, and headed back down the lane toward town. Almost immediately, the quiet of the lane was disturbed by crunching wheels and pounding horses as a buggy raced toward me. In an instant I thought of Walter, who was notoriously reckless with the reins of horses in his hands, and then of a carriage once driven by a guilt-driven man who almost ran me off a bridge. I dashed into the shrubbery that lined the road, putting as much distance as possible between me and the buggy. I was safely out of harm's way but preoccupied by the bramble snagging the trim on my skirt when the horse neighed a few feet away. I glanced up just as the driver snapped the reins wildly, high above the horse's head. The horse was missing a tooth.

Oh my God! I thought, my shock reflected on the driver's face, his eyes widening when our eyes met. I stood frozen, my skirt hitched up higher than was decent, my mouth agape as, if I didn't know better, the ghost of Frank Hayward drove by. Except this man was clean shaven and didn't have a scar on his eyebrow. And then I remembered the orderlies from the asylum. As the carriage raced by, I realized that I was watching a terrified, persecuted man making his escape from that heinous institution.

"Go!" I yelled, waving my arms, cheering him on, my skirt still caught in the bramble. "Get as far away as you can!"

I stared at the back of the carriage until it disappeared around a bend. Then I freed my skirt and headed back down the lane toward town. *He has nothing to fear from me,* I thought, knowing full well I wasn't about to tell anyone whom I'd seen.

Chapter 7

When I finally arrived back at the St. Charles Hotel, despite having picked up the streetcar at N. 22nd Street, my legs were tired, my feet were sore, and my mind was completely exhausted. I'd crammed an entire childhood of memories into one day. Unfortunately many of those memories were tainted by the grief and sadness of what was to come. I'd never been a carefree child, but after losing first my brother, then my mother, and finally my father, I'd strived to refrain from showing much emotion. It's a trait that has served me well in my profession. Yet even as I pushed the door to the hotel entrance, I could feel the memories of the day overwhelm me. The sorrow threatened to engulf me, as if I'd lost my father all over again. I wanted to get to my room to type.

But I can't even do that, I thought. If I had my typewriter, the rhythmic clicking of the keys would've calmed me down. But I didn't have it with me. When I was leaving for St. Joseph, Lady Phillippa had seen my typewriter among my hatboxes and travel cases. She'd insisted that I leave it behind, as I'd no work to do at the funeral. I'd never been without my typewriter since the day my father gave it to me. I'd tried to explain to Lady Phillippa that, despite all my travels, my typewriter was no worse for wear. And yet she'd been right; I'd no reason to bring it. And I've missed its presence ever since.

I'm never leaving my typewriter behind again, I thought as I crossed the lobby.

The hotel lobby was simply furnished with an oak registration desk, several oak rocking chairs along the opposite wall, a wide staircase to the right of the desk with red carpet running up the middle, and a block and leaf patterned ingrain carpet partially covering the polished wooden floor. The room was completed by several brass wall lamps, a wrought-iron umbrella stand by the door, and a cobalt blue vase filled with dried hydrangeas on the painted plant stand.

"Miss Davish?" Was someone calling my name? As I was slow to react, he called out again. "Excuse me, Miss Davish?"

I turned toward the registration desk, cluttered with untidy stacks of newspapers, a brown leather register book, and a half-empty tea cup with tiny orange roses. In his late sixties, the clerk behind the desk was a small, thin man with a very round face and thinning gray hair. He squinted at me despite wearing spectacles. His name tag read, P. PUTNEY.

"Yes?" The old man smiled, reminding me of my beloved, long-dead Irish grandpa.

"Two letters arrived for you while you were out." His hands shook slightly as he handed them out toward me. One letter was typewritten with no return address. The other was in a hand I recognized immediately.

"Walter," I whispered to myself. What wonderful timing. "Thank you," I said to the clerk, though part of me said it silently to another as well, almost 1,500 miles away.

Despite my exhaustion, I returned to my room as quickly as I could, grabbed my letter opener from its place on the table (even with no work to do, my letter opener was always placed where I could retrieve it in an instant), and sliced open Walter's letter. Most of the letter was inquiring after me, my journey, my health, and my feelings about being home again. He wrote how much he missed me and how his mother was slowly adjusting to the idea of our courtship. It soothed me, his words washing over me as if I were in his embrace. I read it three times before I realized that he'd requested a favor in his postscript: to bring back a souvenir from the house where Jesse James was killed. Ever since that fateful day, April 3, 1882, when the outlaw was shot in the head by Bob Ford, St. Joseph has been ghoulishly synonymous with the death of the outlaw. The house has been the leading tourist attraction almost since the day he died. I'd never visited myself and never planned to.

Only for you, Walter, I thought, setting down Walter's letter to open the second letter.

I'd been so delighted to see Walter's letter that it hadn't occurred to me to question whom the second one could've been from. In fact, the more I thought about it, the more disturbed I became. No one, besides Walter and Lady Phillippa, knew I was staying here. I looked at the envelope. The typewritten address read: MISS HATTIE DAVISH, ST. CHARLES HOTEL, CHARLES STREET, SE. COR. 5TH, ST. JOSEPH, MO. There was no return address, but the postmark read: ST. JOSEPH, MO, 5 P.M., AUGUST 25, 1893. It was sent yesterday right after the funeral. I sliced open the envelope and pulled out a single sheet of paper. It was plain white paper, available at any stationery shop. And at first I couldn't read a word. It was written entirely in an esoteric system of short-hand. I translated it slowly, pulling up memories of the different shorthand systems I'd learned over the years. And even when I'd finished I was uncertain if I'd translated it right. It read: *Please don't leave anytime soon. All is not as it should be. You can help.*

I was stunned. What could it possibly mean? What wasn't as it should be? My thoughts went immediately to Frank Hayward's funeral. Could I have been right, that the man they buried wasn't Ginny's father? But Ginny identified him, and who would know him better than his own daughter? No, that couldn't be it. But if that wasn't it, what else could be wrong? Could it be that Frank Hayward's death wasn't an accident, that he was deliberately trampled by a horse? Did it even have anything to do with Frank Hayward? I looked at the letter again.

Now what do I do? I wondered for the second time today. Do I pursue this, assuming it has something to do with Frank Hayward's death, or do I ignore it? If it did have something to do with Frank Hayward's death, I wasn't certain Ginny would approve of my meddling. But if it was independent of the Haywards, it's possible that I could be of some service to someone. But whom? And what did they expect me to do? Again I regretted not having my typewriter. I pulled a piece of stationary out of the drawer that read, *St. Charles Hotel, Charles Street,* dipped my pen in the inkwell, and started a list.

1. Who sent the letter?
2. Who would know such obscure shorthand?
3. How did they know I was staying here?
4. What does "All is not as it should be" mean?
5. Does it have something to do with Frank Hayward's death?
6. If not, then what?
7. Why does the sender believe I can help?
8. Can I help?
9. Should I help?
10. Is there someone following me?

The last question on my list took me by surprise. I'd simply written it down without thinking. But yet twice today I'd sensed that someone was watching and following me. I added another question to the list.

11. If so, why?

I had no idea. Was it all a figment of my imagination? Had the events of the past year shaken my courage and made me fearful and suspicious without cause? I'd overreacted to the asylum orderlies. I'd looked behind me on the street to find no one there. And I'd questioned the identity of Frank Hayward's corpse.

Oh my God, I'm losing my mind! I thought. What would Sir Arthur think? Who wants a secretary who questions her own sanity? I dropped my head into my hands, letting out all of the grief, the confusion, and the sadness that I'd held in since the moment I'd arrived. I drenched my handkerchief before I caught a glimpse of the anonymous letter on the table. That wasn't a figment of my imagination.

As I caught my breath, I glanced at myself in the mirror: curly strands of hair askew from the knot, red, bleary eyes, glistening streaks of tears running down my face, my nose in need of a good wipe, a thin streak of dirt smeared across my forehead. I was a mess. I retrieved a dry handkerchief, wiped my face, dabbed my nose, and then looked again at my list. There's something here. There's something going on. It's not all in my mind. Relief coupled with embarrassment flowed through me as I focused on who might have sent the letter. It had to be someone who either attended the funeral or knew I was there. Although the funeral was well attended by Mr. Hayward's friends and neighbors, how many would be skilled in archaic shorthand? It must've been someone from Mrs. Chaplin's school. But why?

I can't think of this right now. I dropped the list on the nightstand next to my bed. My curiosity had been piqued, but the day had been wrought with emotion; I couldn't comprehend dealing with this new development with such a muddled, weary brain. It was enough that I trusted myself again. And I had no intention of poking around again into the affairs of others. If nothing else, my momentary lapse reminded me that little good came from such irresponsible behavior. No, I'd come to St. Joseph to offer my support to my dear friend at a tragic time in her life. And even that proved ill-fated.

Refusing to think about the mystery letter for one more moment or to contemplate what wasn't "as it should be," I pulled out a new piece of hotel stationery. I spent the remainder of my evening writing to Walter, including a promise to acquire the souvenir from the Jesse James house. At the time, it seemed the simpler task.

Chapter 8

If I thought responding to Walter's letter would be enough to soothe me, I was terribly wrong. The words of the mysterious letter echoed through my mind all night. As did images of my mother, my father, and Frank Hayward, all lovingly laid to rest in their coffins. Bodies of those I'd found crammed into a steam trunk, lying in a pool of blood in a cave, crumpled on the steps of a Civil War statue, or sprawled on the floor of a millionaire's office haunted me as well. After each dream, I woke with a start and attempted to fill my mind with images of the colorful plants I'd collected or of serene hikes I've taken over the years. Instead, I pictured my parents' graves and the orderlies from the asylum as they drifted from gravestone to gravestone. Finally, it was late enough to give up the pretense of sleeping and get dressed.

I examined my new plant specimen before stepping out for a hike. I planned to hike along the river and then across the iron bridge, but before I'd gone two blocks down Charles Street I had the same uneasy feeling someone was watching me again. As before, I looked about me and saw no one besides peddlers heading to Market Square with their produce.

"Who are you?" My shout was rewarded with a scowl by the driver of a passing gig. I listened to the fading clip-clop of the horse's tread until it was taken over by the clanking of an approaching streetcar. It was no use. Whoever it was, they weren't going to reveal themselves to me.

"Whoever you are, stop following me!"

Yesterday I'd been frightened and sad, but today I was angry. I was angry that Ginny didn't appreciate the effort I had made to get here. I was angry that I could no more go on a leisurely stroll through the city of my birth without wondering, worrying if someone was following me. I was angry that someone thought they could send me an anonymous note and expect me to comply with their wishes. I was angry that even to my friends at Mrs. Chaplin's school, of all places, my accomplishments as a secretary had been overshadowed by my association with socialites and murderers. When I'd set out on this journey, this wasn't the homecoming I was expecting.

"*Un, deux, trois, quatre, cinq, six, sept, huit, neuf, dix.*" I counted as I turned around and stomped back to my hotel.

I'd counted to *deux cent trente-trois* by the time I arrived, much calmer than minutes before. And then I heard the clerk call my name as I headed toward the dining room for breakfast.

"Another letter for you, Miss Davish," Mr. Putney said.

Oh, no, not another one, I thought, warily taking it from his shaking hand. I turned it over and was relieved to see a well-formed hand on the envelope and the return address of Mrs. Chaplin's school. It wasn't from the anonymous shorthand writer after all.

"Thank you, Mr. Putney." He bobbed his head as he lifted his teacup to his lips. I continued to the dining room, and after being seated and served oatmeal with a side of pears, toast, and coffee, I sliced open the letter with my fruit knife. It was an invitation, or reminder, of the day's planned "Lake Party," with me as its guest of honor. A carriage would be sent to pick me up at one o'clock.

That gives me time, I thought.

After breakfast, and Mass at the Church of the Immaculate Conception a few blocks away, I walked to the Hayward family home, a small, two-story redbrick house with a bay window, a small side porch, and a mansard roof on South 12th Street. The exercise did me good. Not once did I sense someone following me. It was a welcomed relief; I was already anxious about seeing Ginny again.

But I had to talk to her. I was uncomfortable with attending a party the day after my friend buried her father. I wanted to make sure that she didn't object. I also hoped to discuss the mysterious letter. She knew more about Mrs. Chaplin's school now than I did. Maybe she'd be able to shed some light on who might've sent it and why. Despite the black crape tied with white ribbon on the door, the housekeeper, an elderly woman who had been working for the Haywards longer than I've known them, invited me in to see Ginny when I arrived.

"Good morning, Mrs. Curbow," I said, as she indicated for me to follow her into the parlor. All evidence of the funeral was gone except the portrait draped in black crape and the lingering scent of flowers. Instead I noticed several books lying out on the side table. One was a shorthand dictionary.

"So good to see you again, Miss Davish," the housekeeper said. "I've heard all about your escapades, working for Mrs. Mayhew, traveling all over, and of course all about the dead—" Mrs. Curbow grimaced as she realized what she'd been about to say. "What I mean to say is . . . I bet you've seen more marvels than there are on the midway at the World's Fair."

"I don't know about that, but you're right. Life has not been dull for me since I left home. It's good to see you too, Mrs. Curbow, though I do wish it had been under happier circumstances." The old housekeeper nodded.

"Yes, it's a shock about poor Mr. Hayward."

"How's Virginia taking it?"

Mrs. Curbow furrowed her brow and pressed a finger to her pinched lips. "I've been more mixed up than an egg in a meringue, but Miss Hayward . . . not quite as I would've suspected," she said finally.

"What do you mean by that?"

"Hattie," Virginia, the topic of our concern, said as she entered the room. Despite the slight frown on her face, unlike me, she appeared well rested. "You may go, Mrs. Curbow." She waited for the housekeeper to leave. "I'd thought you'd gone back to Newport."

"No, not yet." Concern clouded Ginny's countenance. "It's one of the reasons why I called."

"Really? What is it now? Did you remember another mark on my father's face that's no longer there?" I was taken aback by the spitefulness of her words.

"No," I said, almost whispering.

I'd never heard Ginny speak to anyone this way. Was it the death of her father or my transgression at his funeral that caused her to speak to me with such malice? I didn't know. Either way, I swallowed hard several times before getting up the courage to speak again.

"Mrs. Chaplin and the new president's wife have arranged a 'lake party' in my honor for today. I thought it inappropriate to attend it this soon after the funeral, so I wanted your advice."

"Oh!" Ginny closed her eyes and sighed. She opened them again and stared at me. She opened her mouth slightly as if she were about to say something, but she didn't. Instead, she began twiddling with her locket.

Did she write the anonymous note? I suddenly wondered. We took shorthand class together all those years ago. And there was a shorthand dictionary on the table. But if so, why not simply ask me for my help?

Without another word, she walked to the parlor door and opened it. I followed her, knowing when I'm being dismissed. "Father would have wanted you to go to the lake, Hattie." I nodded. "Thank you for calling and your consideration of my feelings." The coldness in her voice belied her words.

"Can I do anything to help, Ginny? Anything?" I placed my hand on her arm as she held the door open. If she'd written the note, I couldn't leave without giving her one last opportunity to ask for my help. I had to know that I'd done everything I could to bring her some peace. But she flinched when I touched her and I had my answer. I pulled my hand away.

"Good-bye, Hattie."

"Good-bye, Virginia." She winced at my use of her full name and yet she said nothing.

I stepped through the door but couldn't resist a quick glance over my shoulder. She was already turning away. It broke my heart to see her filled with such sorrow and not be able to bring her some respite. But why did she look so relieved?

Chapter 9

I was in no mood to be merry after returning from Ginny's house. Yet when the surrey arrived for me, the gaiety of the three girls crammed in the back seat was infectious. All between sixteen and twenty, the students each wore a broad smile, rouge on their cheeks, and by the plethora of feathers, flowers, and ribbons, their best hats. Before I had a chance to arrange myself properly next to the driver, one of the girls burst into a squeal of delight. They all began speaking at once.

"Isn't this glorious, Miss Davish? A lake party!"

"I heard Mr. Upchurch mention music and maybe even dancing!"

"The rumor is Mrs. Chaplin provided the drinks and they include champagne!"

"I wish I had a beau to invite."

"Won't the others be green? We get to ride with the guest of honor!" They stared at me as if I were Annie Oakley or the Princess of Wales. "What can you tell us about Mrs. Mayhew, Miss Davish?"

With that the girls all quieted down, leaning forward in anticipation, hoping not to miss a word. I couldn't help but smile. I was still baffled as to why this party was in my honor, but I was beginning to understand the appeal I had with the young students. How naïve I'd been taking the position of social secretary to one of the country's most famous women. I'd never guessed that what-ever she did was news, and that included hiring me. As Lady Phillippa had predicted, I'd be forever connected with the name, for better or worse.

"What would you like to know?" I asked the girls.

I spent the majority of the ride beguiling them with the extravagant world I was briefly a part of, the grandiose and gaudy Rose Mont, the "cottage" the Mayhews owned in Newport, the lavish garden parties with live peacocks wandering about, the hats that could cost me a month's wages, and the ball that was attended by royalty. As they should be, being students at Mrs. Chaplin's school, they were attentive to my every word, merely interjecting the occasional exclamation of disbelief. When I was through, I finally had the opportunity to ask them about themselves.

"What do you intend to do after you graduate from Mrs. Chaplin's?"

To my astonishment, all three girls, in unison, answered, "Be a private secretary like you."

Of course, I couldn't blame them after I'd spent almost a half hour telling them about the glamorous world of the Mayhew household. But I was unique. Girls who graduate from Mrs. Chaplin's work as typists, stenographers, or if they're especially adept, secretaries in offices, factories, or for the government. Few will become secretaries for wealthy individuals. I was extremely lucky to have met and impressed Sir Arthur Windom-Greene. Without his patronage, I wouldn't be heading to a party held in my honor. But who was I to disillusion them? Our fortuitous arrival through the gates saved me from having to do so.

"We're here!" one of the girls announced, sending the azure blue ribbon from the back of her hat flapping in the wind as she craned her neck out the window to see. I took the moment to look about me as well.

I'd been to the lake a few times when I was a little girl. It used to be a quiet place to picnic and fish. But as the surrey approached I saw the area was now a full-fledged resort with two- and three-story hotels, dozens of cottages, and countless rustic cabins. The St. Joseph Boating Association had built an elaborate clubhouse with four round towers and a porch that encircled the entire building. There was now a small amusement park, as well as the Lake Shore Driving Park, which, one of the girls informed me, held horse racing.

Has everything changed? I wondered.

"Miss Davish is here," someone shouted as our carriage pulled up to an enormous circular pavilion embellished with false dormer windows and a turret topped with a flagpole. The flag waved in the gentle breeze at least thirty feet above us.

I was aghast to see over a hundred people, perhaps the full complement of Mrs. Chaplin's school: students, instructors, former teachers, and their husbands. And at the forefront of them all was the man with the thick burnsides I'd seen comforting Ginny at the funeral.

"Welcome, Miss Davish." He offered his hand as I alighted from the carriage. "Asa Upchurch, school president, at your service."

So that's who he was. I'd heard Mrs. Chaplin had retired but hadn't learned the name of her successor. Not wanting to offend my host, I took his offered hand and stepped down. But Mr. Upchurch didn't relinquish my hand when I was free of the surrey but raised it to his lips. I could feel the blood rising in my cheeks.

"Yes, you're very welcome here, Miss Davish." He finally released his hold on my fingers. Everyone applauded.

Why was everyone making such a fuss? I had to ask. "Why are all these people here, Mr. Upchurch?"

"To honor you, my dear girl."

"But why?"

The middle-aged woman with the dimples stepped next to Mr. Upchurch. He introduced her as his wife.

"Because my dear," Mrs. Upchurch said,

"you're what every one of our girls aspires to, a successful, influential, competent, respected, independent woman. You took your education from Mrs. Chaplin's and made yourself into someone we can all be proud of."

"You're referring to my work with Mrs. Mayhew, aren't you?" I sighed.

I wanted to believe it was due to the efficiency, loyalty, and discretion I accord all my employers, but I'd learned of late that notoriety is more powerful than competency. Of course, it could have nothing to do with Mrs. Mayhew either and everything to do with my successful discovery of two murderers. (I'd uncovered a third, but no one would read about that in the papers anytime soon.)

"Of course. To us you're famous, Miss Davish, and there are many, many people who want to meet you." Mrs. Upchurch immediately took my elbow and proceeded to introduce me to everyone as we made our way through the crowd. Over and over the scene was repeated to my chagrin.

"Miss Davish, this is Miss McGill, our new office management instructor." A young woman with thick, jet-black hair, a long, prominent nose, and hooded eyes thrust out her hand.

"Pleased to make your acquaintance, Miss McGill."

"The pleasure is all mine, Miss Davish."

Occasionally Mrs. Upchurch would put an added pall over the entire exchange by saying,

"And you remember Mrs. LaMont, don't you, Miss Davish? You met her at the funeral."

By the time I'd made it halfway through the crowd, despite the nodding heads, smiling faces, and well wishes, I was feeling overwhelmed and morose. The frequent references to the funeral and the endless interrogation on the subject of Mrs. Mayhew made me want to leave the crowded party and hike alone along the lake.

Either by design or because she'd sensed my mood, Mrs. Upchurch suddenly announced, "We have another surprise for you, Miss Davish." I winced at her words. I wasn't fond of surprises and her words reminded me of the disastrous outcome of the last surprise someone sprung on me. "There's someone special here who's eager to see you again." At that same moment, the band began to play.

Like last time, I thought, picturing Walter break into a smile the moment he saw me at the ball in Newport. *Maybe that particular surprise wasn't terrible after all.*

And then the band began "Buffalo Gals," one of my favorite tunes. What a coincidence. I hadn't heard it in such a long time and no one here could possibly know how much I'd loved this song in my youth. I smiled.

"Yes, Mrs. Upchurch, who is it?" She pointed toward the stage where the band was playing.

A man, accompanied by Mr. Upchurch, climbed

the stairs and walked to the center of the stage to the cheering of the crowd. I couldn't believe my eyes. As handsome as ever with perfectly groomed short, shiny blond hair, piercing blue eyes, and a mouth that was always slightly curved up in a smile, his confident deportment matched his self-assured, casual demeanor as he waved at the crowd.

This is why I hate surprises, I thought, trying to keep my face from revealing the anger and bitterness welling up inside of me.

"Give a warm welcome to a man that needs no introduction," Mr. Upchurch shouted above the music as he patted the man on the back. The crowd applauded as Mr. Upchurch relinquished his spot to the newcomer who, to the delight of the gathering, sang:

As I was walking down Felix Street,
Felix Street, Felix Street,
A pretty girl I chanced to meet,
Under the silvery moon.

St. Joe gals won't you come out tonight?
Come out tonight, come out tonight?
St. Joe gals won't you come out tonight,
And dance by the light of the moon.

"It's Nate Boone," Mrs. Upchurch said, stating the obvious. I knew all too well who he was.

"He's in town visiting and when Asa told him you would be in town, he insisted on being a part of the festivities. Isn't that wonderful? Aren't you delighted? Aren't you surprised?"

Nate continued to sing:

I asked Hattie if she'd stop and talk,
Stop and talk, stop and talk,
Her feet covered up the whole sidewalk,
She was fair to view.

St. Joe gals, won't you come out tonight?
Come out tonight, come out tonight?
St. Joe gals, won't you come out tonight,
And dance by the light of the moon.

What cheek, I thought but said nothing out loud.

"I never knew he was such a good singer, did you, Miss Davish? He's simply marvelous, don't you think? We were very excited when he offered to appear. You were dear friends with Nate Boone, weren't you, Miss Davish?"

Not getting the response she expected, the poor woman continued to try to elicit some positive reaction. But she wasn't going to get it. If anything, it took everything I had not to walk out of the pavilion, disappointing everyone who had come for a pleasant day at the lake, take the carriage back to town, and catch the first train back to Newport.

It's what I should've done in the first place, I thought. Then I wouldn't have had to see him again. And what did Mrs. Upchurch mean, "When Asa told him you would be in town?" No one in St. Joe, with the exception of the person who sent me the funeral notice, knew that I'd be here. Did Mr. Upchurch send me the funeral notice?

Before I could ask, Nate finished the song. Not caring if I offended anyone, I covered my ears. I was not going to listen to the last verse.

I asked her if she'd be my wife,
Be my wife, be my wife,
Then I'd be happy all my life,
If she'd marry me.

St. Joe gals, won't you come out tonight?
Come out tonight, come out tonight?
St. Joe gals, won't you come out tonight,
And dance by the light of the moon.

"Miss Davish, are you ill?" As I lowered my hands, I saw sincere concern on Mrs. Upchurch's face.

"No, I'm fine."

"Good. Oh dear, I do believe we missed something."

She was right. Nate had been talking and all we heard was, "Don't you think?"

People applauded or shouted their agreement.

To what, I didn't catch, but as many of the girls were staring and grinning at me, I had no doubt it had something to do with me.

"Now everyone give her a cheer and smile." The crowd happily obliged. "Hope you liked that last song, Hat. Here's another one you might enjoy." Nate picked up his trombone and the band began playing the "Washington Post March."

"Isn't he dashing?" one of the students said to me. "I didn't know you knew Nate Boone too. You know everybody. You're so lucky!" I nodded politely but held my tongue.

Unlike me, Nate Boone was a bona fide celebrity. He was a member of John Philip Sousa's band and had traveled the world, playing to popes, royalty, and crowds of thousands everywhere he went. And since my mother knew his father, we inevitably grew up together. I don't have any memory of a time I didn't know his name, Nathan Orson Boone. We were the same age and we played together as children. We were in the same class at school and walked there together every day. We hiked and skipped rocks on the river's edge together. We read the same books, liked the same foods, and sang the same songs.

And as we grew up, we grew closer. Although I'd never told anyone, he was my first kiss, behind his music teacher's, Mr. Pryor's, house. When we were sixteen and too naïve to know better, we declared our love and vowed to marry.

His father was thrilled. My father never got the chance to give us his blessing. Before I could tell him, he got sick. And that's when everything changed. As I struggled to take care of my father and go to school at Mrs. Chaplin's, Nate was thriving in the music world. He played in the local brass band and then joined a traveling band as its top soloist. We continued to write, but his letters grew more and more infrequent and then they stopped altogether. I continued to write but never received a reply. Then one day, bereft and knowing no one else I could turn to, I wired him about my father being sent to the asylum. It was one of the darkest days of my life. He never responded. My father died days later. Soon after, I read about Nate having been recruited by Sousa to join his band in the newspaper. I couldn't rise above my own grief to wish him well, to forgive him for abandoning me, for not even responding to my telegram. I haven't been able to stomach listening to Sousa tunes ever since.

Is that how Ginny feels toward me? I wondered as I watched Nate take a bow and step down into the crowd. He was heading straight for me.

"You look fabulous, Hat," he said, using his pet name for me. He playfully flicked his finger at the ribbons on my hat.

"Thank you, Mr. Boone." He frowned. Mrs. Upchurch did as well.

"Now, now, Hattie old girl, is that any way to

greet your old best buddy?" He reached out to embrace me. I took a step back.

"If I recall, you gave up that distinction years ago. Now if you'll excuse me, I see a former teacher I'd like to talk to." And to the surprise of Nate Boone and the chagrin of Mrs. Upchurch, I turned my back on them both and walked away.

Chapter 10

"And then she hired Monsieur Upchurch." Madame Maisonet pointed her cane across the pavilion at the aforementioned president. "Much to Malinda Gilbert's chagrin." I glanced at Miss Gilbert, who was scolding a student who held a glass of champagne in her hand.

"Why would Miss Gilbert object? Isn't Mr. Upchurch a capable president?"

"*Oui, oui*, quite charming and quite competent. *Bien sûr*, there have been those strange incidences lately, but that couldn't possibly reflect poorly on Monsieur Upchurch. No, no, indeed, it's nothing like that. No, *ma chère*, you must remember Malinda from your days here at the school. She hasn't changed a bit." Of course I remembered Malinda Gilbert. She'd been an excellent teacher, albeit a bit gruff in her manner. That certainly hadn't changed; I'd already had two uncomfortable encounters with her. Nevertheless I hadn't been surprised to find she was still teaching all these years later. There had never been a single rumor of Miss Gilbert having a beau. In fact, she'd made her ambitions well-known.

But what did Madame Maisonet mean by 'strange incidences'? I wondered.

"She always expected to succeed Mrs. Chaplin, didn't she? We all did. What happened? Why was Mr. Upchurch hired instead?"

"Who knows?" Madame Maisonet shrugged.

"But . . . ?"

"Well, I do know that Madame Chaplin was hesitant to retire in the first place. I too know that Monsieur Upchurch wisely continues to consult her on certain matters. Perhaps Madame Chaplin was concerned that Malinda would not be congenial with such an arrangement. And then there are the financial troubles. I hear Monsieur Upchurch excels in financial matters."

"What financial troubles? From the number of students I've seen, the school seems to be thriving."

"It's gossip, *ma chère.* I don't know any more." She suddenly lifted her hand to the side of her mouth, shielding her words from being read. "Though Monsieur Hayward's name has been associated with those rumors."

"In what way?" This was the first time I'd heard any ill about the dead man.

"He was the school's bookkeeper, after all."

Madame Maisonet nodded knowingly. I couldn't believe it. I remember Frank Hayward as a loving father, a fair teacher, and a conscientious employee.

Madame Maisonet put her finger over her wrinkled closed lips as two girls, students I'd met after the funeral, approached, each offering me a silver tray, one containing flutes filled with champagne and the other containing a variety of desserts: cheesecake, pound cake, sponge cake, plum cake, pastry biscuits with dollops of stewed fruit, fruit turnovers, and jam puffs. I declined the champagne but happily took a slice of plum cake and an apple turnover. Madame Maisonet's mention of Frank Hayward reminded me of something.

"By the way, madame, when did you learn that I was coming home? It seems everyone knew I was coming before I did."

"I have no idea. Someone told me you were coming for Monsieur Hayward's funeral and that we were to have this party, but for the life of me I can't remember who it was. Does it matter? Ah, Mademoiselle Woodruff." The old lady waved over a short, plump young woman with close-set brown eyes, a round face, and thin pale lips who was passing by. She had a noticeable scar across her chin. The young woman stopped, wrapping her arms around her ample bosom as if giving herself an embrace. Her unadorned black dress, in contrast to her porcelain skin, was an instant reminder that not everyone was enjoying a lovely day at the lake. "Have you met Mademoiselle Davish yet?"

"I saw you at the funeral, Miss Davish, but we haven't been introduced."

"Mademoiselle Woodruff came to the school not long after Madame Chaplin retired," Madame Maisonet said. "Our newest shorthand instructor."

"Nice to make your acquaintance," I said. The young woman nodded her head but said nothing more.

Despite the levity of the conversation about us, the music (the band was playing "Daisy Bell," to which, I hated to admit, I'd been tapping my toes), the sunshine reflecting on the lake, and the warm summer breeze, Miss Woodruff seemed immune to the lightness of the day. Her eyes were puffy, her manner slow and solemn. She was at a party but obviously wishing she were somewhere else.

"Mollie, *ma chère*, are you all right?" Miss Woodruff nodded but couldn't lift her eyes to look at the old lady. "And why do you wear black?"

Miss Woodruff's head jerked up. "Mr. Hayward is dead, Madame," she said with surprising conviction.

"Yes, *ma chère*, but you needn't wear black anymore. Only the family is so obliged."

To our surprise, as well as to those around us, Miss Mollie Woodruff cried out, "Oh!" and threw her hands over her face, and ran out of the pavilion. She barely missed colliding with a man carrying a large tray of dirty champagne glasses.

"Now what was all that about?" the elderly French teacher said as we followed Miss Woodruff's retreat with our eyes. I shook my head in answer to the rhetorical question. "She can be a silly girl, that one." She shrugged. "*Tant pis.*" Oh well.

"Were she and Mr. Hayward close?"

The old lady shook her head. "Not that I know of."

As I'd been speaking with Madame Maisonet, I'd been occasionally looking around at the group gathered: clusters of girls, giggling, whispering, drinking, dancing, and teasing one another over Nate's perfectly timed winks, while the instructors stood alone or in small groups huddled together sipping their champagne and scrutinizing the students for any inappropriate behavior. Miss Corcoran, her shoulders slumped, dabbed raspberry jam from the corner of her mouth. Therefore I saw when Asa Upchurch abruptly swallowed a full glass of champagne, handed the glass to a waiter, patting the man on the shoulder, and left his wife's side. He casually strolled across the pavilion, through the crowd, and stepped out onto the lawn. He continued until he reached a small whitewashed shed next to a hedge of tall viburnum bushes. He glanced about as if making sure no one was looking before disappearing behind the shrubs.

There's a proper place to do that, I thought, appalled by what I suspected the president of Mrs. Chaplin's school of doing.

But he was gone for less time than it would take and when he reappeared his face was red. He tugged at his burnsides as if he was trying to rip them off his face. Something had happened to upset him in that short span of time. But what?

Watching Mr. Upchurch make his way back, I caught a glimpse of movement out of the corner of my eye in the direction of the hedgerow. As I turned to look, another man stepped out from behind the shrubs and strode rapidly in the opposite direction. I never saw his face, but I recognized the Panama hat he was wearing.

Surely it's not the same man I ran into at my father's shop?

As I considered the possibility and wondered what he'd been doing behind the bushes, an image of Frank Hayward popped into my head.

"By the way, madame," I said, turning back to my former French teacher, "and this is going to sound a bit odd, but when you were at the funeral, did you ever question that the man in the coffin was Frank Hayward?" The old lady peered at me, one of her thick eyebrows slightly raised.

"*Oui*, you are right. That is an odd question. So the rumors about you are true, Mademoiselle Davish."

"Rumors about me?"

"That you've become a hawkshaw, a sleuthhound, *un détective*." I smiled, relieved that's all she was referring to.

"I've had the opportunity to help investigate crimes lately, yes. But you didn't answer my question."

"*Mais no*, I didn't, because I don't want to encourage you in any way. Sleuthing is not a ladylike endeavor."

"But . . . ?"

The elderly lady leaned in closer. "But . . . I agree Mr. Hayward did not look himself. Even with the disfigurement and reconstruction, I'd wondered." She leaned back again and shrugged. "*Mais mon Dieu*, my goodness, but who else could it be?"

Chapter 11

"It distresses me to say it, but he might have met with trouble had he lived," Asa Upchurch said. I'd been mingling in the crowd when his comment caught my attention. He was standing with a group of teachers, his wife at his side.

"Why do you say that?" the English teacher said quietly.

"You know as well as I do, Miss Corcoran, that there have been strange incidents at the school lately."

"Yes, but what does that have to do with Mr. Hayward?" Miss McGill, the office management instructor, asked.

"I will not speak ill of the dead but . . ."

"Oh, Miss Davish," Mrs. Upchurch said, spying me. She interrupted her husband before he could say more. "Are you enjoying the party?"

"Yes, thank you, Mrs. Upchurch. But I couldn't help overhear Mr. Hayward's name being mentioned."

"Mr. Upchurch was telling us how he came across Mr. Hayward the day he died," Miss McGill said. I knew full well that wasn't the topic of conversation, but I was interested nonetheless.

"Really, Mr. Upchurch? I'd be grateful for you to tell me the tale. I'm afraid I've been having doubts whether the man in the coffin was indeed Frank Hayward." The women gasped.

"Miss Davish!" Miss Corcoran admonished.

"Who else could it be?" Miss McGill said. That's what Madame Maisonet had said.

"Of course it was," Mr. Upchurch declared. "As Miss McGill said, I found him myself. I was driving when I saw something ahead, sprawled out near the side of the road."

"Where was this?" Miss Corcoran asked.

"Near Sherwood's coffee and spice shop on

South Third. I'd stopped there on my way home."

"And then what?" Miss McGill asked.

"As I drew closer, I realized that it was the body of a man. I halted my horse, wrapped the reins around a nearby pole, and raced over to the fallen man's side. There was blood splattered beneath him and he wasn't breathing or moving. Finally, I drew the courage to turn him over, and was shocked by the grisly wounds, his nose was smashed, his jaw shattered, his cheekbones crushed. I was grateful I hadn't yet eaten my supper. Then I wiped away enough blood and grit to recognize the face. It was obviously Frank Hayward."

"Why do you say it was obviously him?" I said. "As you say, he'd suffered ghastly facial wounds. How did you know for certain it was him?"

"Because . . ." The president hesitated, searching for his reason. "Well . . . it looked like him. So, of course, I dragged him into my buggy and brought him to the Hayward house. Miss Hayward herself identified the man as her father. So it obviously was him. And like I was saying before, it was probably all for the best."

"How can you say that?" I was mortified.

Miss Corcoran held her fingers over her mouth in shock. She still had jam on her cheek. "Are you possibly perhaps insinuating the rumors about the school's financial troubles are true and that Frank Hayward, as the bookkeeper, was involved?"

"Like I said before, dear lady, I don't want to speak ill of the dead but . . ." Mr. Upchurch pulled his arm from around his wife's waist and leaned forward.

"I think that's enough solemn talk for now," Mrs. Upchurch said. "Miss Davish, have you tried the refreshments?"

As she led me to a table laid out with elaborate picnic fare—fried chicken, egg and anchovy sandwiches, cheese and lettuce sandwiches, several different cakes, stewed fruit, pickles, butter and biscuits—I couldn't help but feel dismayed and confused. I'd come home to comfort my friend, not uncover a scandal. I absentmindedly took a jam puff, popped it into my mouth, and excused myself from Mrs. Upchurch's company. I found an empty chair at the edge of the pavilion and pulled out my notepad and pencil from my chatelaine bag. I jotted down a quick list.

1. Was Asa Upchurch insinuating that Frank Hayward was in some way responsible for the school's financial   troubles? If so, how?
2. Could this be what Ginny had hinted about in her last correspondence?
3. Did Ginny suspect her father's involvement in some criminal activity?
4. Could any of this explain Ginny's attitude toward me?

5. What were the incidences Mr. Upchurch referred to?

6. How can I make my excuses and leave?

"Vandal!"

Suddenly the gathering hushed and the music stopped in the middle of playing "I'll Take You Home Again, Kathleen," another favorite of mine from my youth. It always reminded me of my mother. Despite my bitterness toward Nate Boone and my displeasure at seeing him again, I had to admit he knew how to charm me. With the exception of the obligatory Sousa pieces, which I regard as grating noise, Nate had played all of my favorite music. No one else would know why he'd chosen to play "Sweet Genevieve" and Strauss's "The Blue Danube," but I did. But he was going to have to do far more than play Gilbert & Sullivan songs if he was seeking my forgiveness.

"What's going on here?" Mr. Upchurch moved through the crowd toward the source of the cry. I jumped up from my spot and joined the others who stepped in behind him. He led us to the edge of the pavilion where waiters had stacked wooden bottle crates and food boxes, many labeled, CLEMENS BAKERY. Following the waiter who had sounded the call, we rounded the stacks to find at least a dozen empty glass bottles strewn about on sodden grass.

"What's the meaning of this?"

"Mr. Upchurch, sir, someone's emptied all of the remaining champagne bottles onto the ground," the waiter replied.

"Could it, maybe, possibly, have been an accident?" Miss Corcoran asked. The waiter raised an eyebrow and shook his head.

"No, the bottles were secure in their crate. Someone intentionally removed them and poured the champagne into the grass."

"This is all your fault, Asa Upchurch," Miss Gilbert said, stomping her way through the crowd, finger wagging in incrimination. "None of this would've happened if I were in charge."

"Ah, Miss Gilbert." Mr. Upchurch raised his hand in an attempt to touch the woman's shoulder. Miss Gilbert glared and took a step back. Upchurch continued as if nothing had happened. "I regret this unfortunate act of vandalism, we will all miss having one last glass of champagne, but we're in a public park; who knows what miscreants are about."

"You should've planned ahead, preventing such a thing from happening."

"How could I have foreseen such an event? If you're clairvoyant, a talent you have kept well hidden, I will gladly take your recommendation for prevention in the future." Mr. Upchurch smiled at those around him, but Miss Gilbert ignored Mr. Upchurch's lighthearted jibe.

"And what about the fire in the etiquette classroom? Or the money earned at the annual spring bazaar that was stolen? Are you saying you're not responsible for those either?"

"Not personally, no. In fact, I was telling some of the ladies that maybe Frank Hayward . . ."

Thankfully Miss Gilbert ignored Mr. Upchurch's insinuation and continued after taking a breath. "Or the vandalized typewriters? The missing pages from the new shorthand dictionaries? Are you denying responsibility for those as well?" Before he could reply, Miss Gilbert stepped within inches of the president, her height matching his own. "And the 'misplaced' enrollment documents? Are you denying responsibility for the missing documents?"

"I think you misjudge me, Miss Gilbert." Mr. Upchurch placed a hand on her arm. She shrugged it off but stayed where she was. "As president, I take full responsibility for everything that occurs during my tenure. However, I will not be accused of negligence by one of my own staff in public. I believe you owe me an apology."

"Missing enrollment documents?" someone whispered behind me.

"I hadn't heard about the fire, had you?" someone else added.

"Did he say Frank Hayward stole the bazaar money?" another whispered. I turned to see who might have said the last comment, but all eyes were on Mrs. Upchurch as she pushed her way through the gathering crowd.

"Excuse me. Excuse me."

"I will never apologize to you, Mr. Upchurch!" Miss Gilbert declared. Mr. Upchurch sighed and shook his head.

"That's enough, Miss Gilbert," he said. "I don't think this is the time or the place to be discussing school affairs. We have a reputation to uphold, after all."

"Well, then, if it's our reputation you're concerned about, maybe we should reconsider the management of the school and hire someone else to be president!"

"I think you've said your piece, Malinda," Mrs. Upchurch said, stepping between her husband and the typing teacher and waving to one of the girls serving. "Here," she said, taking one of the last glasses of champagne off the tray, "have a drink and enjoy the party."

Malinda Gilbert turned her nose up at the offering and stormed back through the crowd. Mrs. Upchurch nodded at Nate, who began playing again, this time "Beautiful Dreamer." Before I could question Mr. Upchurch about Miss Gilbert's accusations, he had offered his wife his arm and escorted her in the opposite direction Miss Gilbert had gone.

What a party, I thought. At least now I knew what strange incidents Madame Maisonet had referred to. I felt certain that Frank Hayward wouldn't have had anything to do with such pettiness. But then who would?

It's none of your concern, Hattie, I told myself as I made my way back to the table for more sponge cake.

Unlike the boisterous ride to Lake Contrary, my return trip was quiet and alone. Much to my hosts' chagrin, I decided to leave early. I had no intention of speaking to Nate Boone again, or listening to Miss Gilbert complain about Mr. Upchurch's management of the school, or hearing one more comment insinuating that Frank Hayward had something to do with the school's rumored financial troubles. I'd agreed to go to the lake party because Mrs. Chaplin insisted my presence would be a boon to the grief-stricken students and instructors. I'd hoped to enjoy myself. But I should've known better when the lady herself declined to go. I never was one for school politics and scandals, even when I was a student and current with all of the rumors. In the end my being there merely set the stage for an unwanted reunion with Nate, disturbing rumors about Frank Hayward, and more questions about working for Mrs. Charlotte Mayhew.

I admit the lemon cheesecake was delicious (though I could've walked over to Prinz's on Edmond for the best cheesecake in town). And it was lovely to see the lake again, but I hadn't a moment to hike and explore it on my own. However, the party had mostly cemented my feelings that it was time to return to Newport. At least that's what I was thinking when I inquired at the hotel desk for any mail.

"Here you are." Mr. Putney handed me three letters and a telegram.

I glanced at the letters, immediately recognizing Walter's handwriting on one and Miss Lizzie's, a dear old lady who had befriended me recently, on the other. Seeing their letters boosted my spirits. And then I glanced at the third letter. It was typewritten with no return address exactly like the anonymous one before it. I ripped it open. It read in standard shorthand:

For the good of the school, please help us.

Who's sending these letters? I wondered with a mixture of dread and annoyance. At least it confirmed my suspicions that someone from the school was sending them. But why? And what did they expect me to do?

I had turned to go to my room when the clerk said, "Are you going to open the telegram?"

Distracted by the anonymous note, I'd barely noticed the telegram. "Yes, thank you, Mr. Putney." I pulled it out from beneath the letters I was holding.

"It's lucky you got here when you did. The telegram scarcely arrived five minutes ago over the wire."

It was marked "URGENT." I immediately ripped open the envelope. It was from Sir Arthur.

THE WESTERN UNION
TELEGRAPH COMPANY
NUMBER *309* SENT BY *CM*
REC'D BY *WT* CHECK *25 paid*
RECEIVED at *3rd sw cor Edmond Aug 27* 1893
Dated: *Newport, Rhode Island*   *5:38 pm*
To: *Hattie Davish St. Charles Hotel,*
St. Joseph, MO

Arrived in Newport.
Expect you no later September 7.
Research all on General Thompson
before returning.

A Windom-Greene

I shook my head at his careless sense of urgency. And then I sighed. In an instant my plans to leave St. Joseph as soon as possible, tomorrow if I could secure a ticket, had changed. *At least now I have something constructive to do,* I thought, cheering up slightly.

"Nothing too bad, I hope?" the clerk said, curious but concerned.

"No, thank you, everything is as it should be." Mr. Putney nodded, genuinely relieved. "By the way, you don't happen to know who"—I glanced down at the telegram—"General Thompson is, do you?" Although I didn't recognize the name, knowing Sir Arthur, I could easily guess.

"You mean Jeff Thompson, former mayor of St. Joseph, known as the 'Swamp Fox of the Confederacy'?"

"Yes, I suspect that is whom I'm referring to. Do you know where I can find him?" The clerk's eyebrows rose in question.

"Sure, and you can go visit him anytime you like."

"Really?" Maybe the research Sir Arthur required wouldn't hold me in St. Joseph much more than a day after all.

"Sure. Mount Mora is open every day, dawn to dusk."

"Oh! Of course." I'd forgotten that he was the infamous Confederate general buried there.

My shoulders sagged as the reality set in. Without a personal account from the man himself, I could be here for days. I glanced down at Walter's letter, suddenly missing him terribly. I hoped it contained better news.

Chapter 12

Who else could it be?

That question haunted me all night. After reading the letters from Newport, I spent the evening writing replies and went to bed filled with thoughts of Walter playing tennis every day at the Casino and Miss Lizzie's report that the Mayhew household had unexpectedly abandoned Rose Mont for Europe days before. And yet it wasn't thoughts of Walter or the Mayhews that crowded my restless mind. As the tune of "I'll Take You Home, Kathleen" played over and over in my head, I dreamt one dream over and over all night. Champagne, by unknown hands, was poured over my head as Madame Maisonet poked me with her cane and asked, "Who else could it be?" I woke many times throughout the night and each time her question echoed in my brain. Finally, an hour before dawn, I couldn't take it anymore. I rose, and in an attempt to occupy my mind with productive thoughts, I sat down at the desk. Once again, I dipped my pen in ink and jotted down what I might do to satisfy Sir Arthur's request. Depending upon how much had been recorded about General Thompson, I could be in for several long days of research.

Good, I thought. To return to a routine of

focused and productive work would benefit me far more than the reminiscing and conjecturing I had witnessed of late. And yet even as I dressed for an early-morning hike, the image of Frank Hayward in his coffin and the voice of Madame Maisonet asking "Who else could it be?" returned.

And the thought returned again and again, as it had in my sleep, as I hiked north along the river. Even as I stood on the bluffs, with one of the best views of the city, which is why they built Fort Smith here during the Civil War (with the cannons aimed at the city), I couldn't shake the idea that the man in Frank Hayward's coffin wasn't Frank Hayward.

But why couldn't I shake it? Because the dark, overcast sky was dampening my spirits? Because I'd mistaken on which side of his face he'd had a distinct scar? Because Ginny's grief wasn't as visible as mine had been? Or was it because I was desperate to give my friend something I could never have, her beloved father back? It didn't matter. I couldn't change the truth, and I'd been childish and selfish thinking I could. Frank Hayward, like George Davish, was now beyond our earthly reach. All that was left for me to do was accept the fact and get to work.

But then why can't I stop hearing Madame Maisonet say, "Who could it be?"

I spent most of the day visiting the library, City Hall, and the courthouse, poring over books, newspaper clippings, and records about General Meriwether Jeff Thompson. I was pleasantly surprised how much I learned in a short time. Beyond the basics—his birth, his death, his marriage, his children, his occupations, and his places of residency—I was also able to uncover intimate details. Before the war, Thompson was a land agent and leader in developing the Hannibal and St. Joseph Railroad, as well as the Pony Express. But he was also the man who brought the Civil War to St. Joe. As mayor at the outbreak of the war, he led a mob to remove the U.S. flag from the post office. The act was so controversial he was forced to flee the city, eventually joining the Confederacy. There he gained the nickname the Swamp Fox by spending much of the war leading ragtag Confederate guerillas on forays through the swamps of the South. While a prisoner of war in Charleston, he took up writing poetry and, unlike anyone else, carried a white-handled bowie knife stuck out perpendicularly from his belt on the middle of his back. But the strangest detail I'd uncovered all day was that General Thompson had proudly supplied, and reclaimed afterward, the rope used to suspend John Brown from the gallows.

Sir Arthur will be thrilled, I thought.

Pleased with my day's work, I emerged from the courthouse into a clear, blue sky and brilliant sunshine. I felt my spirits lift. I walked the two blocks north to 516 N. Fifth Street, General Thompson's former residence. A maid answered the door and was able to confirm that the house had long since been sold to a family who had no connection to the Thompsons. Satisfied I'd done all that I could do, I happily forwent the streetcar and briskly made my way back toward my hotel, taking a quick detour when I spied a vendor's wagon parked down the block (I hadn't eaten anything all day).

I can leave for Newport tomorrow, I thought, as I glanced down the street. I noticed the sign for Sherwood's spice shop.

And then I froze. A woman, less than twenty yards away, was stooped over, staring down at the ground. A gray squirrel scampered across the yellow awning above her head, scrambled down the side of the brick building, and bounded across the street. She didn't notice. She was obviously searching for something she'd dropped in the road, but that's not why I stopped. She was standing in the exact spot that Asa Upchurch said he found the dead body of Frank Hayward. I immediately approached her.

"Excuse me, ma'am?"

She looked up at me, her eyes blank. Graying yellow curls popped out from under her floppy straw hat with a simple gray velvet bow, sunspots marked her face, and her shoulder stayed slightly hunched over even when she stood. Her deep-set blue eyes, deeply wrinkled at the corners, couldn't focus. Was she blind? I wondered.

"Are you looking for something? May I help look?"

"Yes," she said, bobbing her head as she looked about her as if for the first time. "Yes, I'm looking for my husband, Levi."

Taken by surprise, I almost retorted, "In the road?" But luckily I caught myself and asked instead, "Does your husband work around here? Can I take you to him?"

"No, he works at the Excelsior Wagon and Carriage Works on Lafayette."

"But you're on South Third and Charles Street, ma'am." I was still under the impression that her sight was poor. Then she looked me in the eye.

"I know. You see, I've been at my sister's." She hesitated as if she'd finished her tale. She looked about her again and continued as she took in the buildings surrounding us. "When I came home, Levi was gone. He's been anxious lately, you see, and I worry about him."

"Have you checked at the hospitals?" She nodded. "Then what brought you here?"

"Someone at Ensworth Hospital said that a man fitting my husband's description was rumored to have been found dead here several days ago." I tried to keep the shock from my face. Frank Hayward? Could he have had a wife no one knew about? Could he have had a false identity? Had Ginny suspected?

"There's nothing here now, I know, but I was hoping someone saw something or could tell me something that might help me find Levi." And then she pulled a photograph out of her leather shopping bag. "This is him, my husband, Levi Yardley, taken many years ago." She held it up for me to see. I gasped but couldn't bring myself to say a word.

I knew it!

"What is it?" she said. "Do you know something about my husband? Please, please tell me if you do?"

I took the photograph from the woman's hand and looked at it more closely. Even without the aid of my monocular, I could see the uncanny resemblance. For with the exception of a bulbous nose and the scar missing from his eyebrow, Levi Yardley was the very image of Frank Hayward.

I wasn't going crazy after all, I thought.

But what should I say to this poor soul? For despite being vindicated for my suspicions, I still didn't know if I was right. I didn't know which man was dead or which man was actually buried in Frank Hayward's grave or which man recently escaped from the Lunatic Asylum. Could it all be the same man? Could the bulbous nose be a disguise? Was Frank Hayward really Levi Yardley and vice versa? I'd come across men who had false identities before. Or was it a mere coincidence that the two men resembled each other? I didn't believe in such coincidences. Something was definitely suspicious here. But what? Could one have been mistaken for the other? Could Levi Yardley have been the missing patient from the State Lunatic Asylum and mistakenly buried in Frank Hayward's place? If so, where was Frank Hayward? I had a sick feeling in the pit of my stomach, envisioning myself cheering on who I'd thought was an escapee from the asylum. Could that actually have been Frank Hayward? Or Levi Yardley? I didn't want to believe Frank Hayward was capable of killing Levi in order to fake his own death. But it was possible. Or was it the other way around? If so, why? At least one of them had been admitted to the asylum, after all. My head hurt puzzling it out.

"Please, if you know something," Mrs. Levi Yardley pleaded, grabbing ahold of my arm.

"I don't know much, Mrs. Yardley, but I can tell you all I suspect. Is there somewhere we can talk? It's a little complicated."

How little I knew what an understatement that would turn out to be.

"Then we must go to the asylum and determine if it was my husband who escaped!" Mrs. Yardley insisted after I explained my suspicions to her.

We'd found a small restaurant a few blocks away. I ordered a plate of beef, fried potatoes, cabbage, and apple pudding. I was starving. We both ordered coffee.

We? I had no intention of going to that place ever again. I told her as much.

"Please, Miss Davish. I must know what's become of Levi."

"I understand, Mrs. Yardley. If our places were reversed, I'd have to know as well. But he's your husband. Why must I go?"

"I can't go alone." She shook her head violently. "I had a friend that struggled a bit after the birth of her fifth child and they sent her to the state asylum. I never saw her again."

"What does that have to do with me going with you?"

"What if they won't let me leave?"

I wanted to tell her she was foolish to think such a thing, but I couldn't. She had every reason to be afraid. I'd been there before, and after reading a list of reasons for admittance that included everything from immorality and grief to novel reading and uterine derangement, I held the same fear. And I knew they could do it without anyone's consent.

"Don't you have family or a friend who could go with you?"

"No, Levi and I moved here from Omaha a few months ago. We don't have family in town.

Our children are all grown with families of their own. And we haven't made any friends yet. I know you as well as I do my neighbors. It's not like home where we had lots of friends. I still don't understand why Levi made us leave. He had a good job working for the Elder Carriage Company." She reached across the table and grabbed my hand in both of hers. "Please, Miss Davish, will you go?"

No, I told myself. *I can't go back there. I swore I'd never go there again.*

And yet my heart ached for this poor woman. Would I plead with a stranger for help if it meant finding the truth about a loved one? About my father? And too, I couldn't deny the pull of curiosity. Could this be a strange case of mistaken identity? I hadn't heard of Frank Hayward spending any time in the asylum and assumed Levi Yardley was the escaped patient. But if so, why hadn't he contacted his wife? Hadn't I seen him in the buggy making his getaway? Or had I? Could Levi Yardley be the man whom Asa Upchurch found in the street? Could he be the man in Frank Hayward's coffin? If so, I'd been right to disturb Ginny with the news. But then where was Frank Hayward? I had to find out.

And yet I still couldn't believe my own ears when I said, "Very well, Mrs. Yardley. I will accompany you to the asylum." The woman sighed in relief.

"Please call me Bertha."

"Very well, Bertha," I said, standing. I placed coins on my bill, snapped my purse closed, straightened my hat, and said, "Let's go find out what happened to your husband."

Chapter 13

It hadn't changed a bit. After hiring a cab, the mile walk beyond the last streetcar stop being too strenuous for Mrs. Yardley, we drove beyond the city limits on Frederick Avenue until we came to pasture and farmland. Horses grazed as men in denim overalls drove a caravan of Bain wagons toward a distant orchard. Dairy cattle, chewing their cud and swishing their tails, watched as we passed. Dozens of men in old woolen suits and women in gray linen aprons, their backs bent, took no notice of us as they harvested fruits and vegetables from gardens that stretched for acres. We had arrived at State Lunatic Asylum Number Two. I never discovered where Number One was; I didn't care. Surrounded by a deceptively pastoral scene, this institution, with its redbrick four-story building sprawling over a quarter of a mile long, capped with numerous cupolas and wings that stretched out on either side of the center, like some large raptor about to take flight, haunted my nightmares. And here I was again.

This time I wasn't leaving without answers.

As we pulled into the semicircular drive, lined with trees shading the many wooden benches and swings scattered about, Mrs. Yardley leaned over, and said, "Are we in the right place, Miss Davish? It looks like a city park."

"Don't let the illusion fool you, Mrs. Yardley." Before long, she understood what I meant.

We disembarked from the cab and headed up the path to the main entrance. Bertha Yardley's expression soon reflected my own trepidation. Before reaching the front doors, we passed a row of men in plain blue suits with white shirts but no ties, rocking incessantly, their chairs lined up parallel, instead of perpendicular against the wall. Several had their arms cuffed to the armrests of their rocking chairs. Mrs. Yardley unconsciously moved closer and took my arm.

"Miss Davish, what do we do?" she said when the closest man waved to us, his fingers wiggling independent of each other, a blank stare upon his face.

"You might wave back if you want or keep walking. He means you no harm."

I'd seen this scene before, and far, far worse, but time had diminished its hold over me. Yet as we neared the front door, my heart fluttered and I grew light-headed. I forced myself to take deep breaths, imagining Walter, and not Mrs. Yardley, holding my arm. I took one last deep breath and pulled at the door. It refused to open.

"What's wrong?" Mrs. Yardley's voice was slightly higher pitched than usual.

"The door's locked." I didn't remember the door being locked in the middle of the day.

"Then we must knock." Without conferring, we knocked at the door simultaneously. We looked at each other and chuckled nervously. And then Mrs. Yardley grew serious. "We will find him, won't we, Miss Davish?"

"Yes, we will. And if he's not here, we won't leave until we know what's happened to him." And then the door opened.

"May I help you?" A young woman in a plain light blue cotton dress and white apron of a nurse's uniform stood in the doorway.

"Yes," Bertha said, as I peered beyond the woman's shoulder to the hallway beyond.

Uncluttered by chairs, hat stands, tables, or furniture of any kind, the wide hall stretched toward a grand oak staircase at its end, the main access to the upper floors. Several doors, accented by oak molding and lead glass transoms, stood open and inviting. Light from a large ornate brass chandelier high above reflected off the spotless decorative tile floor as a woman in a light gray wrapper pushed a floor drag over and over across the same few feet of tile. It was bright, it was clean, and it was tranquil, and yet I hoped I'd never have to step into that hall again.

"I'm looking for my husband, Levi Yardley. I think he may have been a patient here."

"Please come in." The young nurse opened the door wider and stepped aside.

"No," Bertha said, to my utter relief. "No, I'd prefer to stay here if that's all right." She pulled out the photograph of her husband. "If you could take a look at this and tell me, I'll be on my way."

The nurse frowned. "Very well. If you'll stay a moment, I will ask Nurse Simmons to assist you." Bertha nodded.

The man who had waved to us rose from his chair and shuffled toward the open door.

"No, Henry. It's not time to come in yet. Go back to your chair," the nurse said. Henry, without uttering a word, turned around, still wiggling his fingers about in front of him, and headed back to his rocker. The woman, satisfied Henry wouldn't follow, turned and disappeared into the first doorway on the right.

"I hope it's all right by you, Miss Davish, but if I don't have to step foot in this place, I'd rather not."

"It's more than all right, Bertha. It's sound judgment. And please call me Hattie." She nodded, but her smile quickly vanished. "Are you well, Hattie? You look a bit pale."

"I'm fine." I smiled, remembering all the times I'd told Walter the very same thing. Of course, he knew better.

"Hello, I'm Nurse Simmons." This nurse was also in her early twenties, with shiny blond hair, wide-set blue eyes, and teeth too big for her mouth. "The duty nurse said you were inquiring about your husband, Mrs. Yardley?"

"Yes," Bertha said, showing the nurse the photograph. "Was he a patient here?" The nurse didn't even give the photograph a glance.

"Yes, Mrs. Yardley, your husband was a patient here."

"Was?"

"Yes, I'm afraid to say he is no longer with us."

"No longer with us? Oh my God! Are you saying my husband's dead?" Bertha cried, squeezing my arm.

"No, no, Bertha, I think she means he escaped," I said, patting her hand.

"Oh!" Bertha sighed in relief.

The nurse seemed a bit taken aback by my statement. It hadn't been a question. "Yes, I'm afraid you're right. And you are?"

"Miss Hattie Davish."

"Well, Miss Davish and Mrs. Yardley, Mr. Yardley is currently the subject of a citywide search. He escaped a week ago and is considered possibly dangerous. He was admitted for mental excitement in the first place."

"By whom?" Bertha asked. "He's been a little anxious lately, yes, but nothing he hasn't been able to cope with before."

"Many patients find it hard to reveal the truth, even to their loved ones, but Mr. Yardley had been seeing the doctor for several weeks before he was admitted to the asylum."

"Who was the doctor?" I asked. "How can you admit someone without gaining permission from the family, let alone notifying them?" This is exactly what had happened to my father. After suffering from illness for months at home, he was finally beginning to recover. And then one day, without my knowledge or permission, Father was admitted to this place. He lasted but a few days in here.

"Mr. Yardley admitted himself, voluntarily," Nurse Simmons said.

"Then why did he escape?" I asked. The nurse had nothing to say.

The smell of carbolic acid, urine, and the metallic scent of blood accosted me every time I stepped foot in the room. I felt ashamed holding a hand-kerchief to my nose. I peered over the stooped figure of the doctor to see the lump beneath the sheets in my father's bed. The doctor raised his arm, holding a shiny steel syringe with a six-inch needle attached. I gasped at the sight. Startled, he dropped the syringe and swiveled around to face me.

"You shouldn't be here, Miss Davish," he said. "Your father's very unwell."

I glanced at the table beside his bed. The silver tray my mother used to use for special occasions was crowded with a full pitcher of water, a partially filled glass of water, brown glass bottles with cork stoppers and white paper labels glued to the front, and unlabeled glass tubes filled with blue pills. And then I saw what was on the washstand: a metal bowl filled with dark, bloody water and partially submerged steel instruments of what purpose I couldn't imagine.

"Yes," I said. "And he seems to be getting worse."

Several months ago, my father began complaining of headaches. Soon he was waking, shouting in the night, his forehead damp and his body shaking. When I'd ask what was ailing him, he'd say, "I'm fine." When I asked if he was dreaming of his time in the war, he'd tell me, "Go back to bed, Hattie." I could only guess what had occurred to trigger some distant memory that haunted him now in his sleep. I was concerned for him but as he rose every morning as if nothing had happened, I went about my daily life as usual. Until one day, after several weeks of nightly terrors, he refused to rise from his bed. Except for the day we buried my mother, it was the only day in my life that he'd not gone to the shop. With the help of the housekeeper, I was able to nurse him while still attending Mrs. Chaplin's school, until the day I came home to find a doctor examining my father. I never learned how he knew to come by. When I asked, Father turned his head away and the doctor didn't deem it necessary to explain anything to a seventeen-year-old girl. He came twice a day for three days, each time insisting that my father should "get the help he needed." My father would thrash in his bed, yelling, "Never, never." For the first time in my life I was frightened of my father and for my father. When the doctor left, Father would grab my hand, sometimes squeezing it too hard.

"Remember, we're not quitters, you and me. I'll get better, but I have to stay out of that wretched place. Promise you won't let them take me." I had no idea what place he was talking about. I assumed he meant the hospital.

"I promise."

When my father continued to refuse to leave his home, the doctor arranged for a special doctor to visit, Dr. Hillman, one who had more experience in "this type of mind disease." When I'd asked what he meant, he'd merely patted my head, and said, "Poor child." Dr. Hillman had continued to arrive in place of the first doctor from that day on. I couldn't see how his experience was helping. As far as I could tell, since in his care, my father's decline had been rapid and frightening.

A groan came from the bed, and ignoring the demands of the doctor to leave, I made my way to my father's side and sat on the edge of the bed. Wrapped in the sheets like a mummy, all I could see of him was his head. He was pale, having not stepped outside for weeks, and his hair, not drying properly after the washing I'd attempted the night before, was sticking up at random angles. He needed a shave and a haircut. I brushed the hair away from his eyes.

"Father? It's Hattie, Father." His eyes darted around until they came close to looking at me.

"Mary Margaret?"

"No, Father, it's Hattie, your daughter."

"Oh, Mary Margaret, forgive me. Forgive me. I can't find your fiddle." And with that my father began to sob hysterically. I'd never seen my father cry.

I laid my hand on his shoulder. "Father, it's all right. Mama's fiddle is in the closet."

"Forgive me, but I don't know what I did with it."

"It's right here," I said. "I'll show you." I stood up, intending to retrieve my mother's violin, when, without warning, his tears turned to shouts and he began thrashing about.

"Get it off! Get it off!" He tried to pull his

hand loose from the sheets but couldn't. Frustrated, he began thrashing about.

"Blazes! I can feel them crawling on me. You there," he said, scowling at me. "Can't you see them? Get the damn things away from me!" I started to shake. I didn't know what upset me more, to hear my father cuss for the first time in my life or the fact that I saw nothing but the white sheets on his bed.

I took a few steps back as the doctor rushed in to administer something to calm my father down. He lifted a part of the sheet, revealing my father's bare leg.

"Damn you to Hell," Father screamed as the doctor jabbed the needle deep into the thick thigh muscle. I turned, overwhelmed with nausea, and fell to my knees. As I emptied the contents of my stomach on the floor, I heard my father moan and grow quiet. In my head, he said, "We're not quitters, you and me." But my head was spinning so much that I didn't flinch when I felt a hand on the back of my shoulder. As I struggled to take a deep breath, my ribs feeling crushed against my stays, I shrugged the hand off.

"Now, now, Miss Davish, it's time we arrange for your father's admission to the asylum."

"No." I wiped my mouth with a handkerchief before facing the doctor. "Father said he doesn't want to go. Besides, you've made him worse with your treatment."

"I have years of experience working with this disease. Trust me. I'm confident that if I can oversee his treatment day and night, his condition will improve."

"But he doesn't even recognize his own daughter." Suddenly the rage my helpless father had felt filled me. I leaped to my feet. "Out!" I screamed, pointing to the door. "Get out!"

"Now, Miss Davish, be rational."

"I am. I never want to see your face again."

"Your father requires arduous medical attention. What will you do, nurse him yourself?"

"He was better off when I did! Now go!" I strode over to the door, yanked it open, and waited. The doctor collected his instruments, slowly cleaning them one by one before returning them to his case. When he finally closed the lid on his bag, he looked up at me as if to say something but instead strode out the door, shaking his head. I slammed the door behind him.

I went over to my father, freed both his arms from the sheet, and wiped the drool dripping down his face. I dabbed his forehead with a cool rag lying in a clean bowl of water beside the bed.

"Hattie?"

"Yes, Father." I was elated that he knew who I was. But the feeling wouldn't last.

"Hattie? Where's my girl, Hattie?"

"She's right here, Father," I said. "And she's not going to let anyone hurt you again."

"Who was the doctor?" I asked. The nurse still hadn't given us a name.

"Dr. Hillman. He's in charge of the nervous patients."

"Dr. Hillman?" Had I heard her right? The cursed man who had admitted my father and had overseen his treatment all those years ago? I expected to feel the room sway, but instead I felt a wave of anger flow through me and my face flushed.

"Yes, Dr. Cyrus Hillman," the nurse said.

"If he was Mr. Yardley's doctor, Bertha," I said, "your poor husband didn't have a chance." And before I knew what I was doing, I pushed past the nurse, strode into the hall, and began looking at the nameplates on the doors. Not seeing what I was looking for, I rushed toward the stairs.

"Hattie?" Bertha called from the doorway as I ascended the stairs. "What are you doing? Where are you going?"

"I'm going to find Dr. Hillman and find out once and for all what happened to my father!" I shouted without looking back.

"Don't you mean my husband?" she said, as she scuttled through the door to follow me.

Intent on finding his office, I hadn't realized my mistake. I merely nodded and continued on, but unlike the hallway below, the doors on the second floor were all closed. And then suddenly it was there, the name I was looking for. Without a moment of hesitation, I placed my hand on the doorknob and turned it.

"Hattie, what are you doing?" Bertha called, having reached the top of the stair.

"Follow me, Bertha. Dr. Hillman has some questions to answer."

"What's the meaning of this?"

Dr. Cyrus Hillman, sitting behind a small oak desk, looked up from the paper he was reading. Oak bookshelves lined the wall behind him, populated mostly with medical books and rows and rows of medical journals. On the opposite wall were two metal filing cabinets and a wooden hat rack, with a single tan derby hanging from a hook. Several high-backed wooden side chairs were scattered about the room, and a Hermann Herzog landscape painting of a river scene hung on the far wall. With dark circles beneath his eyes and patches of gray in the temples of his dark brown hair and his neatly trimmed beard, the man before me was older and more tired looking than I remembered. Yet, I could never forget the gaze from his deep-set eyes.

"I'm sorry, Doctor," Nurse Simmons said.

"They were asking about Mr. Yardley and then shoved their way by me."

"This is highly irregular. You've interrupted my work. I must insist that you please leave."

I didn't move. I couldn't say a word. My anger, and with it my courage, had abandoned me the moment I heard his voice. Then I stared at the photographs. An entire shelf on the bookcase behind the doctor was dedicated to a row of silver-framed photographs of smiling dark-haired children. How could the man who killed my father be a father? The idea further unsettled me. Luckily Bertha Yardley wasn't so dumb-struck.

"We're not leaving until I know what's become of my husband." Bertha advanced on him. "Why did you admit him? What was wrong with him? Where's he now? Did he escape from here? Tell me, Dr. Hillman. I want to see my husband!"

"I'm sorry, Mrs. Yardley, but I cannot discuss my patients without a careful review of their files and certainly not under duress. Make an appointment and I will do my best to answer your questions. Nurse Simmons, if you would escort these women back downstairs, I'd be much obliged." He looked back down at the paper on his desk. I couldn't stand by in silence any longer. I joined Bertha at the edge of the physician's desk.

"Do you remember me, Dr. Hillman?" I managed to say.

Without looking at me, he said, "Were you a patient?"

"No, but my father was. George Davish? Do you remember him?"

"Of course. How is your father?"

"Dead, thanks to you." His head jerked up to glare at me. That got his attention, I thought.

"I'm sorry about your father, but I did everything I could. He was a very sick man."

"If you remember my father, Doctor, why did you ask how he was?"

"Because all of my patients are very sick men. Now please, as you can see"—he indicated the papers on his desk—"I have work to do."

"And we have unanswered questions," Bertha chimed in. "Is it true my husband escaped from your care here?"

"If I answer, will you leave me in peace?" She nodded. I didn't. Now that I was close enough that I could smell the Macassar oil in his hair, I never intended to leave this man in peace.

"Very well. The truth is, Mrs. Yardley, neither your husband nor anyone else has recently escaped from these walls. It's been known to happen, yes, but not in a very long time." The doctor shuffled through the files on his desk before finding the one he wanted. He picked it up and perused the contents. It was labeled, LEVI YARDLEY.

"But, Doctor?" Nurse Simmons said.

133

"Your husband," Dr. Hillman continued, ignoring the nurse's protest, "was suffering from a severe case of business nerves." He put the file down but didn't look up. Instead, he shoved the file into a desk drawer. "I admitted him, treated him, and then released him. That's all. He was here for a few days and then left."

"But he wasn't at home when I came back from my sister's," Bertha said. Dr. Hillman looked at the distressed woman.

"I'm sorry, Mrs. Yardley, but I don't keep track of my patients after they leave."

"If no one escaped recently, why were there orderlies in town searching for a missing patient?" I asked. "And why did you say it was Mr. Yardley they were looking for, Nurse Simmons?" Nurse Simmons opened her mouth but said nothing.

"Nurse Simmons must've misunderstood. I've answered your questions and have nothing more to tell you. Now, if you'd be so kind and let me return to my work."

Bertha and Nurse Simmons retreated quietly, but I couldn't let him have the last word. I leaned on the desk, my heart thumping in my chest, and stared at him until he looked up.

"What is it? I've told you all I know."

"Have you? We'll see about that." I enjoyed the scowl on the man's face, before turning my back on him to leave.

Chapter 14

"You know what Dr. Hillman told Levi Yardley's wife?" Nurse Simmons huddled in a circle of nurses standing outside the nurse's office as Bertha and I descended the grand staircase. After several of the nurses inquired about what he'd said, Nurse Simmons declared, "That he released the patient, that Levi Yardley never escaped."

To the protests and astonishment of the nurses, Nurse Simmons nodded. "I know, I know."

"You don't believe him?" I asked, approaching the nurses.

"Were you eavesdropping, Miss Davish?" Nurse Simmons said.

"No, I couldn't help but overhear your entire conversation with the acoustics in this hall." I pointed up to the tin ceiling tiles.

"You certainly weren't whispering," Bertha added. Several nurses nodded. Nurse Simmons shrugged.

"Well, I'd no reason to. It's ridiculous for Dr. Hillman to claim he discharged your husband, Mrs. Yardley. Why else would the asylum staff be searching for Mr. Yardley all over the city? I don't know why he'd say such a thing."

"Don't you have records of such things?" I asked.

"Of course." Nurse Simmons gestured for us to follow her. She led us down a flight of back stairs and into a room marked RECORDS above the door. Every wall was lined with tall, black metal cabinets. Each drawer of every cabinet was labeled. Nurse Simmons walked over to a cabinet on the far wall and pulled a drawer out labeled "Y." She scanned through several files until selecting the one she wanted.

"You see, this is for Mr. Yardley and there are no discharge papers here."

"May I see?" Bertha eagerly reached for the file that could tell her more about her husband's condition and his time spent here.

"No, I'm sorry." Nurse Simmons hurriedly refiled the folder and slammed the drawer shut. "The files are restricted to staff. But at least we know for sure that Dr. Hillman wasn't being truthful."

"I wonder why?"

"That's what I'd like to know, Miss Davish." Nurse Simmons indicated for us to precede her out of the room. "He's normally meticulous about everything. I can't see him making such an important mistake."

I was the first one through the doorway. I turned my head to ask Nurse Simmons another question when Bertha yelled, "Look out, Hattie!"

I twisted around and nearly collided with a stretcher carrying the remains of a deceased patient. I stopped less than an inch short of touching the pale, waxy arm that flopped out as the orderlies jerked the stretcher sideways to avoid me. The hallway tilted and spun as I grappled for something to hold.

"Hey, careful, lady," one of the orderlies warned as the other carefully returned the arm to its place at the dead man's side.

Ironically I'd seen several dead bodies of late and all in much more distressing positions, but the draping of the sheet, the rhythm of the orderlies' feet as they carried their load past us, coupled with the smell of formaldehyde that I hadn't noticed until now, was enough to unhinge me. I recalled seeing my father being carried out like that. For a moment I saw nothing but the tiny bumps in the whitewashed plaster wall. And then everything went black.

"Walter?" I said, slowly opening my eyes. I felt the warmth of someone's body against me. But instead of Walter, I was looking up into the face of Nurse Simmons; I was lying partially in her lap. "Oh!" I gasped, and sat up with a jerk.

"Please move more slowly, Miss Davish." I ignored the nurse and pushed myself up, making every effort to stand. I brushed my skirt off and glanced about me. The stretcher was nowhere to be seen.

"What happened?" I asked, readjusting my hat.

It had slipped to the side of my head when I fell.

"You fainted, Hattie," Bertha said.

"You're extremely lucky I was able to catch you before you hit your head."

"What? Yes, thank you, Nurse." I was still a bit befuddled.

"I think you should lie down. You still look very pale."

"No, thank you." My heart throbbed and my fingers and toes were tingling, but I wasn't about to let her believe I needed aid. I might not be allowed to leave.

"But you may be ill, Miss Davish. It would be for your own good. I'm sure we have an empty bed we can—"

Bertha placed her hand on my arm. "Thank you for your concern, Nurse, but Miss Davish is fine. We will be going now." I gave Bertha a weak smile, grateful for her intervention, but I had no intention of leaving—yet.

"Actually, I think one more visit to Dr. Hillman's office is in order, don't you?" Bertha looked surprised, but then nodded. She followed as I pushed past Nurse Simmons before the nurse could object. "Aren't you coming, Nurse Simmons? He lied to you too."

After a moment of hesitation, the nurse followed as Bertha and I ascended the stairs. When we arrived at his office, I knocked several times with no response. Thinking my knocks were too timid, Bertha leaned over me and pounded on the door, causing the door to open of its own accord.

"Dr. Hillman?" I called as I pushed the door slightly to see more inside. Still no response.

"Dr. Hillman, you lied to us. Where's my husband?" Bertha pushed the door open all the way, eager to step inside. She stopped a few feet past the threshold as the nurse pushed past both of us.

"I'm sorry, Dr. Hillman but—" Nurse Simmons stopped mid-sentence. I couldn't see the doctor's desk without peering over Bertha's shoulder.

"What is it?" I suddenly pictured another office in Newport where a dead man lay sprawled out on the floor. "What's wrong?" Bertha looked back at me, her lips pursed in frustration.

"The room's empty," she grumbled. "The liar's gone!"

Despite the desire to confront Dr. Hillman, I'd never been so relieved to feel the sway of horses pulling a moving cab in my life. Feeling the fresh air on my face as I sat close to the open window, I no longer felt the nausea rise in my throat. My heart had settled back into a more peaceful rhythm and I could sit up without the fear of falling. I watched as the gargantuan building receded from sight.

That was too close, I thought. If the nurse had

truly known how distressed I'd been, I might never have been allowed to leave. If I never saw State Lunatic Asylum Number Two again, I wouldn't mind.

And then I caught a glance of Bertha. Her head hung low as she wrung her hands over and over in her lap. Our quest had been only partially successful and we'd uncovered more questions than answers. Bertha's husband might have indeed been the escaped patient, but where was he now? I pulled out my notebook and pencil.

1. Where is Levi Yardley?
2. Was that him I saw in the buggy on Lover's Lane?
3. If so, why hasn't he contacted his wife?
4. Could he be injured and mistaken for Frank Hayward?
5. Or was Frank Hayward the inmate mistaken for Levi Yardley?
6. Either way, where is Frank Hayward?
7. Who's buried in Frank Hayward's grave?
8. Why did Dr. Hillman lie?

"I hope we don't ever have to go back there again," Bertha whispered, as I put my notebook away.

"Don't worry, Bertha. We won't." Even as I said the words and took the woman's hands in mine, a knot formed in the pit of my stomach. I was lying and I knew it. Someone was going to have to confront Dr. Hillman and find out the whole truth.

We didn't speak again until we reached the St. Charles Hotel. I offered her money to pay for the cab, but she refused. Instead, Bertha flung her arms around me.

"Thank you so much for helping me, Hattie."

"You're welcome, Bertha, but I'm afraid I haven't helped very much. I wish I could've done more." The driver opened the door and offered me his hand. I gladly took his help and alighted from the cab. I turned to face Bertha, huddled in the darkness of the cab.

"At least we know something about Levi. It's a start and I couldn't have done any of this without you. Here, take this." She leaned out the window and thrust the photograph of her husband into my hand.

"But—"

Before I could say another word, she tapped on the roof of the cab and it drove into the flow of traffic. I looked at the photograph in my hand. One of the edges had bent and a crease cut across the top of the man's head. I was struck again by Mr. Yardley's resemblance to Frank Hayward.

Where are you? I wondered, not knowing myself which man I referred to. And then instead of returning to my room, I headed for the nearest streetcar stop.

141

• • •

"I'm sorry, Miss Davish, Miss Hayward isn't at home," the housekeeper said, shaking her head. I'd returned to Ginny's house hoping to learn whether her father had spent any time recently at the asylum. I knew I couldn't rest until I confirmed, without a doubt, that it was Levi Yardley who had escaped that dreadful institution and not a case of mistaken identity.

"In my day, a daughter wouldn't leave the house this soon after a father died. If I remember right, you stayed in for weeks after your father passed." I winced at her comparing my mourning to Ginny's, but chose not to comment.

"That's all right. Maybe you can help me, Mrs. Curbow."

"If you think I can."

"Do you know if Mr. Hayward had been away at all in the days before his death?"

The housekeeper shook her head and stared for a moment at the band of black crape around her arm. "No, bless his soul, dear man. He was as reliable as the sun, going every morning but Sunday to Mrs. Chaplin's school and coming home every night on time for dinner. Well, every night except . . ." I waited, but she didn't say more.

"Yes, I'm sorry," I said. "Did a doctor visit recently?"

"No, as far as I knew that man was as healthy

as a horse. Oh!" Her hand flew up to cover her mouth, appalled by her slip of the tongue. "I don't know what's gotten into me. One moment he was here and the next he was gone." She leaned toward me a bit. "I saw him the morning of his death, you know."

"Did you?"

"Yes, I handed him the lunch I'd packed for him. It was probably his last meal: cold boiled beef, bread, butter, pickles, and a few lemon jumbles. If I'd known, I would've packed him a meal Grover Cleveland would've envied."

"Thank you, Mrs. Curbow." My suspicions were confirmed; Levi Yardley must've been the asylum patient and not Frank Hayward. "You've been a big help."

She nodded sadly, still thinking of the inadequacy of the leftover beef. "Should I let Miss Hayward know you came by?"

"No, you needn't trouble her. I'll send her my good-byes."

"Oh, here." The housekeeper reached for a plate on the table covered with a linen cloth. "If I remember right, you used to eat nothing but sweets. We have too much; Miss Ginny could never eat it all." I took the plate and peeked under the cloth. There were several pieces each of apple pie and squash pie. I caught my breath.

"Thank you, Mrs. Curbow. That's . . . very thoughtful." I struggled to maintain my composure. The old woman's kindness had startled me.

Far kinder than Ginny has been, I thought.

"Good-bye then to you, Miss Davish. I wish your return had been for a happier occasion."

"So do I."

I walked the distance to my hotel, hoping the brisk walk would help me shake the melancholy I'd begun to feel the moment Mrs. Curbow closed her door. Instead of thinking about Ginny and her inexplicable reversal of feelings toward me, I concentrated on the questions still buzzing in my head. True, I'd confirmed that Levi Yardley was the escaped patient, but we still didn't know where he was. And sadly, it wasn't my business to find him. I pulled the photograph of him from my bag as I walked up the hotel steps. The resemblance to Frank Hayward was still unnerving. I'd accompanied Bertha Yardley and helped her with her inquiries out of a sense that Frank Hayward might've been involved, or so I told myself. Yet Ginny had expressly asked me to stop questioning her father's death. So why did I help Bertha? Why did I subject myself to such distress for the sake of a stranger? An image of the dead body being carried out on the stretcher flashed through my mind.

"These arrived for you, Miss Davish." Mr. Putney's announcement interrupted my morbid thoughts. He thrust two hand-delivered cards toward me. I took them and frowned. Again I didn't recognize the handwriting.

Now what? I thought. Who else could possibly want something from me? At least it wasn't another one of those anonymous letters.

I pulled the first card from its envelope and immediately regretted my uncharitable thought. It was signed by several of the instructors from Mrs. Chaplin's school, inviting me to a luncheon tomorrow to speak with their best pupils. Since I wasn't able to leave town until Sir Arthur was satisfied with the research I'd done, I could gladly accept. Helping one student find her way in the world would go far in redeeming my otherwise ill-fated trip back home.

I looked up at Mr. Putney and smiled as I pulled the second card from its envelope. He smiled back, leaning forward over the edge of the desk.

"Good news?"

"Happily, yes." I opened the second envelope and then groaned.

"Spoke too soon?"

"Yes, I'm afraid so." The second was from Nate Boone, inviting me to dine with him. I glanced at the tall, oak clock against the wall. Luckily it was already too late to respond.

"Thank you, Mr. Putney," I said, folding the cards up. "Could you arrange to have coffee, cold meat pie, and toast sent to my room?"

"In for the night then, Miss Davish?"

"I am."

I hardheartedly visualized the vexation on Nate Boone's face when he realized I wasn't coming. "Thank you, Sir Arthur," I said under my breath. Writing up what I'd learned about General Thompson was the cure I needed after an unnerving afternoon and I had a good excuse to stay in.

"I have much work to do, Mr. Putney. Do you have a typewriter I could borrow?"

Chapter 15

"Gus, is that you?"

Unable to find a typewriter I could use at the hotel, my plans to stay in for the night changed. After a quick telephone call to Mrs. Chaplin and a short streetcar ride to the school, I'd happily settled myself at one of the student typewriters in Miss Gilbert's classroom, a square room with white walls, highly polished oak floors, and two dozen desks perfectly lined up in three rows. The night watchman Gus, a silent, broad-shouldered man who wore his cap low over his eyes, had let me in before continuing with his rounds. Simply being surrounded by the sturdy machines put my mind at ease and for several hours I'd heard nothing but the reassuring rhythmic tapping of the keys as I worked. It was the most peaceful

I'd felt since I'd arrived. And then I heard foot-steps. I glanced at the clock hanging on the wall. It was nearly one o'clock in the morning.

"Gus?" I called again, and rose from my chair.

There was no answer. I walked to the open doorway and peered into the dark hall, lit only by the sharp electric light streaming from the classroom. A figure, a woman dressed in dark clothing, was disappearing around a corner. I looked up and down the hall and saw no one else. Leaving my work in the classroom, I followed her. Having some experience before, I knew how to step lightly and keep my presence unknown. It took a few moments for my eyes to adjust to the dark hallway, but when I caught up to her not far from Mr. Upchurch's office, I could easily see by the dim light of her lantern. I hid in the deeper shadows of a doorway as the woman stopped outside an office a few doors down. She glanced about her before entering the room. I couldn't clearly see her face, she'd pulled the veil from her hat down over her eyes, but from the feather plume that fluttered as she walked, to the row of buttons on her kid gloves, everything she wore was black.

Ginny?

I slipped down the hall, stopping shy of the door. All the doors in the school were ornamented with a brass plate, but as the woman had taken the lantern with her, I couldn't read it in the darkened hallway. Only the slices of light beneath the door and through the crack where she'd left the door slightly ajar seeped across the floor. I felt around for the plate on the door and traced the engraved letters with my finger, F. HAYWARD. Why would Ginny sneak into her father's office at night? I peered through the gap as the figure moved about frantically from desk to bookshelf to filing cabinet, pulling open drawers, turning over papers, and rifling through books. For a moment the figure's fingers lingered over a pasteboard pencil box left on the desk. She slid it open. Two of the gray slate pencils were missing.

What is she looking for?

And then she looked up. It wasn't Ginny. I jerked my head back, flattening myself against the wall, and held my breath.

"*Un, deux, trois.*" I counted silently, hoping she hadn't seen me. When I reached ten, I dared to let out my breath. Since she hadn't called out or come to the door to investigate, I assumed she hadn't caught me spying. Yet I still didn't move. Instead, I listened as she continued her search. And then I heard another set of footsteps heading in my direction from down the hall. These were much heavier and steadier than those made by the woman inside the office. A thin light glowed from the same direction.

Gus.

In response, I heard the distinct sound of breath blowing out the lantern and footsteps approaching the door. The woman's ragged breath was inches from me as she peered into the hall. Could she hear me breathing? What would she do if she found me here? Why didn't I confront her? She slowly pulled the door closed and the moment was lost. Soon Gus would find me hovering outside Frank Hayward's door. I felt my way to the nearest door—luckily it was unlocked—and slipped inside. We waited, in our respective rooms, the woman and I, for several minutes as the heavy footfalls of the night watchman grew louder. The approaching light illuminated dust particles floating through the open transom as Gus passed by. And then the light and the sound of Gus's steps grew fainter until there was silence and darkness again.

He doesn't even know we are here, I mused. *No wonder the incidences keep occurring.* But why had I hidden from Gus instead of making him aware of the intruder's presence?

I cracked open my door and waited but a few moments more before I heard more than saw the woman streak by me, her boots clacking against the wooden floor, as she ran in the opposite direction from Gus. I stepped into the hall and listened to her hasty retreat before finding my way back to the blinding light of Miss Gilbert's classroom. I sat behind the typewriter once again, but unlike before, couldn't bring myself to work. My hands hovered over the keyboard until my fingers ached. I stared at the letters between them, DFGHJK, wondering what Miss Woodruff was doing in Frank Hayward's office.

"If you could, perhaps, maybe, give the girls one piece of advice, Miss Davish, what would it be?" Miss Corcoran, the English instructor, asked, stabbing a stewed tomato from her plate. "That is, if you'd be so kind?"

After returning from Mrs. Chaplin's school in the early morning hours, I managed a few hours' sleep. I awoke well after sunrise and had to forgo any leisurely hike. After a light breakfast of coffee, toast, and butter, I telegraphed Sir Arthur, packaged the research I'd finished typing up last night, and made my way to the post office.

How ironic, I thought as I entered the imposing stone building with a six-story clock tower on the corner of Eighth and Edmond. It was here that General M. Jeff Thompson supposedly pulled down the flag at the onset of the Civil War. And now I was mailing Sir Arthur what I'd uncovered about the general.

When I emerged from the post office, I made my way back toward the Pacific House Hotel, where I'd been invited to lunch. Miss Woodruff would be in attendance and all of my thoughts were of her as I crossed at the corner of Seventh and Francis. Suddenly, I felt that all too familiar feeling that I was being watched. With at least a dozen buggies navigating the intersection and countless pedestrians, on both sides of the road, going about their day, I saw no one staring at me. I'd continued on my way and had tried to ignore the hairs raised on the back of my neck. Yet the feeling never left, even when I'd joined the ladies for luncheon.

"My father used to say, 'The customer gets what the customer wants.' "

I was happy to have an excuse not to eat the stuffed pheasant and potatoes I'd been served. With Miss Woodruff seated directly across from me, I had little appetite.

"And in our case, the customer is our employer. It's essential that you understand your employer and strive to give him or her exactly what they expect."

"I don't understand," Miss Meachem, one of the students, said. She had a stubby little nose and numerous blemishes on her high forehead. "Doesn't an employer who hires a typist want a good typist?"

"Of course they do, but often they expect far more than simply the fastest typist they can get." The girl blushed at my reference to her reputation as being the fastest typist in the school. "You need to determine what beyond the basic skills is expected of you."

"Perhaps, maybe you could give us an example?" Miss Corcoran said. "If you wouldn't mind?"

"Of course. For example, if your employer expects loyalty, you need to give them every reason to believe in you. If your employer expects you to be discreet, never give them reason to doubt you. If your employer expects you to be humble, never speak out of turn, never."

"But why isn't being a fast typist enough?" Miss Meachem asked.

"Because we women need to be competitive in the workplace. There are many fast typists. You need to excel beyond that. Simply put, be the best at your assigned tasks, act exactly the way they expect, and they won't know what they did without you, and more importantly, won't be able to imagine anyone taking your place."

"Is that what you did, Miss Davish? You're obviously speaking from experience. Do you do whatever your employer demands?" Miss Gilbert twisted my words, making me sound unscrupulous.

"No, Miss Gilbert, I don't do whatever an employer demands. However, I do speak from experience. I've had to learn on my own that employers expect more from their personal secretaries, people they have given access to their most personal and confidential affairs, than simply someone who works in a typing pool. As a personal secretary, you're the buffer between your employer and the world. There's no set job description. You have to be flexible, capable, and motivated."

Despite my retort, the next several questions from the girls were more in line with Miss Gilbert's.

"Have you ever been asked to do anything immoral?"

"Do you hold secrets that could compromise your previous employers' life or livelihood?"

"Have you ever had to fight off unwanted advances?"

"No, of course not," I lied. I could've said yes to all three questions, but I didn't want the students to misunderstand the nature of my work. They were already thinking the worst. "It's a business arrangement, ladies, a job," I said. "You work for an employer. You do your best to meet their expectations, but they don't own you."

"So you say," Miss Gilbert mumbled under her breath, chewing on a fingernail.

"Is there anything else you would like to ask Miss Davish before dessert is served?" Miss Woodruff said, giving Miss Gilbert a sideways glance of disapproval. I'd avoided her glance during the luncheon, but now I took the opportunity to study her. Except for the dark circles that stood out against her pale skin, she seemed at ease. But what had she been doing in Frank Hayward's office last night?

A girl raised her hand. She was wearing a pretty straw hat with a rosette of wide satin ribbon and a bunch of orange silk flowers.

"Yes?"

"I was wondering, Miss Davish, if you could tell us some of the non-secretary work you've done lately."

"Non-secretarial work? I'm not sure I understand."

"She's talking about the snooping into murders you've been up to lately," Miss Gilbert said, snidely.

"Oh." I was afraid that's what she meant. "Well, it's another example of performing to the best of your abilities when you're required to do more than type. A few of my employers have requested my aid at such times and I met the challenge. In fact, I used many of the skills I learned at Mrs. Chaplin's to help me."

"I'm sure you did," Miss Gilbert said.

"I did, in fact. So, girls, learn everything Miss Corcoran, Miss Woodruff, and all of your teachers can teach you. If you learn to think, observe, and organize, you can do anything."

"And now for dessert," Miss Woodruff said, as the bread pudding with brandied peaches was served.

"Speaking of dessert, wasn't that Nate Boone scrumptious?" Miss Meachem said. I'd taken a bite of the bread pudding, which almost immediately soured in my mouth. I set my fork down.

"Did you know Miss Davish and Mr. Boone were childhood friends? And the tale was that they were even engaged?" I was stunned by Miss Gilbert's audacity. "Oh, look at Miss Davish blush. It must be true." My face reddened even more as everyone gawked at me and I tried to quell my anger at Miss Gilbert's teasing.

Un, deux, trois, I counted in my head.

"Really?" Miss Meachem said.

"I don't think Miss Davish's private life is a topic for discussion," Miss Woodruff said. "It's not anyone's place to examine whom and why we love." Cupping her hand over her chin, Miss Woodruff glanced down at a red splotch where a tomato had dripped onto the white linen tablecloth. She was still dressed in black crape.

"Thank you, Miss Woodruff." I was sincerely grateful and yet baffled by her unexplained behavior.

"Well, then, let's discuss why on earth Mrs. Chaplin chose to hire Mr. Upchurch when she retired."

"I don't think that's an appropriate topic either, Miss Gilbert, especially in front of the students," Miss Woodruff said.

"It concerns them as much as it does us how this school is managed. I think if Mrs. Chaplin were to know what was going on . . ."

"What's going on?" a student asked.

"I think Miss Gilbert's talking about all the 'incidents,'" Miss Meachem whispered behind her hand.

"Yes, incidents," Miss Gilbert said. "More like acts of negligence and incompetence. None of these 'incidents' would've occurred if I were president."

"You mentioned them at the lake. What do you think is going on?" I asked.

"I think it's a string of unrelated coincidences," Miss Woodruff said. "No one can fault Mr. Upchurch for the classroom fire—"

"Poor management," Miss Gilbert interrupted.

"Or the missing pages from the shorthand textbooks? Or the emptied champagne bottles?"

"Again poor management."

"What about the missing money?" Miss Corcoran said. "Goodness gracious! You don't think our president stole that, do you?"

"From the rumors I've heard, Mr. Hayward might've had something to do with that," Miss Meachem said coyly behind her hand.

"That's a hurtful lie!" Miss Woodruff shot up out of her seat and slammed her palms flat down on the table.

The girl shrank back, her mouth agape as the glassware wobbled precariously for a moment. The entire table fell silent. The clinking of silverware and the muffled words of the other diners' conversations filled the void. Miss Gilbert merely raised an eyebrow.

Is Miss Woodruff always this peculiar? I wondered. She persisted in wearing black, I'd discovered her rifling through papers in a dead man's office, and now her eyes blazed as she leaned over the table, challenging anyone to speak ill of that same dead man. Why would Mrs. Chaplin employ someone unstable?

Miss Woodruff knows something. The thought struck me so unexpectedly I gasped.

"That may be, Miss Woodruff," Miss Gilbert said slowly, "but either way, the rumor gives more credence to what I've been saying. Mrs. Chaplin's School for Women, under the management of President Asa Upchurch, has become a place of gossip, thievery, and vandalism. I don't think that's at all what Mrs. Chaplin intended."

"No, of course, it isn't," Miss Woodruff said. She sat down, her face flushed with embarrassment. She again covered the scar on her chin with her hand. "Forgive me, girls. I haven't been myself lately."

"If I may, I would have to agree with Miss Gilbert. There does seem to be an instability about the school since Mrs. Chaplin retired," Miss Corcoran said. Miss Gilbert smiled in triumph. "But I'm not sure, and it's only my opinion, but I don't think that Mr. Upchurch has anything to do with it." Miss Gilbert stopped smiling.

"Tell me then, Miss Corcoran, who or what is responsible, if not President Upchurch?" Miss

Gilbert demanded. The timid English instructor blanched and immediately stared at the napkin in her lap.

"Does Mrs. Chaplin know what's going on?" I asked.

Miss Woodruff shook her head. "We don't think so."

"Why haven't you told her, Miss Gilbert?" She shrugged at my question and took a sip of her coffee.

Why not tell Mrs. Chaplin? I wondered. Miss Gilbert had certainly taken every available opportunity to voice her displeasure in Mr. Upchurch's management of the school. Did she think she jeopardized her chances of replacing Mr. Upchurch if she played the role of tattletale? She certainly didn't hesitate to divulge my secrets. Or did she fear the danger of being the bearer of bad news? Was she waiting for someone else to step forward?

"You could tell her," Miss Gilbert said, setting her cup down. Her pronouncement shouldn't have come as a surprise. I should've known. Why else invite me to luncheon? She didn't want me to advise her students, she wanted me to intercede with Mrs. Chaplin on her behalf. "We all know you're her darling, her prize student, her star. She'd listen to you."

"Mrs. Chaplin is retired," Miss Woodruff said. "Do you really think we should be bothering her with such matters?" She looked expectantly at Miss Gilbert, who then turned her attention to me. All eyes followed.

"What say you, Miss Davish?" And there she had me. We both knew Mrs. Chaplin well. We both knew that the old matron, if presented with such news, would take immediate action. She was one to have a hand in everything that occurred at her school. It was still difficult for me to imagine her retiring to the peace and quiet of her back parlor.

"Yes, Miss Woodruff," I said. "I do think Mrs. Chaplin would want to know that all is not well at the school."

"You agree to tell her then?" Miss Gilbert said, triumphantly, as I looked into the expectant, adoring eyes of the students at the table.

"Yes, Miss Gilbert, I will tell her." The table burst into a flurry of talk as the students speculated what Mrs. Chaplin would do once she heard about the incidents at school, about how she would react, and how they were glad it wasn't they who had to break the news.

I merely glared at Miss Gilbert, who raised her coffee cup to me and smiled before taking another sip.

Don't blame Miss Gilbert, I thought, forcing myself to return her smile. *You got yourself into this mess.*

Chapter 16

"Thank you for inviting me, Miss Corcoran." Everyone pushed back from the table and prepared to leave. "I enjoyed this very much."

Especially the bread pudding, I thought. It was one of Father's favorites. I hadn't had it with brandied peaches since leaving home.

"Oh my, thank you, Miss Davish, for being so accommodating. If I may say so, the girls were inspired and will have much to think on after listening to your adventures and advice."

"I do hope I helped." I noticed over the English instructor's shoulder that Miss Woodruff was the first to reach the dining room exit.

"Miss Woodruff, may I have a quick word?" She waited for me by the door. "If you'll excuse me, ladies."

"What is it, Miss Davish?" Mollie Woodruff said.

"May we go somewhere where we won't be overheard?" Her eyes widened at my request, but she didn't hesitate to respond.

"If you think it best."

She led me down the hall to a small parlor. Furnished with an oak parlor suite, covered with blue and gold heavy silk tapestry and two side tables, it was quiet and empty.

"What is it, Miss Davish?" Miss Woodruff said the moment she stepped in the room and closed the door behind her. Her eyes were wide with worry. I indicated for her to sit, but she shook her head. "Tell me. What's wrong?"

"I saw you last night."

"Saw me?" She tilted her head slightly. "Saw me where?"

"At school. In Mr. Hayward's office." She twisted her neck, almost looking over her shoulder, avoiding my gaze. She again covered her chin with her hand.

"Oh."

"Why were you there? What were you looking for? What did you find?" She sank into the nearest chair and looked up at me.

"I couldn't let it go on. It's not right." I grabbed a side chair, placing it opposite her, and sat down.

"What's not right?"

"You've heard the rumors. What else could I do?"

"What are you talking about? Which rumors?"

"About Frank, of course, rest his soul." She dropped her head and stared into her lap.

"What about Mr. Hayward?"

She looked up at me, her brows knitted. "You're not daft, Miss Davish. Haven't you heard a word I've said?" I didn't want to remind her that she was the one being obtuse.

"I'm listening very carefully, Miss Woodruff.

Please tell me about what's not right. Tell me about Mr. Hayward." Did she too believe that Frank Hayward wasn't in the casket? But if so, why was she still wearing black? Why was she wearing black anyway? What did she know that she wasn't telling me?

"It's not right that he should be accused of wrongdoings. He was an honest, decent, conscientious, hardworking man, devoted to his daughter and to his school." Miss Woodruff's passion for her subject grew with every word. "I can't have him blamed for something he didn't do!"

"No one wants to see an innocent man falsely accused, but what does that have to do with your foray into his office in the middle of the night?"

She looked at me again as if I were the daffy one. "To get rid of any more evidence. Before anyone else finds it."

More evidence? What could she mean by that?

"But if he's innocent, there would be no evidence," I said.

"Exactly. I found nothing." Before I could ask her what she meant by any "more evidence," she twisted her head toward the door. "Did you hear that?"

I glanced toward the closed door and we listened. All was quiet. I had heard something, like something rubbing against the door, but it had stopped. Had I been followed even in here? I

162

wondered. I jumped up, crossed the room in a few steps, and threw open the door. No one was there. I glanced down the hall in both directions. An elderly couple, hunched over with their arms entwined as much for mutual support as for affection, had their backs to me. At their pace, they had passed the door long before we heard the sound.

"Excuse me." I overtook them easily.

"Oh" and "My" were exclaimed at my sudden approach, their deeply creased faces turned to greet me.

"I didn't mean to startle you, but did you happen to see anyone in the hall a moment ago? Particularly outside the parlor door?"

"Just a lady, like you," the old man said. His wife nodded in agreement.

"How was she like me? Was she young, thin, brown hair?"

"Maybe not so thin," the wife said. "You must eat more, dear. And not young, but you aren't that young either, are you?"

"No, I'm not." I was trying to be patient. I needed to know if someone had been eaves-dropping on our conversation and if so, why? Maybe I could finally discover who'd been following me. "Anything else you can tell me about her?"

"She definitely had brown hair," the husband said. "Or maybe it was blond."

"And she wore a . . ." the wife said.

"Yes?" I hoped to get something, anything that would help me identify this mystery woman. "A particularly patterned dress? A hat with distinguishing flowers?"

"She wore a straw hat. Yes, that's it. And it had a ribbon about it and some flowers on it."

Like every other woman under the age of eighty, I thought. The wife herself wore a narrow, black, high-set bonnet, fashionable when I was a little girl twenty years ago. I wanted to shout in frustration, but instead said, "Thank you for your help." At least I knew that there was another person, a woman, in the hall around the time Miss Woodruff and I heard the sound at the door.

"Well, they weren't very helpful," I said, entering the parlor, "but at least we know—" I stopped mid-sentence. The parlor was empty. Miss Woodruff was gone.

I returned to the dining room in search of Miss Woodruff, but she and Miss Gilbert were gone. I accompanied Miss Corcoran, Miss McGill, and the students back to Mrs. Chaplin's, all the time wondering what Miss Woodruff meant by "more evidence." After a quick search, it was obvious she hadn't returned to the school. But I wasn't about to waste the trip. I pulled out the photograph of Levi Yardley and I headed for President Upchurch's office.

"Can I help you, Miss Davish?" Miss Clary, the president's secretary, looked up from her typing.

She sat behind a Remington set on a small walnut desk in the outer office, simply furnished with area rugs with geometrical patterns of green and white scattered about the room. Behind the desk were two doors, one labeled, PRESIDENT, on a brass plate, the other, slightly ajar, led to a storage room. Several new posters from the World's Fair hung on the walls.

"Yes, I was wondering if Mr. Upchurch was in?" I approached her desk. A souvenir spoon with the famous Ferris Wheel imprinted on it sat next to a steaming cup of coffee.

"Yes, he is. Please follow me." She pushed back from her desk and walked to the president's office. She knocked loudly once and then opened the door. "Mr. Upchurch, Miss Davish is here to see you."

Asa Upchurch looked up from his large, elaborately carved mahogany desk and smiled. Sunlight streamed through the tall double windows behind him, making the room brighter than I'd expected with mahogany paneling and numerous mahogany bookshelves.

"Ah, Miss Davish, what a delight. Thank you, Miss Clary." Mr. Upchurch rose from behind his desk as his secretary left. He approached me and then touched my arm slightly while indicating for me to sit. "Please, please, have a seat." He sat on the edge of his desk as I picked the armchair closest to me. "I want you to know what a treasure you are to this school."

"Oh, I don't think—"

"Now, now, no denials, young lady. Mrs. Chaplin said you'd be modest." He leaned over and patted my shoulder. "You're undoubtedly the best student we've ever had. And what with all that's been going on, you've no idea what a boost in morale your visit has given the students and teachers alike."

"Thank you, Mr. Upchurch." I tried to sound gracious when I felt quite awkward. "I'm glad I could help."

"Yes, you most certainly did help. Now, what can I do for you, Miss Davish?"

I revealed the photograph Bertha Yardley had given me and handed it to him. "I wonder if you recognize this man?"

Mr. Upchurch took the photograph and studied it briefly before looking back up at me. "I'm sorry, but I can't say that I do. Who is he?"

"His name is Levi Yardley."

"Levi Yardley," he repeated, looking carefully at the photograph again. "No, his name isn't familiar either. Why do you ask?"

"Because except for his nose, I think he looks extremely similar to Frank Hayward."

"Really?" A slight frown stretched across Asa Upchurch's face as he continued to study the photograph. "Yes, I guess he does." He shook his head as he finally handed it back to me. "Is he a relation you're trying to track down for Virginia? I didn't see him at the funeral."

"I think maybe you had but didn't realize it."

"Oh?"

"Could it be possible that the man you saw in the street, the man you thought was Frank Hayward, was actually this man, Levi Yardley?"

"Oh now, my dear Miss Davish, I don't mean to sound critical, but no. I know Frank Hayward. I worked with the man six days of the week. I wouldn't make such a terrible mistake. No, no, I can't even imagine such a heinous thing."

"What are you talking about, 'heinous thing'?" We both turned at the voice to see Mrs. Upchurch entering the office, wearing the latest style dark plum velvet wrap and matching silk gloves I'd seen in Herr's department store window. It would've cost me a month's wages. "Hello, Miss Davish. Enjoying your visit?"

"It's been interesting." She smiled down at me, her dimples deepening, and then approached her husband, who kissed her cheek.

"What heinous thing, Asa?"

"No need to trouble yourself about it, Emily," her husband said. "Miss Davish and I were discussing the funeral. Sad business, that. What can I do for you, dear?"

His wife ignored his question and looked back

at me. "What heinous thing, Miss Davish?" I glanced at Mr. Upchurch for permission to answer his wife's question. He tossed his head and threw up his arms in mock dismay.

"Whatever my wife wants, my wife gets," he said, playfully dramatic. His wife smirked at her husband's acquiescence.

Perhaps he was attempting to shield his wife from distress, but I couldn't approve of his light-hearted treatment of my concern. *This is nothing to joke about,* I thought.

"I was speculating that perhaps Mr. Upchurch had been wrong about the man he found dead in the street."

Emily Upchurch's smile instantly vanished from her face. "My, my, that is serious. What would make you think such a thing?"

"I can't dismiss the resemblance of this man," I said, handing her the photograph, "to Frank Hayward. His name is Levi Yardley."

"Where did you get this?"

"The man's wife. Do you know him?"

"Yes, in a way, I do." A thrill ran through me and I stood up. Mr. Upchurch's eyes narrowed and his face reddened.

"Emily, you couldn't possibly know this man."

"Oh, but I do, Asa." His wife continued to stare at the photograph. "I saw him the other day arguing with someone in the middle of Charles Street." She looked up at her husband and then at me. "He seemed quite oblivious to the traffic doing their best to avoid him." She handed the photograph back to me. "Are you saying this is the man we buried instead of Frank Hayward?"

"No, no, dear, of course not," her husband said, even as I nodded.

"Really?" she asked me. "Then where's Frank Hayward?"

"I don't know." It was the question that had haunted me since the minute I doubted the identity of the man in the casket.

Asa Upchurch smiled at me while shaking his head. "Well, I do, dear ladies. Frank Hayward, rest his soul, is dead and buried in Oakland Cemetery. We all saw him with our own eyes. I assure you, Emily, Miss Davish, it wasn't this Levi Yardley I found in the middle of Third Street. It was Frank Hayward."

"But I've no doubt that this is the man I saw in the street." Mrs. Upchurch pointed to the photograph in my hand.

"I don't doubt that you did, my love, but that doesn't mean he was the man I found. The two men obviously were in the area of Charles Street and Third at different times and for different reasons. Unfortunately, it was Frank, and not Mr. Yardley, that suffered the worst consequences."

How could President Upchurch believe what he was saying? Spoken out loud, such a coincidence seemed preposterous. Did he truly believe what he said or was he rationalizing away his part in burying the wrong man?

"Besides, even if you question my judgment," he said, "which would be a blow, dear Emily, how can you question Miss Hayward's? She too knows the man that I found, the man that we buried, was her beloved father."

"It is a conundrum," his wife agreed. "I don't doubt your judgment, Asa."

"Thank you, dear."

She continued as if he hadn't spoken. "Or that of Virginia's, though she was indeed distressed enough to make a mistake. But—"

"But what?"

"I do marvel at such a coincidence," she said. I nodded in agreement. "Two men, who resemble one another, both finding themselves, for whatever reason, in the middle of Charles Street traffic."

"I found Mr. Hayward in the middle of Third Street," her husband corrected.

"Yes, but near the corner of Third and Charles."

"Very well, but may we all agree that this is an extraordinary coincidence and nothing more? For the good of the school, let's not talk of this again." His wife nodded her head slowly but was obviously still giving the subject more thought. "We wouldn't want to undo the good you've done, Miss Davish."

"No, of course not," I said.

"Good. I knew you'd understand." President Upchurch flipped open his gold pocket watch. He walked back behind his desk and snapped the watch closed before sitting down. "Well, now, ladies, I've enjoyed our visit, but the school won't run itself, you know. So if there's nothing more?"

Mr. Upchurch picked up a pen, dipped the nib in ink, and held it over the paper he was reading when I arrived. "Thank you for your visit, Miss Davish. Safe travels back." A small drip splashed to the page. "Darn it!" Upchurch tried to blot the drip.

Mrs. Upchurch waved her hand, indicating for me to follow her toward the door. "We will leave you to your work, dear." He nodded without looking up.

"Thank you, Mr. Upchurch," I said. It was all I could muster with my mind muddled by his artful dismissal of my concern. Did he truly believe in such a bizarre coincidence, or did he not believe his wife saw Levi Yardley like she claimed? Or could he not admit, even to himself, that he'd made a terrible mistake? Either way, he seemed secure in his belief that he buried the right man. I wished I could be that certain.

Once in the outer office with the door closed behind us, Emily Upchurch said, "I really do think you're on to something, Miss Davish." Miss Clary continued to type, appearing to ignore us.

"You do?" I was relieved to know I wasn't the only one.

"Yes, absolutely. I know what I saw. Yet Asa could be right. It all could be a fantastical coincidence. Either way, it's a mystery, and I do love a good mystery. If there's anything I can do to help, please ask."

"Actually there is something you might be able to do. Can you describe the person Mr. Yardley was arguing with?"

"Yes, I can. In fact, he was the one that caught my eye in the first place."

"Why's that?"

"Because he was wearing a white coat over his street clothes. He seemed to be trying to convince the other to return to the safety of the sidewalk."

"What did he look like, the man in the white coat?"

"He was in his early to mid-forties, tall, thin, with a Roman nose, dark brown hair, graying at the temples—"

"Did he oil his mustache and beard?"

"Why, yes, he did. But how did you know that?"

"The same way you knew Levi Yardley. I've seen him before." Mrs. Upchurch had described Dr. Cyrus Hillman.

Chapter 17

I couldn't leave Asa Upchurch's office fast enough. I had to get back to the asylum and confront Dr. Hillman. After parting with Mrs. Upchurch in the hall, I pulled out my notepad and pencil and scribbled a quick list.

1. Why had Dr. Hillman lied about not knowing what happened to Levi Yardley?
2. What were the two men arguing about?
3. Did Dr. Hillman witness Yardley being trampled?
4. Why didn't he come forward when the body was misidentified?
5. Why is Asa Upchurch so certain he discovered the right man in the road?
6. How could Ginny misidentify her own father?
7. How could they not be wrong?
8. Where is Frank Hayward?

"Do watch where you're going, Miss Davish," a voice boomed. I looked up from my list into the amused face of Mrs. Chaplin. "If I recall, you always were one lost in reverie and oblivious to your surroundings. Watch your step, young lady, not your book!"

"Yes, Mrs. Chaplin." I felt very much the chastised student again.

Mrs. Chaplin! I'd completely forgotten my promise to Miss Gilbert that I'd have a word with the retired matron. But I had to see Dr. Hillman.

"I'm glad to have run into you, though not literally, of course."

"Oh?" I said, still struggling with my conflict. I needn't have, as Mrs. Chaplin made the decision for me.

"I feel we haven't had a proper conversation since you returned. The funeral wasn't the appropriate setting, of course."

"No, ma'am."

"I'd like you to dine with me. Then we can have plenty of time to discuss literature, life, and the state of the world's affairs."

"I'd enjoy that but—"

"I will not take no for an answer, young lady. My carriage is waiting."

"Then thank you, ma'am. I'd enjoy that." I meant it. I'd much rather spend the evening in my old mentor's company than go back to the asylum.

Mrs. Chaplin was an intelligent, well-read, charismatic woman whom I'd enjoyed countless evenings with. Although we were being trained as typists, secretaries, and stenographers, Mrs. Chaplin insisted we also learn life skills, basic bookkeeping, basic sewing, cooking and house-keeping skills (which I failed miserably), as well as proper dining etiquette, dancing, and conversation skills. She would host these lessons at her home, overseeing the instruction herself. She was a firm but fair teacher who enlightened us, with the lessons as well as with discussions ranging from politics to world travel to art. I credit her more than any other with my success. If it weren't for her, I'd probably be languishing in a typing pool. I'd never have found the courage or the requisite breadth of knowledge to interact with the variety of people I've worked for. It was because of her that I was here today. If not for her insistence that I take further book-keeping instruction from Frank Hayward, I'd never have met either Mr. Hayward or Ginny. Oddly, I only recently had an opportunity to use those skills.

As we turned up Francis Street and the horses climbed the hill toward Mrs. Chaplin's stately home, I felt relieved not to be going to the asylum. Now that the urgency had left me, I was in no way anxious to return. Dr. Hillman must be held accountable for his lies, but the truth was I needn't be involved. It wasn't my responsibility. After dinner tonight, I'd write Bertha Yardley explaining what I'd learned, but that would be the end of it. Let her pursue this matter. I sat back satisfied with the unexpected rescue and resolution to my predicament when suddenly I thought, *But what was Mrs. Chaplin doing at the school in the first place?*

●●●

Dinner was lovely. Over plates of filet of beef with mushroom sauce, cold duck, green peas, string beans, mashed potatoes, salad of lettuce, and olives, Mrs. Chaplin was as engaging and informative as I remembered, regaling me with her recent visit to the World's Fair. (*Am I the only person who hasn't attended?*) The apple pudding, one of Mrs. Chaplin's signature dishes, was delicious. Eventually the conversation turned from the acquittal of Lizzie Borden, the deadly tornado that hit Charleston, the Duke of York's recent wedding, and the possible repeal of the Sherman Silver Purchase Act to reminiscing about time at the school. We spoke briefly about Ginny.

"Do you know what Virginia's going to do now that her father's dead?" I asked.

"I offered her a position at the school, but she refused me."

"Did she say why? Did she say what she was going to do?" Without a husband or a personal fortune, a single woman's prospects were slim. She had an education, at least, I thought. I said as much.

"Yes, but she doesn't seem to be making any plans to use it," Mrs. Chaplin said. "I don't know, Hattie. Between you and me, I worry about that girl. She needs to be looking to her future now."

I waited throughout dinner, unsuccessfully, for an opportunity to bring up the school's current troubles, as I'd promised. I still hadn't mentioned it when Mrs. Chaplin guided me to her parlor, a comfortable room with a high ceiling, mahogany paneling, plush tapestry covering the parlor suite, and a small fire crackling in the grate. When she left me to supervise the after-dinner refreshments with her maid, I relished browsing the stacks of books that were scattered throughout the room. The few I picked up included *The Firm of Girdlestone* by Sir Arthur Conan Doyle, John Churton Collins's *The Study of English Literature: A Plea for Its Recognition and Organization at the Universities*, *Might Is Right or The Survival of the Fittest* by Ragnar Redbeard, and Sir Richard Burton's *Land of Midian (Revisited)*.

And then, while pulling a copy of *Life on the Mississippi* from the bottom of the stack, I knocked the books to the floor. I hurriedly picked them up, restacking them until I noticed a stack of papers under the tea table. Unlike the books, these were not in neat piles but haphazardly stuffed behind the tablecloth. The aberrant piles were so out of character from everything else in Mrs. Chaplin's house that I didn't hesitate to retrieve one of the papers from the clump. It was a page from a shorthand dictionary. I picked out another paper. It was identical to the first, page 187, which ran from *sick-bed* to *sinful-ly*. I grabbed another and another and another, creating a similar pile of random papers on the floor next to me. Sheet after sheet was identical to the first. Hadn't there been an incident at the school where the new shorthand dictionaries were all missing the same page? I pulled the remaining papers from beneath the table, adding them to the pile next to me, and stacked them neatly together. I placed the stack on the table.

Mrs. Chaplin stole the pages from the new dictionaries? Why?

I picked up the Mark Twain book I'd been attempting to retrieve when I created this mess. Directly below it was *Burns' Phonic Shorthand: For Schools.* Many of the pages were bent at the corners and the brown cloth had flecked off from most of the spine. It was twenty years old, and yet when I opened it up to a random page, I immediately recognized the style. This was the same archaic shorthand style from the anonymous letters I'd been receiving. I was stunned. I sat down in a chair, the Burns book in my lap, and waited for Mrs. Chaplin to return. I didn't wait long.

"Here we are." Mrs. Chaplin handed me a cup of coffee. "I wouldn't have been so long but Lettie misplaced the—" She stopped mid-sentence when she noticed the book in my lap. I glanced at the stack of papers on the table and she followed my gaze. "Oh, I see." I'd never heard her speak so quietly.

"Mrs. Chaplin?" I waited for an explanation. She dropped into the nearest chair.

"You were one of my best, if not the best, Hattie Davish. I should've known you'd find me out sooner or later. But then again, that's why I did it, you see." She stopped as if that explained everything.

"No, Mrs. Chaplin, I don't see." I set the Burns book on the table.

"You obviously realize that I'm the one that sent you the anonymous letters to your hotel." I nodded.

"And the funeral notice." I was guessing.

"Oh, figured that out too, did you? Well, yes, but I bet you didn't know that I'd begun planning the lake party before you even arrived? Don't tell Emily Upchurch, though. She thinks it was all her idea."

"But why?"

"Because I knew you would come."

I shook my head in confusion and frustration. "I don't understand. Why did you want me to come? And why be secretive about it? Why not write me in your own hand and ask me to come?"

"Would you have made the cross-country trip for Frank Hayward's funeral if I'd simply asked?" I began to answer yes, then hesitated. She was right. I thought I'd come for Ginny's sake, but if I was being honest the intrigue of the mystery behind the funeral notice letter probably did more to persuade me to come than I'd like to imagine.

"I don't know. But why was it important that I

come in the first place? I obviously brought cold comfort for Virginia Hayward. Did you too suspect the dead man wasn't Frank Hayward?"

"What? No. What crazy idea is that? Of course not! What are you talking about?"

"You mean you sent me the funeral notice for another reason?"

"I sent you the notice because I need to know what's going on at my school." That wasn't what I expected. "There have been a string of unfortunate incidents. And they may seem petty to you, but who else would investigate them for me? Isn't that part of what you do now?" It seemed Miss Gilbert was wrong; Mrs. Chaplin knew about the problems all along.

I picked up the stack of the torn-out shorthand dictionary pages. "But what about these? I found them under the tea table." Mrs. Chaplin took the stack from me.

"See, that's precisely the sort of thing I'd hoped you do, find clues, find answers. Unfortunately I already knew about these."

"Did you tear them out of the books?" I couldn't believe I was accusing my former head matron, my former mentor, of defacing books, but the evidence was undeniable.

"No, no." She shook her head, dismissing the idea. She set the stack on the table again. "No, these came to me anonymously, stuffed in a large envelope."

"Anonymously?" This was becoming an all too common form of communication.

"Yes, that's how I got the idea to write to you. No one but you would be able to translate the Burns' shorthand. And of course, the challenge of it would further intrigue you and persuade you to come."

How well she knows me, I thought. Perhaps better than I knew or would like to admit to myself.

"So will you help me?"

What else could I say to the woman I owed so much but, "Of course, I will."

"Good. Now where do we start?"

"Obviously you're aware of the dictionaries, but do you know about the fire at the school?" She nodded. "And the other acts of vandalism, the stolen typewriter keys and the emptied champagne bottles at the lake party?"

"Yes, I know about all that as well as the missing applications and stolen bazaar money." Somehow Mrs. Chaplin had been kept well-informed.

"Have you heard the rumors that the school is in financial trouble?" Her face blanched. She obviously hadn't heard about that. "And that Frank Hayward's name has been connected with possible criminal activity?" I didn't like repeating the rumor, but Mrs. Chaplin deserved to know everything I did. She'd founded the school by herself over twenty years ago with the money her late husband left her. She'd been a rich, educated widow, with grown children and nothing to do.

She shook her head slowly; then she squinted at me. I remembered her doing that when I'd yet again burned the roast in cooking class. She wasn't happy. Taking me by surprise, she suddenly stood.

"Let's go!"

I scrambled to my feet and I followed her lead as she headed toward the door without further explanation. Never one to suggest frailty, Mrs. Chaplin moved with a swiftness I found hard to match.

"Where are we going?"

"To the school, of course. I think it's time I came out of retirement, don't you?"

"I admit I wondered why you retired in the first place. But why go to the school now?"

"After apple pudding and such enlightening conversation, I have a sudden hankering to look at the accounting books." She smiled like the Cheshire cat. She hadn't lost any of her wit, her charm, or her determination in her old age. I admired her more in this moment than ever before.

With my help, she clambered into her ladies' phaeton carriage. "But why do you need me to tag along?"

I hoped it wasn't to drive. It was one lesson

Mrs. Chaplin hadn't taught and I'd been glad, having always given horses a wide berth. And considering what happened to Levi Yardley (yes, I told myself it was Levi Yardley and not Frank Hayward who was trampled), I was right to do so. I'd held the reins of a horse once, and even that had given me a fright. Luckily she took the reins herself. Though I hadn't been surprised that she refused to wait for her driver, again I hadn't anticipated her response.

"You always were the better bookkeeper, of course." And with that she snapped the reins and we were off.

"Who's there?"

Mrs. Chaplin and I'd arrived at the school well after dark. Without a single light emanating from within the building, the only illumination we had to guide us was the electric glow of the street-lamps. Mrs. Chaplin had fumbled in the dark with her key.

"Let us in, Gus," Mrs. Chaplin said. "I'm having trouble with my key."

"Mrs. Chaplin?" a man's voice said through the door.

I wondered, since Mrs. Chaplin was supposed to be retired, how Gus recognized her voice. She probably visited the school far more than she'd admitted. Oddly, his voice sounded familiar to me, though I distinctly remembered on my first foray to the school after dark that Gus had not uttered a word.

"Yes, yes. It's me. Miss Davish and I would like to come in. Please unlock the door."

The sound of jingling keys and then a *click* signaled that he'd unlocked the door, but when Mrs. Chaplin opened it and stepped inside, Gus was nowhere to be seen. She immediately headed for her former office.

"Gus is a bit odd, isn't he?" I told Mrs. Chaplin about how he hadn't spoken to me before.

"He seems perfectly competent to me." I didn't tell her that Miss Woodruff had rifled through Frank Hayward's office while Gus was on duty.

"When did the school start requiring the need of a night watchman?" Had the incidents at the school been more rampant and dangerous than I'd been told?

"After the fire in the classroom. The firemen determined it had been set deliberately. After the money from the students' annual bazaar was stolen, the fire was the last straw. Mr. Upchurch was right to hire him."

"But what if the incidents are being caused by students or teachers that are here during the day?" Mrs. Chaplin stopped in midstride and I nearly bumped into her.

"What are you saying, Hattie? That someone at the school may be doing all this?" I was surprised the thought had never occurred to her.

184

"Yes, I've even heard several people mention Frank Hayward's name. It's very possible. I can see a stranger stealing money or even setting fire to the school. But who else would tamper with enrollment documents, typewriters, and shorthand dictionaries but someone associated with the school in some way?"

"But nothing else has occurred since we hired Gus." I shook my head and reminded her of the champagne incident at the lake. She put her hand to her cheek.

"I'd forgotten about that." She continued again down the hall. "I'd hate to think that you're right, Hattie, but that's why I got you to come, isn't it? You have more a mind for this criminal activity than I do."

I grimaced at her "compliment." Luckily she had her back to me. I've been unfortunate enough to have crossed paths with a few murderers, but that didn't qualify me as an expert of criminal activity. I opened my mouth to voice my objection but thought better of it. Mrs. Chaplin was still talking.

"So it could be anyone: a student, a teacher, a maid, a cook . . . a secretary." She turned back to measure my response and laughed. I tried to smile, but I didn't want to encourage her. I think she was actually enjoying herself. I could imagine, if I were living the life of a retired widow, how bored I'd be. But I wouldn't recommend sleuthing to fill the days. "Here we are," she said as we reached the president's office.

Mrs. Chaplin grappled with her string of keys, found the one she was looking for, and unlocked the door. I was surprised when she led me through the outer office, not toward Asa Upchurch's office door but to the now-locked storage room. Again she fumbled through the keys until she found the one she wanted. I studied the jumble of keys in her hand and recognized what they meant. Mrs. Chaplin hadn't truly retired or intended to after all. She hadn't even given up her keys. How involved in the school was she? How does Asa Upchurch handle Mrs. Chaplin's input in, what should now be, his affairs?

With his usual charm, I suppose, I thought. *His charm doesn't work on Miss Gilbert, though, does it?*

My reverie was cut short when Mrs. Chaplin swung open the door, revealing a large closet, lined with bookshelves. One bookshelf was filled from ceiling to floor with day books and ledgers. Mrs. Chaplin walked in and began scanning the ledgers. I took the time to examine the other shelves, filled with typical office supplies: stationery, writing tablets, carbon paper, typewriter paper in several sizes, pens, pencils, rows and rows of bottles of ink, paper clips, rubber bands, rubber erasers, chalk crayons, blackboard erasers, typewriter ribbon, typewriter oil, and type cleaning brushes. I nodded my head in approval. Every clip, every ream of paper was in its place as it should be at a school that trains secretaries.

So it was completely unexpected when Mrs. Chaplin nearly shouted, "One of them isn't here."

"One of what?"

"One of the accounting ledgers, from the time since I've retired, is missing."

"Could it be somewhere else? Mr. Upchurch's office, perhaps? Or in Miss Clary's desk? Could it be in Mr. Hayward's office?"

"It shouldn't be. Everything has its place." I couldn't recall how many times I'd heard that motto. Yet another lesson I'd learned at Mrs. Chaplin's school. "But let us look regardless."

I followed her out of the closet, watched her lock it back up and head toward Mr. Upchurch's office. I followed her in and between the two of us, searched the office for the ledger. When I'd been here earlier, I'd been struck at how simply, yet richly, the office had been furnished. But now as I searched through desk drawers, I realized how austere the room truly was. With the exception of a photograph of his wife on the desk, President Asa Upchurch kept nothing personal in the room—not a plant, not a personal book, not even a hidden bottle of whiskey. He obviously felt strongly about keeping his personal and professional lives separate. It was admirable; he was living by example, as this was something else strongly advocated by the school. Until very recently I'd managed to follow closely to this principle. However, dead bodies and handsome, persuasive doctors tend to complicate things.

"I found nothing." Mrs. Chaplin sighed. "You?"

"No."

"Let's keep looking." And we did. We searched every inch of the outer office, including Miss Clary's desk. We went to Frank Hayward's office, but it had been cleared out of everything.

When had this happened? I wondered. Last night the office still contained books, papers, and more. And who took it all? Miss Woodruff? President Upchurch? Ginny? Miss Woodruff's voice saying "more evidence" sounded in my head. Could there have been something of importance in his office? *The ledger!* I thought. Of course, but where's it now?

"Where could it be?" Mrs. Chaplin grumbled, echoing my thoughts. "Everything has its place!" In her frustration she wasn't seeing the obvious.

"Someone has taken it, Mrs. Chaplin." She looked at me with wide eyes.

"It too has been stolen? Who's doing this? Who's trying to sabotage my school?"

"You think the missing ledger is merely one more incident?"

"Don't you?"

I shook my head. "Maybe, or it could be much more serious."

"You mean someone stole the ledger to prevent us from doing exactly what we intended to do tonight?"

I nodded. "Yes."

"But who? Who would do such a thing?"

I hesitated, not wanting to be the one to voice the name we were both thinking. I looked about me at the empty office of the former book-keeper. Mrs. Chaplin followed my gaze.

"No. Do you really think Frank Hayward would do such a thing?"

"I don't know. I wouldn't have thought so, but if he wasn't the man we buried last week . . ." I couldn't bring myself to accuse him outright. Besides, it was all still supposition. "We still don't know what's happened to him."

"I'd no idea it was this sinister," Mrs. Chaplin said, glancing about the empty room again before stopping her gaze on me. "Oh, Hattie, what have I gotten us into?"

Chapter 18

"Thank God for God," my mother used to say.

I'd always thought it an odd phrase, but over the years I grew to understand what she meant. Many times in my life I've found solace in a holy place, whether it was St. Patrick's in Kansas City, St. Mary's in Newport, or the little chapel in Eureka Springs. I've always come away refreshed, calm, focused, and thankful. This morning, attending Mass at the Cathedral of St. Joseph with its single-squat bell tower and its memories of attending Mass with my mother, was no different.

I'd struggled to sleep last night. When I'd returned from Mrs. Chaplin's home there was yet another dinner invitation from Nate Boone waiting for me. His persistence and impudence was exasperating. And then there was Dr. Hillman. I'd written Bertha Yardley and posted the note before going to bed. Yet despite telling myself that the doctor's lies and his confrontation with Levi Yardley were none of my concern, I couldn't deny the desire to confront the man and hear what he had to say. But it had been the questions about the missing ledger, the disappearance of Frank Hayward, and the undeniable possibility that the two were linked that had kept me awake. Mass this morning soothed my restlessness. And after savoring the scent of incense one last time, I walked out of the cathedral into the bright, warm late August morning at peace again.

It ended the moment I stepped off the streetcar. This time there was no doubt; I was being followed. The feeling of being watched surged through me like electricity. I whirled around, certain I'd confront my mysterious pursuer but yet again found no one but an elderly man, with the aid of a cane, alighting from the streetcar behind me. I apologized to the frightened old man, stepping out of his way, but peered about the street for signs of the person following me. I was rewarded when I spied a man holding his hat on his head as he sprinted down Faraon Street. For a brief moment, I considered pursuing him, but he was fast and already too far ahead. He passed a row of two-story whitewashed brick houses and disappeared around the corner, two blocks away.

A mixture of anger, relief, and confusion rooted me to the spot as other passengers disembarking from the streetcar had to make their way around me. After a disgruntled comment from a nanny herding several small children and a baby carriage that bumped into the back of my legs, I moved out of the way and sat down on the bench. I pulled out my notebook and pencil.

1. Why would anyone want to follow me?
2. Does it have to do with Frank Hayward?
3. Does it have to do with Levi Yardley?
4. Does it have to do with Dr. Hillman and his lies?
5. Is my pursuer doing it for himself or was he hired by someone?

My mind raced as I thought who would want to track my every move. I added names to the list.

6. If hired by someone, who? Nate? Mrs. Chaplin? Ginny?

I let my notebook drop to my lap, distressed that I could be suspicious of people I loved, and considered what to do next.

At least I know I was right, I thought.

Someone has been following me. I wasn't imagining it. Although I hadn't seen the man's face, I was now certain I'd seen him at least twice before. He wore a Panama hat.

"This came for you, Miss Davish," Mr. Putney announced when I arrived back at the hotel. He handed me a folded piece of paper with my name written on it. I sighed. I'd thought confronting Mrs. Chaplin would put an end to mysterious notes. I opened it up. It was from Mrs. Yardley.

Dear Miss Davish,

You have been so kind and helpful I hate to beg one more favor of you, but I don't know who else I can turn to. Would you be so kind as to meet me at the police station this morning? If my husband is dead and buried, I must know. I must lay him to rest in our family cemetery. Then Levi and I can both find peace. But I can't face them alone. My appointment is for half past eleven. Will you, Miss Davish? Will you come?

Your friend,
Mrs. Levi Yardley

How could I refuse?

I looked at the wall clock. It was quarter past eleven already. I shrugged my shoulders at the confused desk clerk before turning on my heel and heading back outside. Luckily the police station, a three-story redbrick castle, complete with turret and pointed roof, was a short walk from the hotel. I entered through the arched doorway, CENTRAL POLICE STATION etched into the stone above. Mrs. Yardley was sitting on a bench staring out the window, but she jumped to her feet the moment she saw me.

"Oh, Miss Davish, I knew you would come." Mrs. Yardley used the almost exact phrase as Mrs. Chaplin. The irony wasn't lost on me.

"Of course, Mrs. Yardley, but how can I help?" Instead of answering me, she glanced over at the approaching policeman. No taller than I, he had very broad shoulders, a square jaw, but almost no neck. His uniform fit snugly over the thick muscles in his arms.

"Miss Davish?" The officer indicated for me to sit next to Mrs. Yardley on the bench. "I'm Officer Quick. Mrs. Yardley said you have something to tell me about the disappearance of her husband." I looked to Bertha for guidance.

"Please, Hattie, tell him everything you know about what happened to Levi."

The officer took the seat beside me and waited. I've had several experiences with police of late.

Luckily in this case, I wasn't directly involved in any way. I could relate my pertinent information to the man and let him take it from there. And the man seemed patient enough to listen to my story. So I did.

Bertha Yardley slowly paced the room, occasionally stopping to glance out at a buggy passing or to squint closely at the World's Fair print hanging near the door. (*I truly am the only person who hasn't been.*) Ignoring her anxiety, I told the officer everything: from my misgivings at the funeral, to my learning about the escaped patient from the asylum, to the nurse's confirmation that Levi Yardley was the escaped patient, to Mrs. Upchurch's identification of Levi Yardley arguing with Dr. Hillman in the street.

Officer Quick sat quietly and listened. Not once did he roll his eyes, shake his head, pick at his fingernails, or display any other dismissive behavior. Instead, he gave me his full attention and gave me every reason to believe he was taking me seriously. After all, I wasn't trying to do his job. It was a refreshing change from times past.

"With both of them missing, I can't prove that Levi Yardley was mistakenly buried as Frank Hayward, but that is my suspicion," I said. "I suspect that because these two men resembled one another so closely that they were mistaken for each other and at least one of them is dead."

Officer Quick nodded his head, placed his

finger across his lips but said nothing for several moments. A few moments too long for Bertha Yardley.

"Well?" She strode across the room and stood over us. "What are you going to do about it?"

The policeman calmly rose. "What do you propose, Mrs. Yardley?"

"Dig him up!"

"Are you formally requesting that I exhume the body of Frank Hayward?"

"No," Bertha said, shaking her hands about her, flustered. "I'm asking you to dig up the body of my dead husband, Levi Yardley."

"Who Miss Davish suspects was buried wrongfully in the casket bearing Frank Hayward's name?"

"Yes."

"If my husband is buried in Frank Hayward's grave, I want his body back. To be buried with his family, not misidentified as some stranger." The policeman nodded but said nothing. Compared to the other policemen I'd encountered, Office Quick was a man of few words. Now I'd learn whether he was also a man of action.

"If what you say is true, Miss Davish, where's the body of Frank Hayward?"

"I have no idea." And then I remembered the incident on "Lover's Lane," when a buggy raced by driven by a man I thought resembled Frank Hayward. That couldn't have been the escaped patient as I'd once thought. Levi Yardley would've already been dead. Could it have been Frank Hayward after all? And what about the man who's been following me? Could he be Frank Hayward? "I can't say for certain he's even dead."

"But his family believes he is, correct?"

"Yes, his daughter identified the body."

"But you think the damage to the man's face misled her."

"Yes, considering how much the two men resembled each other."

"Besides Levi's nose, of course," Mrs. Yardley added. The policeman nodded.

"If Frank Hayward isn't dead," the officer said, "why hasn't he come forward? Why would he prolong the grief of his family?" I shook my head. That's the one question I'd asked myself over and over and still couldn't answer. The Mr. Hayward I remembered adored his daughter. He wouldn't want her to suffer one moment if he could prevent it.

"He too must be dead," Bertha Yardley said. And then I had a thought.

"Or incapacitated in some way."

"How?"

"Like being locked up in the Lunatic Asylum," Bertha said, thinking the same thing I was. I nodded. "One patient for another. If Miss Hayward mistook Levi for her father, couldn't Dr.

Hillman have mistaken Frank Hayward for Levi?"

"But then the nurses would've known they'd found the escaped patient, wouldn't they?" I said.

"Not if Dr. Hillman lied about that too," Bertha said.

"So to be clear," the policeman said, "you ladies think that Mr. Yardley, trampled by a horse, was mistakenly buried for Frank Hayward while Frank Hayward may have been mistaken for Levi Yardley, the escaped patient, and returned to the asylum?"

Bertha and I looked at each other. Having someone else repeat our speculations out loud made them seem fantastical, but nonetheless true. We both nodded.

"So you'll dig up the body?" Bertha Yardley asked. The policeman stared at Mrs. Yardley for a moment and then at me. With an answer not coming forthwith, Bertha added, "You do know that Miss Davish has helped the police solve murder cases? You should take what she says with great consideration."

I cringed. I'd hoped to get through this interview without my past experiences being mentioned. I should've known better. There had been few conversations I'd had since I arrived home where someone hadn't mentioned them. How could I've thought an interview with a policeman would be any different?

Officer Quick said nothing but tilted his head as he regarded me. I felt like he was looking at me for the first time. "I will consult with Chief Broder," he finally said, turning to Mrs. Yardley.

"Does that mean you will dig up Levi so I can bury him at home in Omaha?"

"Rest assured, Mrs. Yardley, we'll look into the matter." He stood, walked over to the door, and held it open for us. "Thank you, ladies, for coming."

"Does that mean I'm going to get Levi's body or not?" Mrs. Yardley asked me when we were outside. I shook my head.

"I don't know, Bertha."

"Well, I'll dig him up myself if I must." I stifled a chuckle at the image of Bertha Yardley grave-robbing in the middle of the night. But then I realized she was in earnest.

"No, Bertha, you must let the police take care of it. You'll get your husband's body back and some much-needed peace of mind."

She nodded, though I wasn't sure if she believed me. And then I realized I wasn't sure if I believed it either. After all, I'd never told the policeman about my pursuer or about the acts of vandalism and theft occurring at Mrs. Chaplin's school. Why? Because I didn't think they were related to what happened to Levi Yardley and Frank Hayward? Officer Quick seemed trustworthy enough. So why didn't I tell him?

"Yes, thank you, Hattie. You're right. Peace of mind, that's what I'm doing all this for," Bertha said, unaware of my doubts.

Me too, I thought. But for whom?

And that question brought me back to Ginny's house, despite her desire for me not to return.

"What do you want, Hattie?" Ginny said, finally, the words coming slow and with difficulty.

I didn't know what to say. She'd been kind enough to see me when Mrs. Curbow informed her I'd come. But I was shocked by the change in Ginny's appearance and manner. A few days ago, she was calm, composed, and, despite dressed in black, had color in her cheeks. Now with deep circles under her eyes, she was pale and her hair was barely contained in a hastily pinned bun. She'd entered the parlor without a word, sat down, and without regarding me once, stared at the floral pattern on the rug to the right of her feet for several minutes. She blinked but twice. I'd come to tell her about the police's involvement, the possibility that her father's coffin might be exhumed, and my concern that if Levi Yardley was found in her father's place, that her father's fate might have been to take Levi Yardley's place, at the asylum. Yet she seemed unfit to hear such news. I had to tell her something.

"Ginny, I have news that may be both a relief and a concern. I don't want to add to your grief, but I think it's important that you know." She gave no indication that she'd heard me or that she wished for me to continue. I had to continue. I owed her that much. "There's a woman, Mrs. Bertha Yardley, who's asking the police to exhume your father's coffin." That got her attention. Her head jerked up and she stared straight into my eyes.

"What? Why would she do that? Why would the police do that?" How did I tell her it was because I'd convinced them that her father wasn't buried in the coffin that bore his name? She'd already forbidden me from getting involved. Our friendship was already strained. If I told her the whole truth, she may never speak to me again.

Then why have I gotten involved? I wondered.

I'd told myself it was for Ginny's sake, but I knew now that she wanted nothing to do with discovering the truth behind her father's death or disappearance as it may be. Or at least she wanted me to have nothing to do with it. So why had I gotten involved? I didn't want to face the truth, so I faced Ginny instead.

"Mrs. Yardley believes that her husband was mistakenly identified as your father." I pulled out the photograph of Levi Yardley. Ginny looked away, leaving me holding the photograph in the air between us. "If you saw this, you'd see why. The two men bear a striking resemblance to one another."

"Did you have anything to do with this, Hattie?" She reached up and clutched her gold locket.

"I met Mrs. Yardley at the site of the accident, where your father was trampled. She was looking for her missing husband and I . . ."

"And you were snooping around where I'd asked you not to." She glared at me. "Doesn't our friendship mean anything to you?" Her accusation stung. She was right to accuse me, but it was for the sake of our friendship that I'd done it.

"Of course it does." She turned her gaze to the far wall. "Ginny, I think your father is still alive."

Ginny gasped and then turned to look at me. Tears ran down her cheeks. Was she feeling the grief and sorrow of her loss or was she crying in relief? I couldn't tell.

"I didn't mean to bring you more pain, Ginny. I thought I could help."

"Please just leave."

"And if they discover that your father is still alive?"

"How cruel are you, Hattie? Get out of my house!" I felt a sharp pain in my chest and my breath quicken as I realized she didn't believe me. She thought I was toying with her. "Get out!"

"I'm so sorry," was all I could say as I retreated from the room.

Grief threatened to overwhelm me as the impact of Ginny's accusation and mistrust grew. Mrs. Curbow gave me a questioning glance as I rushed past her in the hall, a tightening in my chest so unbearable I could barely breathe, let alone mutter good-bye. How could she ever think I'd be so cruel? Have I changed so much that she'd think this of me? I didn't want to consider what it would take for her to believe me. So for now, I simply fled from the Hayward house, determined to get answers from the one person I knew was withholding them, even if it meant going back to the asylum.

Chapter 19

I can't believe I'm doing this.

I'd walked the mile from the end of the streetcar line, in drizzling rain, and was approaching the imposing presence of State Lunatic Asylum Number Two again. This time I was all alone. This time it was personal. Once on the portico, I lowered my umbrella, took a deep breath, and then yanked on the heavy door. This time it opened. I'd assumed the rain had kept the patients inside as I hadn't passed any in the gardens or fields as I had before. Therefore, I expected a flurry of activity inside, but the hall was empty. I approached the open door of the nurse's office and waited for the nurse at the desk to acknowledge me.

"Yes, what can I do for you?"

"I'd like to see Frank Hayward. He's a patient of Dr. Hillman's." She began flipping through a ledger on her desk.

"I don't think . . ." The woman paused mid-sentence. "Let me call Nurse Simmons. She may be able to help you. It may be a few moments. You can wait over there." She pointed to a row of simple, wooden, high-backed chairs against the wall.

"I remember from years back that you once had a conservatory. Would it be possible for me to wait there?"

"It hasn't been used much in recent years, but I can certainly have Nurse Simmons find you there if you'd like."

"Thank you."

"Do you remember where it is? I can't leave my post to show you."

"Through those doors and at the very end of the hallway?" I pointed in the direction I meant. She nodded.

"Yes, the conservatory door should be unlocked."

I thanked her again and opened the doors to the hallway. To my dismay, the hallway wasn't empty. Dozens of rockers, parallel against the wall, creaked as silent, lethargic men rocked back and forth. I kept my eyes straight ahead as I swiftly made my way down the hallway, past the patients and the many open doors leading to their rooms. I had no desire to see anything but the conservatory.

When I pulled the conservatory door open, I

was immediately assailed by the smell of soil, decaying plants, and mold. The nurse was right. When I'd been here last, dozens of plants, including several types of asters, lupines, lilies, citrus trees, and tomatoes, had been flourishing. One of the doctors had believed caring for the plants was therapeutic for his patients. Did the doctor leave or discover he was wrong? But now there was little left but the weeds. I was slightly disappointed not to see the thriving blossoms, but the weeds were exactly what I'd come to see.

I'd always enjoyed the scent and beauty of flowers and had been interested in the hidden language of plants, as many a young girl my age had been. And thus, on the day my father died, I'd sought solace in this place of color and life. I'd strolled under the glass, warm from the afternoon sun, in shock, barely conscious of the beauty around me, when I'd nearly tripped over a humble sorrel plant, a weed growing up through the gravel floor. How had it grown so large? Why hadn't anyone pulled it out? How had it even found its way into this haven of cultivated beauty? And then I'd realized what it meant.

Paternal love. According to the flower dictionaries I'd memorized, the sorrel plant meant paternal love. I'd broken down then, letting out my exhaustion, my fear, my anger, my intense sorrow, and had fallen on my knees to the ground, ignorant of the dirt and litter on my dress or the gravel digging into my knees and palms. My father was dead, but here was a sign that he was at peace. I had no idea how long I'd knelt there not knowing or caring about my physical discomfort. When I couldn't cry any longer, I'd carefully pulled up the sorrel plant and, unpinning my hat, had placed it inside. I'd carried it home that day and haven't stopped collecting plants since. Whenever I miss my father, I pull out that original sorrel plant, preserved in my collection. I haven't looked at it for some time. And despite my hope, I didn't see another one today. Despite all the other weeds including dandelions, broadleaf plantain, and horseweed, there were no sorrel plants growing through the cracks.

"Miss Davish?" I turned to see Nurse Simmons standing in the doorway. I crossed the weed-covered gravel floor and followed the nurse out of the conservatory. "You were asking about another patient, a Frank Hayward?" She closed the door behind me.

"Yes, I wondered if I could speak with him."

She shook her head. "I'm sorry, Miss Davish. I looked through the admittance paperwork and found nothing for a Frank Hayward."

"He's not a patient here?" She shook her head again.

"And never has been. Who told you he was here?"

I evaded her question. "May I speak with Dr. Hillman, please?"

"If it's about Levi Yardley—"

"No, it's of a more personal nature."

"Well, I'm afraid you'll have to come back. Dr. Hillman isn't here today."

"Really?" I didn't want to have to come back again. "Is he visiting patients in town?"

"No, I believe one of his daughters has taken ill. Is there anything I can help you with?"

"No, thank you. You've been most helpful." The nurse furrowed her brow slightly.

"Well, then, I must get back to my rounds. I've already taken too much time away. I know it's irregular, but could you find your own way out?"

"Of course."

"Then I'll leave you. Good day, Miss Davish." The nurse headed down the hallway.

I watched her disappear into one of the patients' rooms less than halfway down before I headed in the same direction. As I passed the room she was in, I couldn't help but glance in. A man in a white nightshirt was sitting on the edge of his bed, his hands wrapped in what looked like a leather muff. His head was turned away as he dodged Nurse Simmons's attempts to coerce him into drinking medicine from a brown glass bottle. I rushed past, not waiting to see the man's inevitable defeat. When I came to the main lobby, instead of leaving, I ascended the stairs and made my way to Dr. Hillman's office. Whether the nurse was telling me the truth or not, I couldn't leave without confirming for myself that the man wasn't here. The door was slightly ajar. I looked about me to make sure I was alone and then peered through the crack in the door. The narrow view it afforded me showed me part of his desk and a bookcase. I couldn't tell if the doctor was in the room. I knocked. No answer. I knocked again, slightly harder, causing the door to open wider. I still couldn't tell if anyone was inside. And still there was no answer. I looked about me again. No one was in the hall as I pushed the door all the way open and slipped inside.

The room was empty. I glanced at Dr. Hillman's desk. It was mainly covered with closed files bearing patients' names. Resisting the urge to organize the haphazard files, I pulled open a drawer. It was filled with various medical supplies: bulb syringes, packets of cotton gauze, a mortar and pestle, and many glass bottles of varying sizes, filled with colored tablets, clear liquids, or powders. I closed it and pulled open another.

What was I looking for? I wondered even as I caught the sight of an open green velvet-lined mahogany box filled with shiny metal instruments: forceps, scissors, tweezers, hooks, knives, saws, drills, and others that I'd never seen before. I slammed the drawer shut as my breath and pulse quickened. Were those the same instruments Dr. Hillman had carried into my father's house? Had they had a hand in my father's demise? Ever since I'd seen the steel drill-like instrument Dr. Hillman considered using to cut a hole in my father's head, I haven't been able to abide the presence of medical instruments of any kind. Even Walter's stethoscope caused me to swoon. And here were possibly the very instruments used on my father. The very thought sent the room spinning. I dropped into the doctor's chair and put my head between my knees.

"Dr. Hillman?" In my position, I was invisible to the person calling at the door. "He's not here. Let's check to see if he's in his treatment room."

I sighed with relief when I heard the door close and footsteps fade down the hall. I slowly sat up, feeling slightly better in the head but incredibly foolish for my predicament. I didn't want to imagine what would've happened to me if I'd been caught. Using the desk for support, I stood up, testing my balance. When I felt sure I wouldn't faint, I took a few tentative steps toward the door. The room seemed to shift beneath my feet and I grabbed the nearest surface, a metal cabinet. I read the labels on all four drawers, PATIENTS: HILLMAN. With something to focus on, I gained my balance and tugged open the filing drawer. I thumbed through the files searching for the name Frank Hayward. I didn't find it. I wasn't entirely surprised. It had been pure speculation on my part that Mr. Hayward was here. But then I noticed there wasn't a file for Levi Yardley either. I went back to the desk and searched the files there. No Levi Yardley.

But I'd seen it! I thought. It must be here somewhere.

I purposely walked over and locked the door. It wouldn't prevent Dr. Hillman from finding me in his office, but it would at least prevent being accidentally discovered by someone else. It was a risk I had to take. I began a systematic search. First I went through all of the cabinet drawers, then all the desk drawers, carefully avoiding the one with the instrument case, and then his bookshelves. I lingered for a moment to study the photographs of the Hillman children: two boys and three girls. I still couldn't reconcile the fact that the man who killed my father was one himself.

These children still have their father, I thought bitterly before pulling myself away and continuing my search.

Nowhere did I find anything with either Frank Hayward's or Levi Yardley's name on it. The last place I looked was a crate shoved far under the doctor's desk. It contained notebooks and loose papers full of statistics and medical notes. I was about to push it back into place when a notebook with the date 1882 caught my eye. The year my father died. I lifted it out and with trepidation, leafed through it, page by page, using my well-practiced eye, for any mention of George Davish. And then I found it. A hand-scribbled note that read:

Patient suffers from melancholia, irritability, nightmares, debility and resulting atrophy, neuralgia of the head, cacospysy and delirium, the latter a possible effect of prescribed treatment. Diagnosis: Neurasthenia. Cause: Unknown, though patient was diagnosed with Soldier's Heart while serving in Union Army. Treatment: Given progressive treatment. Patient exhibited signs of increased irritability, delirium and acute mania. Restraint was recommended to prevent patient from hurting himself. Increased dosage to no effect. Patient suffered from heart failure and died 3:23am, April 3, 1882.

"Feeling better, Father?"

He merely nodded as he sipped his broth. It had been two days since I evicted Dr. Hillman from the house and already Father was improving. Yes, he still seemed melancholy and was very weak after spending weeks in bed, but he no longer shouted, cried, or claimed to see things that weren't there. And he knew again who I was.

"Thank you, my girl," he said, setting it aside. He'd eaten little.

"You need to eat, Father. You need to improve your strength."

"I will, Hattie. I will." He attempted a smile, but the effort seemed too much.

"I hate to leave you."

"You must go to school. There's nothing more important than your education." I smiled. How many times had I heard him say that?

"I'll be back by seven." I kissed the top of his head. He patted my hand before closing his eyes. I could feel a tremor in his touch.

He's so weak, I thought. "Please eat some more, Father."

"Go, my girl. I'll be fine." It was the last thing I heard my father say. I returned from school to find an empty house. Frantically I ran to the closest neighbors and pounded on their door.

"Hattie, Hattie, what is it?" The upholsterer's wife fumbled with the latch before opening her door.

"Have you seen my father today? He's not at home."

"Oh, dear, I didn't see him, but I think I know where he is."

"Where?" She bit her lip as she slowly shook her head.

"Hattie, sweetie, I wasn't sure it was your father or what I could do if it was."

"Just tell me where he is," I pleaded, grabbing one of her hands in both of mine.

"I saw a wagon with two men in blue coats drive away from your house with a man that might've been your father in the back about an hour ago. I think they were from the Lunatic Asylum."

"Oh no." I could barely breathe. And then I was running. I hailed the first cab I came across and directed them to the asylum. When we arrived, I begged for the driver to wait. I dashed through the front door.

"Hey, where are you going?" a nurse yelled at me as I sprinted down the hall, heading for the staircase.

"Father? Father? Where are you?" The nurse grabbed my arm as I searched for any sign of my father.

"Where is he? What have you done to him?"

"Please come back to the office. I'm sure I can help you, but you have to calm down." At her threat, I followed her quietly back toward the nurse's office near the front door. I wouldn't do my father any good if I was locked up here as well. As I passed back down the hall, I noticed that several patients filled a side room and all were either quietly reading or calmly playing chess, checkers, or cards. One man rocked gently as he hummed "Bonnie Blue Flag" to himself.

This isn't what I imagined, I thought, relieved to see the contentment on the patients' faces. But it was so quiet, too quiet. Was it contentment I saw or resignation? Or something quite different altogether?

"Now what can I do for you?" the nurse asked, when we reached the office.

"I'm looking for my father, George Davish. A neighbor said she saw orderlies from here take him away a little over two hours ago." She glanced at a book on the desk, and then consulted another book held in one of the drawers.

"Yes, Mr. Davish was admitted earlier today."

"But why?"

"I can't say. I'm sorry."

"How can you do that? Admit him without my consent."

"It says here that your father has been under the care of Dr. Hillman."

"Yes, until two days ago. But—"

"Dr. Hillman doesn't need your consent to admit his own patient."

"But my father doesn't want to be here. He made me promise not to let Dr. Hillman bring him here."

"I'm sorry. I'm sure Dr. Hillman has the patient's best interests in mind." I couldn't believe this was happening and I didn't know what to do. What could I do?

"May I see him now?"

"No, I'm afraid Dr. Hillman has ordered that this patient be confined for a few days. That means no visitors."

"Why must he be confined? What does that mean? What are you doing to him?"

"I can't say."

"But he was getting better!"

"Calm down and come back on Friday, Miss Davish. You should be able to see your father then."

I barely slept or ate for three days, imagining the worst. When I arrived on Friday, my fears had been confirmed. As the nurse led me down a hallway, down a flight of stairs and through a locked door, I could feel nausea rising into my mouth.

"Right in here." The nurse opened the door to a stark, whitewashed room with no carpet, no curtains, and no adornment except a table covered with a silver tray lined with syringes, needles, forceps, and other steel instruments. I caught a glimpse of my father, constrained with leather straps to a bed. His hair was unwashed, his eyes were bloodshot, and his teeth were clenched. When he saw me, if indeed he could, he screamed. The nurse suddenly stepped in front of me and with outstretched hands, barred my way.

"Father!" I yelled, trying to shove past her. As

I did, Dr. Hillman stepped into view, grabbed my arm, and thrust me backward.

"What's the meaning of this, Nurse?" Dr. Hillman closed the door behind him, and shut out my view of my father. I could still hear his curses and screams.

"I'm sorry, Doctor, but I thought it would be all right for the patient's daughter to visit now. That's what the chart said."

"You obviously made a mistake."

"What have you done to him?" I demanded. "Let me by. I want to see my father."

"Now, now, Miss Davish, your father is very ill." Dr. Hillman held my arm firmly in his grasp, forcing me back the way I'd come.

"What's wrong with him?" My legs were weak and wobbly, about to give out beneath me. The doctor transferred his hold on me to the nurse, who wrapped her arm around my waist.

"Go home, Miss Davish, and trust me to treat your father," Dr. Hillman said before turning back toward my father's room.

"What have you all done to him?" I gasped for breath. "He was getting better."

"This must be very upsetting for you, but it will all be all right, Miss Davish. Your father is in the best of hands. Dr. Hillman will do everything in his power to help him. Go home and rest. We'll contact you when you can come and visit again." She escorted me back to the waiting cab, patted my hand like a child, and reassured me again that everything would be okay. But I knew she was wrong. I'd promised my father not to let them come, not to let them seal him up in this horrible place. I'd failed him. But I'd no idea how wrong she was. I never saw my father again. He was dead within days.

I stared at the doctor's notes again. Neurasthenia? Soldier's Heart? I knew my father had fought in the war, but he never spoke of it—ever. I never knew he'd been diagnosed with Soldier's Heart. So, the war explained his nightmares and rapid heartbeat. I'd never been told of any illnesses he suffered from. Now I finally knew. Could Dr. Hillman have prevented my father from suffering horribly from this disease? I still believed so. The doctor's treatment even added to Father's suffering. Dr. Hillman had told me to trust him and still my father died. But did he kill him with his negligence, arrogance, and ignorance? Probably not. Could he have saved him? Probably not. With a weak heart, my father could've died anywhere, at any time.

Suddenly I felt light-headed, not in the way that would cause me to faint, but as if a great weight had lifted from my shoulders. I felt calm and relief like I hadn't known in years. To test my new serenity, I pulled open the desk drawer and stared down at the metal objects that a few moments ago held such power over me. I felt nothing. I leaned over, touched the drill, and felt the coolness of the metal. I almost smiled as I slid the drawer shut again. I didn't know what it meant that I couldn't find any record of Frank Hayward or Levi Yardley among Dr. Hillman's records, but I knew what I had found was more than I'd been looking for. I couldn't wait to return to my room and write Walter immediately.

Chapter 20

But that never happened.

As I was leaving, I spotted Dr. Hillman disappearing through a side door. I thought he was treating his sick child at home? Without thinking, I followed after him. In the halls I could easily trail behind the doctor without his knowledge. It was passing the patients rocking in their chairs that proved more difficult. Several tried in earnest to get my attention, waving their hands, jutting a leg out in front of me, or cursing at me. Once, a man grabbed hold of my wrist, the back of his hand damp and glistening with saliva. Unable to stifle a squeal, I yanked my arm from the patient's grasp and stepped as far away as I could get, pressing my back against the opposite wall. I glanced down the hall toward Dr. Hillman, expecting to see him turn, alerted to my presence by my cry. To my astonishment, he ignored the cacophony of noise and continued on his way as if no one were about. I swiftly followed the doctor to a stairwell that he promptly began to descend. I waited at the top until he'd disappeared around the corner of the first flight. I used the sound of his footsteps to track his descent. At the bottom of the stairs, Dr. Hillman was nowhere in sight, but then I spied a set of double doors down the hall closing.

Where's he going? I wondered as I raced to catch the doors before they locked behind him.

Behind the doors was a long, narrow concrete tunnel, lit by evenly spaced bare bulbs hanging from the ceiling. My shadow stretched far behind me, but Dr. Hillman was nowhere to be seen. Luckily the sound of his footsteps echoed faintly ahead. I pursued him, around several turns, once catching a glimpse of his shadow, until his footsteps faded away and all I heard was the sound of my own breathing.

I'll never find him now, I thought, disappointed to have gotten this far without discovering where he was going. But what had I thought he was doing? I'd followed him without thinking. What had I thought to learn? Puzzled by my own behavior, I turned back only to realize that in my hasty pursuit I'd failed to take note of the way back.

And then I heard the wailing.

"Aaaaaaaah, aaaaaaaaah!"

The sound pierced my heart like wind passing through me. Without thinking, I picked up my skirts and ran in the opposite direction. Yet no matter which direction I chose, the howling grew louder. And then someone's sobbing overlaid the wailing and I could barely think. I covered my ears, but to no avail. I had to get away, distance myself from the pain in those desperate cries echoing in and around my head. Before long, I was lost, finding myself in tunnels narrow enough I could touch the walls with my outstretched hands. I stooped over to avoid brushing my hat against the damp ceiling or knocking into a hot electric bulb. Water puddled on the floor along the walls and the air became increasingly fetid, the odor of unwashed bodies, mold, and traces of chloride mingling together. I put my handkerchief to my nose and continued on. And then all went silent. I stopped and listened. Nothing.

Thank goodness, I thought, letting out pent-up breath. I waited for several moments, listening, waiting for the cries to return, but the silence remained. Emboldened by the quiet, I took a few steps around yet another corner of another tunnel and in the sudden dimness tripped over the wrought-iron leg of a bed. No electric bulbs lit the dark; only a single kerosene lamp flickered halfway down the tunnel.

What's a bed doing down here? I wondered as I

struggled to my feet. I brushed the dirt from my skirt and then readjusted my hat with one hand, mindful to keep my nose covered. *I must've found an old storage area.*

And then the tunnel exploded with the eerie howls of a man in turmoil. I froze, chills shooting up my spine as the outline of a figure writhed in the bed next to me. The sound of chains rattling accompanied the distressed person's next wail. Like having to see an upturned carriage up close, I stepped forward. Before me was a man, not much older than me, wearing a cotton nightshirt, once white but now so threadbare it was almost transparent. The sleeves hung above his elbows. The outline of a mermaid or a strangely shaped fish tattooed with India ink on his flabby forearm wiggled its tail every time he moved. His scrawny legs were bare. He had no sheet or coverlet to protect him from the damp. His head had been shaved bald. His eyes bulged out as he stared at me, rattling the chains that secured him to the wall even as he lay prostrate in the bed. His tongue hung loosely from his mouth as he opened it to wail again. I covered my ears again.

The poor, wretched creature was beyond any help I could give him, but seeing him gave me hope. With a patient sleeping here, attending nurses must not be far away. I left his side, hoping to find an exit nearby. As I approached the light, I could see that the wailing man wasn't alone. The entire tunnel was lined with beds, occupied by other men chained to the wall. One man whimpered and rocked himself side to side while another simply followed me with unblinking eyes as I passed.

What's wrong with them? I wondered, remembering the list of reasons for admittance I'd seen: political excitement, religious enthusiasm, bad whiskey, or snuff eating? I shuddered to think it could've been something as innocuous as any of that.

And then I pictured my father here, chained to the wall, abandoned. Were these patients being treated or punished? Were they here left to die? As I passed yet another bed, a man, rattling his chains as I approached, lunged at me. Despite knowing he couldn't reach me, I screamed and leaped back as far away from him as I could. I misjudged the width of the tunnel; my back smacked against the hard concrete of the opposite wall, crumpling the brim of my hat and knocking the breath out of me. I slumped over, trying to catch my breath. Suddenly every patient began rattling their chains, yelling or moaning. Even with my hands over my ears, the noise was unbearable.

"Help! Please! Somebody help me!"

My feeble cries simply added to the cacophony of the others. I slid down the wall to the damp floor. I hugged my knees to my chest as I whimpered in fear; I was as trapped as they were. And then a blinding light shined out from an opened door partway down the tunnel. I hadn't even seen it.

"Hey! You on the floor. What are you doing down here?" a woman said. All I could see was her outline against the light. "You need to get back to your own ward."

She thinks I'm a patient!

Without a moment of hesitation, I clambered to my feet and dashed by the nurse in the doorway. Carrying a metal tray covered with glass tubes filled with blue tablets, a tin cup, and a pitcher of water, she could do nothing to stop me but yell. I climbed the steps before me in twos and sprinted down a familiar hallway, skidding to a halt on the highly polished floor, just as another patient covered with a white sheet was carried by me on a stretcher. This time I dropped my eyes and focused on anything: the dark smudge that marred the tip of my shoe, the rent in the trim of my skirt, my racing heartbeat, anything but the passing body.

Once the orderlies and the body were gone, I picked up my skirts and ran. I ran, as fast as I never had, past patients lounging in doorways or playing checkers in an alcove, past startled nurses who shouted words of disapproval at my back, past one matronly lady in a wide-brimmed hat waiting patiently in a high-backed chair in the lobby. I ignored all of their scowls and stares, stopping to catch my breath only after I'd shoved open the front doors and could fill my lungs with fresh air. As I stood on the path panting, looking back at the building that had for a short time entombed me, I thought of what had brought me here in the first place.

Dr. Hillman and his secrets be damned! I thought, vowing never to step foot in that wicked place again.

I was still shaking when I stepped into the hushed peace of the Cathedral of St. Joseph. Needing a place of sanctuary, I'd thought of returning to Mount Mora, but that sacred place had been tainted by the specter of the man in Frank Hayward's coffin. Kneeling at my father's grave, I wouldn't be able to set aside all the questions that still remained about Frank Hayward and Levi Yardley. Nor would I be able to forget the terrors I'd just witnessed and my fear that Father once suffered a similar fate. Thus I went back to the cathedral, despite being slightly disheveled and dirty, hoping to find the peace and tranquility I craved. And I found it. I stared up at the ceiling, painted blue with gold stars, and breathed in the incense, still burning in a side chapel. I closed my eyes as rays of sun streamed through the ten-foot-tall glass windows and warmed my face. I cleared my mind of everything—Ginny's rebuke, the troubles at Mrs. Chaplin's, Frank Hayward's mysterious where-abouts, Dr. Hillman's lies, and Levi Yardley's fate. I knelt and prayed, feeling the panic, the fear and loathing that I felt lost in the tunnels under the asylum slip away.

I slipped back into the pew when a fellow parishioner sat down a few rows in front of me. I glanced at the marble statue of St. Joseph with the infant Jesus in his arms, and stared at the flickering candles at its base. It reminded me of the shadows in the asylum tunnels.

I didn't get dizzy or nauseous, I suddenly realized. During the terrifying encounter with the chained patients, I'd felt panic, fear, and loathing. I'd imagined never finding my way out and facing a fate similar to that of the poor, pathetic human beings who had been reduced to little more than rabid animals. But I hadn't once felt the floor tilt or the room spin. I hadn't once needed to prop myself up against the wall or hold on to the rail of a bed.

Could learning about my father's true fate have affected me so deeply, so quickly? I'd been able to face the instrument case in Dr. Hillman's drawer. What else would I be able to face? As I pondered this new idea, I looked about me at the others in the church. Two elderly gray-haired women occupied the second pew as they prayed on their knees, shoulders touching. Another old woman, dressed all in black, knelt in front of the statue of Mary, clutching her rosary. A young man, with a thick mustache and a scowl on his face, sat with his arms wrapped around him, in a pew across the aisle and toward the back. With his hat in his lap, he simply glared at the altar. And then I saw Malinda Gilbert. She was coming out of the confessional, biting her nails. I immediately dropped my eyes and stared at my hands. When I looked up again, she was gone.

Had she seen me? I wondered. I hoped not. If she had, I wanted in no way for her to guess what my first thought was when I saw her. To my shame, I wondered what she had to confess.

Think of your own sins, Hattie, I heard my mother's voice say. As a child I had often voiced my curiosity after seeing someone I knew exit the confessional box. She properly scolded me for my ill-placed inquisitiveness. I'd apologize, hoping it would save me from the consequences, fifteen "Ave Maria" prayers, but it never did. Now, as then, I walked over and opened the confessional door.

"Bless me, Father, for I have sinned. It has been a month since my last confession."

Chapter 21

"This came for you, Miss Davish."

Mr. Putney handed me an envelope and then retrieved a large, heavy packet wrapped in brown paper and string. He chuckled a bit. I was struck again how much he reminded me of my grandfather. "I think we're getting into quite the habit here."

After changing my soiled dress and crumpled hat in my room, I had a light meal in the dining room. I hadn't eaten anything since before Mass this morning. I was passing the desk when he called my name.

"Yes, it does seem that there's something for me every time I return." The clerk nodded, smiled, and giving up any pretense of a lack of curiosity, leaned over the desk a bit. I opened the envelope first.

"He's persistent," I said. "I'll give him that."

"Another invitation from Mr. Boone?"

I nodded. "Some men can't seem to take no for an answer."

"You could say yes?" Mr. Putney shrugged when I frowned at him. "It would stop him from sending you invitations." He had a point.

"I'll think about it. Now what do you suppose is in here?" I examined the brown package and noticed there was no postmark or stamp on it. It couldn't be from Sir Arthur then. But whom was it from? "Was this hand-delivered?"

"They both were. Do you think it's from Mr. Boone too?" I looked up at Mr. Putney. I'd never thought of that.

"There's one way to find out." I ripped it open.

"A ledger?" the clerk said, eyeing the tall brown book. "I'm guessing it's not from Mr. Boone then. Something for your work, I suppose?" I barely heard him as I flipped open the ledger and found a note inside the cover. I read it quickly.

Dear Miss Davish,

Per Mrs. Yardley's request, we're sending you this ledger found with the body of her late husband, Mr. Levi Yardley. She insisted that you were the one to place it in the hands of its proper owner. If you're in need of assistance, I am your servant, Officer Daniel Quick.

"No, Mr. Putney, this is possible evidence of a crime."

"Really?"

"Yes," I said, absentmindedly, for my mind was swirling with the implications of both the ledger and the note.

The police must've exhumed the casket as Mrs. Yardley requested and had confirmed without a doubt that it was Levi Yardley and not Frank Hayward in the coffin.

Poor Bertha, I thought. At least now she knows the truth.

But how? Mrs. Yardley couldn't simply say, "That's my husband." Normally that would be all that was necessary, but hadn't Asa Upchurch and Ginny also identified the same body as Frank Hayward? Did the police have other ways of knowing for certain that it was Levi Yardley? I'd once read a story in the newspaper several years ago about how the famed Dr. Alexandre Lacassagne in France had used anthropometrics, tooth patterns, and bones to identify a body found in a river four months after the man's death. Had the St. Joseph medical examiner used similar techniques? Either way, I'd been right. Levi Yardley had been the man buried in Frank Hayward's place. But that also meant that Ginny and Asa Upchurch were wrong. But how? How does one misidentify one's own father? And then I imagined my father in his casket: his head shaved, his body gaunt, his eyes and cheeks sunken. If I hadn't known better, I might not have recognized him either.

Poor Ginny, I thought even as I contemplated what discovering the fate of Levi Yardley meant. What's happened to Frank Hayward? And what does this ledger have to do with his disappearance?

"You're involved with the police, aren't you?" Mr. Putney's question pulled me out of my thoughts.

"No, not really."

"But you do know who this ledger belongs to?"

"Yes, I do."

"And you think it's a clue to a crime?"

I nodded as I skimmed through the pages of the ledger again. It was definitely the missing ledger from Mrs. Chaplin's school. Someone had hoped to bury it with Frank Hayward, or at least who they thought was Frank Hayward. But that would mean Mr. Hayward himself couldn't have stolen it, or if he had been involved, he had had an accomplice. Whoever stole the accounting ledger brought it to the funeral. Ginny? I thought. No, we were at odds, but I couldn't believe it of my friend. She'd never be involved in something like this. Mrs. Chaplin? No, she seemed genuinely shocked to find the ledger missing. The more I considered the gathering, the more I realized almost anyone could've hidden the ledger in the dead man's coffin.

I pulled out my notebook, set it on the desk beneath Mr. Putney's curious eye, and began to jot down every name of the staff and students from Mrs. Chaplin's in attendance at the funeral.

1. Ginny
2. President & Mrs. Upchurch

Miss Gilbert. I stopped writing when I got to her name. She went to confession today. I blushed again at my sacrilegious curiosity. But . . . could she have done it? But why? Why would anyone want this ledger to disappear forever?

I flipped through it again and immediately realized that the first few pages were written in a different hand than the remaining pages.

Why hadn't I seen this before? I thought.

Two different handwriting styles meant two different people made entries into the ledger. But why? Frank Hayward had been the bookkeeper. Who else would've made these entries? Ginny, perhaps, helping her father for some reason? I glanced at the second set of handwriting. I knew Ginny's handwriting from the many years of letters I'd received from her, but I didn't recognize this handwriting at all. I began to examine the tables of numbers, dates, and lists of inventory more carefully. Nothing struck me as being out of the ordinary until I reached entries made in the second hand.

Wait a minute, I thought, making a quick calculation in my head. *Something's wrong.*

"Speaking of crimes," Mr. Putney said,

disrupting my train of thought, "have you seen today's headline?"

"What?" I said, trying to regain my focus. Something was wrong with this book. I needed a little more time to examine the figures in detail.

"The headline in tonight's paper." The desk clerk held up a copy of the *Herald.* It read:

One man murdered, another man missing. Dead man buried in another man's coffin.

I snatched the paper from him and read the first lines of the story.

Today Coroner Whittington caused the coffin of Mr. Frank Hayward, of St. Joseph, previously buried in Oakland Cemetery on August 25, to be exhumed due to suspicions of mistaken identification. Chief Broder of the city police confirms that the coffin contains the body of Mr. Levi Yardley, newly arrived from Omaha, and not that of Mr. Hayward. An autopsy was conducted and police uncovered no evidence that Mr. Yardley was trampled by a horse as originally supposed. The wounds the dead man suffered from were the result of some other form of trauma. Police will not comment on actual cause of death but are continuing their investigation into the suspected murder of Mr. Yardley and the whereabouts of Frank Hayward. According to police, Frank Hayward is their prime suspect.

"Oh no!"

"What is it?" Mr. Putney asked, confused.

"Keep this in the hotel safe for me, would you please, Mr. Putney?" I snatched up the ledger and handed it to him. He took it with trembling hands.

"Of course." He hugged the ledger tight against his chest. He leaned forward as far as he could over the desk. He lifted his spectacles and squinted hard at me. "Are you caught up in this police business in some way, Miss Davish? Are you in trouble?"

"You have no idea, Mr. Putney." Then without another moment's hesitation, I turned my back on the wide-eyed clerk and headed straight out the door.

"I'm sorry, miss, but Officer Quick has gone home for the day. Can I help you? Is there something you would like to report?"

I'd headed straight for the police station after leaving the hotel, but I hadn't given any thought to the fact that it was late evening. Of course he wouldn't be there.

"No, actually, I came to inquire about the murder of Levi Yardley."

"Oh? Do you have information about the death, miss?" The policeman, a lanky fellow with stubble on his chin, began shuffling papers around on the desk.

"Actually, it was my information that led the police to exhume Frank Hayward's coffin. But I'd no idea Mr. Yardley had been murdered. We'd all been told that he'd been trampled by a horse."

"Ah, here it is." He snatched up a piece of paper. "Are you Miss Davish?"

"Yes, I am." I was slightly startled he knew my name.

"Officer Quick left this note notifying me that you might stop by." It was one thing that the policeman knew my name; I'd given evidence after all. But how would Officer Quick know I'd be back?

"What else does your note say?"

"That you might want to know more details about the case." Again, how would he know that?

"He's right. I do. What can you tell me?" The policeman studied the paper in his hands.

"Says here to tell you that we're still investigating, but we can confirm that the disfigurement to Mr. Yardley's face wasn't caused by a horse. The body is still being examined, but we suspect Mr. Yardley didn't die a natural death."

"Is that all you can tell me?"

"What more do you want to know?"

"The newspaper said that you suspect Frank Hayward of the murder. Is that true?"

"It's not technically a murder yet. As Quick

says, we're still investigating. I wouldn't believe everything you read in the paper."

"I'd like to help with the investigation." The policeman opened his mouth but before he could object, I added, "Frank Hayward is the father of a dear friend. We now know that he's missing. He too could be dead or at least in danger."

"Miss Davish." The policeman tried to interrupt me.

"And I have experience in these things." I inwardly cringed even as I said it. I never imagined I'd use my past encounters with murder as justification to help investigate another one. "And I could—"

"Yes, Miss Davish, I know." He successfully startled me into silence.

"You know what?"

"That's also on this note from Quick." The policeman waved the sheet of paper in the air. "Says here you've been involved in murder investigations in both Arkansas and Illinois." Officer Quick had obviously checked up on me. That's how he guessed I'd be back making inquiries. I now had a record of doing such things. But he'd missed my involvement in the murder in Rhode Island.

No need to enlighten him, I thought.

"So?"

"So the answer is no thank you. Officer Quick and his team are more than capable of conducting this investigation. This isn't some small town in the Ozarks, Miss Davish. We've been solving murders in St. Joe for decades. I watched as the convicted murderers hung over there by the old Patee House Hotel. We even lent a hand in the investigation into the killing of Jesse James." He chuckled under his breath before continuing.

"Now that was something! Sheriff Timberlake himself identified the body. He could verify Jesse's known wounds, having known Jesse from the war. Police Commissioner Craig came up from Kansas City. But what a surprise it was! We didn't even know Jesse was in St. Joe. One minute I was enjoying a quiet cup of coffee at the station and the next I was helping to contain the crowds that swarmed the house as word got out."

"But—" I said, but he hadn't finished his tale.

"And can you believe that lots of folks didn't believe us? Thought he'd faked his death or something. It had happened before. First time folks thought he died was in seventy-nine. I'll never forget the editorial that compared Jesse James to a cat with nine lives, saying he'd been dead many times before, only to be resurrected as often. But I was there. This time, there was no doubt. Photographs were taken, in front of witnesses, including me, a full coroner's inquest was conducted, and no less than three doctors performed the autopsy confirming the dead man was indeed Jesse James."

"One of the doctors was Dr. George Catlett, superintendent at the Lunatic Asylum."

"Yeah, how'd you know that?"

I shook my head, regretting having mentioned it. My father had been at the asylum the same day. "Long story."

"Well, anyway, all this is to say we'll contact you if we need to ask you any further questions, but otherwise, we'll do fine by ourselves. It's our job after all. From what I hear, you're a top-notch secretary."

"I do my best." I tried not to sound disappointed, but I was.

"Thank you for your help and interest, miss, but if that's everything, these reports won't file themselves." The officer indicated the tall stack of papers on his desk.

"Yes, of course." I turned to leave and the policeman jumped up and ran around the desk. He reached the door before I did and opened it for me. "Thank you."

"You're very welcome, Miss Davish. Let's hope we don't meet again, at least not under these circumstances," he said, with a lighthearted laugh. I nodded and forced a smile, which turned into a genuine smile when I remembered that I hadn't made any promises. Frank Hayward's where-abouts was a mystery, but I could solve it. It may not have anything to do with Levi Yardley's death, but it would mean the world to Ginny. He may not like it, but Officer Quick won't be able to accuse me of interfering with his investigation.

"We'll see," I said, stepping by the policeman and through the door as his smile was replaced by a furrowed brow and a genuine look of confusion. "We'll see."

Chapter 22

"I'm sorry, Miss Davish," Mrs. Curbow said. "It's late and Miss Hayward isn't seeing any visitors. Not even you, I'm afraid."

If she'd said, "Especially not you," I wouldn't have been surprised. But I couldn't take no for an answer. This was too important. Ginny had to know.

"I'm sorry too, Mrs. Curbow." She frowned and shook her head, misunderstanding me. "Has she seen the papers today?"

"No, of course not. Unless it's crumpled up and wiping my windows, I say newspaper is good for nothing."

"I didn't think so."

"Ah!" The housekeeper cried out as I pushed past her.

"Ginny!" I yelled. "Virginia, I must speak with you."

"Miss Davish, this is highly irregular. Miss Hayward—"

"Must see me," I said, interrupting her. "Ginny! It's imperative I talk to you! I've come from the police." Mrs. Curbow's face turned pale as her hand went to cover her gaping mouth.

"But why?" she asked. I ignored her and yelled again.

"Ginny!" Like an apparition, a figure in a white muslin nightdress and stockinged feet appeared at the top of the stairs.

"What do you want, Hattie?" There was a cold edge to her voice.

"I must speak to you about your father. Have you seen the headlines?"

She dashed down the stairs so fast, the large, ruffled lace collar of her nightdress flapped about her face like wings. Any moment I expected her to trip and fall. She descended the stairs without incident but slipped when she reached the highly polished parquet floor and slid several feet, waving her arms about her before stumbling right into me. I caught her in my arms, surefooted in my heavy-soled boots, which prevented us both from tumbling backward to the floor. She was so close I could smell the Florida water on her skin. Once we would've giggled at her clumsiness, but there was nothing to laugh about now. She immediately pulled away from me.

"What headlines?" she said, brushing herself off.

"You may want to sit down."

"When did you get so dramatic, Hattie? Just tell me." I shrugged and glanced at Mrs. Curbow as if disavowing any responsibility of what might happen next. Mrs. Curbow, her face still pale as a sheet, had her arms wrapped tightly around herself and was rocking slightly back and forth. *Maybe she's the one who needs to sit,* I thought.

"The police exhumed your father's coffin."

"What?" Ginny shrieked, her hands in fists at her sides, her face a combination of fury and, could that be, fear? "When? Why? They can't do that without my permission. How dare they!"

"The coroner ordered it due to suspicions of mistaken identity."

"Hattie," Ginny said through a clenched jaw, "did you have anything to do with this?"

I ignored her question. "And they may have uncovered evidence of a serious crime."

"What crime?"

"Murder."

I caught the expression on Mrs. Curbow's face out of the corner of my eye and had barely enough time to dash to her side as she collapsed. I caught the weight of the old woman and went down with her, landing hard on my knees, but keeping her head from smacking against the floor. Her head rested gently in my lap as I tapped her cheek. Ginny rushed to her side.

"Mrs. Curbow? Are you all right?"

The old housekeeper's eyes fluttered and then

slowly opened. She nodded her head slightly but showed no signs that she was inclined to sit up.

"What murder?" Ginny hissed over the prostrate figure of her housekeeper.

"A man named Levi Yardley. He was the man buried in your father's coffin . . . not your father."

"That can't be." Color drained from Ginny's face. "I saw Father with my own eyes."

"Through the autopsy, the medical examiner determined positively that it was Mr. Yardley and not your father."

"But how could that be? I saw him with my own eyes," she repeated, hanging her head as she stared at the floor.

I shook my head and then remembered the photograph I still had in my pocket. I pulled it out to show Ginny. "As you can see, Mr. Yardley and your father look a great deal alike."

Ginny slowly raised her head, took the photograph from me, and studied it. "Besides his nose of course," Ginny said, wrinkling hers.

"Do you know him or have you ever heard of Levi Yardley?"

"No, never." She handed back the photograph.

"Mr. Upchurch must've mistaken Mr. Yardley for your father when he found him in the street. When he brought him here, you assumed it was your father as well. As you say, with the disfigured nose, it would've been difficult to tell them apart." She nodded, accepting my explanation. "That and the missing scar."

"But you said this other man was murdered?"

"It's not conclusive yet, but that's what the police suspect."

"And my father?" Mrs. Curbow moaned. I shrugged.

"I have no idea. He's obviously missing." I didn't want to voice the possibility that he too could be dead. "Do you have any idea where he might be? Or why he hasn't contacted you?" Ginny shook her head, speechless.

Mrs. Curbow moaned again and began struggling to sit up. We aided her and got her into an upright position.

"Are you feeling better, Mrs. Curbow? Can you stand?" I asked.

"I don't know. My legs feel as wobbly as an uncooked soufflé." I put my arm around her waist and helped her to her feet. Ginny remained crouched on the floor. The housekeeper looked down at her. "Is she all right?" I couldn't answer that.

"Let's get you to a chair." I helped her into the nearby parlor, sat her down, and poured her a brandy from the tray on the sideboard. "Here, drink this. It should help. I'm going to check on Miss Hayward." I left the housekeeper sipping the brandy slowly. Ginny hadn't moved.

"There's more, isn't there?" she asked without looking up.

"Yes."

"Tell me." I told her about the newspaper's claim that her father was a suspect in Mr. Yardley's death.

"My father didn't kill anyone." Ginny looked straight into my eyes for the first time.

"It would explain why he hasn't contacted you."

"But why? Why would he do such a thing?"

"It would certainly be a convincing way to fake one's own death, killing someone who looks just like you."

"No, Father would never do such a thing!"

"He might if he were desperate enough. Could he have been involved with what's going on at the school?"

"What's going on at the school?"

I explained to her about the incidents at the school: the fire, the vandalism, the theft, as well as the missing accounting ledger.

"I knew about some of it. Don't you remember, I even wrote you about it?" I remembered that she'd only written about her concern. She'd said nothing specific. "But this is the first time I've heard about a ledger gone missing."

"The ledger was found buried in your father's coffin alongside Levi Yardley."

"And there's suspicion that my father was involved?" I nodded. "With what? Stealing bazaar money? Dumping champagne into the grass?

Ripping out pages from shorthand dictionaries? Hattie, that's absurd. And to think you believe he's capable of killing someone over such pettiness. . . ." Her face reddened with anger.

"Actually he's suspected of embezzling money from the school."

"No! My father loved the school. He'd never do anything to harm Mrs. Chaplin or the school's reputation. He certainly wouldn't steal from it."

"There's one way to prove it."

"What's that?"

"Do you have a sample of your father's handwriting?"

"Of course, but how is that going to help?"

"Please, Ginny, indulge me." Ginny stood up and walked into the parlor. I followed her. Mrs. Curbow was still clutching the brandy glass between two hands. It was almost gone.

"Are you well, Mrs. Curbow?" Ginny asked. The housekeeper nodded but said nothing and took another sip.

Ginny pulled an envelope out from one of the pigeonholes from a secretary placed in the corner of the room. "Here's a letter he was writing to a friend the night before he died. He never finished it."

"May I?" She handed me the letter.

I skimmed it, looking at the formation of the letters and not the content. I didn't need to match it to the first pages of entries in the ledger.

I recognized it as Mr. Hayward's hand. Then who belonged to the second hand?

"Thank you." I handed the letter back. "The handwriting in that letter confirms that your father made the first few pages of entries in the ledger. From what I saw, there was nothing suspicious about them."

"Then everyone will know he did nothing wrong," Ginny said.

"Not necessarily. Until the police discover who killed Levi Yardley, or until your father reappears and clears his name, the police will suspect him."

"No, Hattie, no. You know my father. He'd never harm anyone."

"The fact remains, Ginny, he's missing, and until we find him . . ." I hesitated. I caught myself from saying "alive or dead."

"What?" The desperation in Ginny's voice was heartbreaking. She reached for her locket that wasn't there.

"Until we find him, he'll be a suspect. It was his coffin the dead man was found in, after all, with one of his ledgers beside him."

"But he didn't do it, Hattie. He didn't do any of it."

"Then where is he, Ginny?"

Her shoulders sagged and she shook her head violently. I knelt down beside her and put my arms around her. She clung to me. Mrs. Curbow, revived by Ginny's need, set down the empty brandy snifter, stood up, and came to stand next to Ginny's chair.

"Now, now, Miss Hayward, it'll all be all right." She handed Ginny a handkerchief.

"I'm so sorry, Hattie," Ginny said. "I'm so sorry."

"It's okay." I said it over and over. She shook her head again.

"You tried to tell me. You tried to be a good friend and look how I treated you. I spurned your aid and now look what's happened."

"It's okay." I was relieved that Ginny finally understood my motives.

I'd only wanted to help. But I also couldn't help thinking that some of this was my fault. If I hadn't questioned the man in the coffin's identity in the first place, maybe Ginny would be better off. But no, without my questioning, Mrs. Yardley would always have wondered what had become of her husband, a killer would've never been sought, and Frank Hayward would've been left to his current fate, whatever that may be. No, I did what I had to. It didn't mean I had to like the pain I'd caused, though.

I gently pushed Ginny away and looked her in the eyes. "Can you tell me anything about where your father may be or why someone would put the ledger in his coffin?"

Mrs. Curbow, who had sat at the end of the

settee nearest Ginny, scooched to the edge of her seat and stared expectantly at her. Ginny hesitated. At first I thought she was catching her breath, trying to hold back tears, but something in her manner, the way she looked away, the way she searched the room with her eyes as if looking for answers, made me wonder.

"No, I'm sorry. I have no idea." And then she looked up, a strange look in her eye. "When I gathered his things from his office, I didn't find anything unusual, nothing that didn't belong to him." So that's why Frank Hayward's office was empty. "But I could guess who might've stolen the ledger."

"Who?"

"Asa Upchurch or Malinda Gilbert."

"Why them?"

"They were competing for the head position. Maybe one of them wanted to hide something that would lessen their chances." Maybe, I thought. "And then there's Miss Woodruff. She was acting particularly strange at the funeral. Like she had something to hide."

"You noticed that too? She was overly distraught and emotional. I thought she simply was mourning the loss of your father."

"She hardly knew my father."

"But then why steal the ledger?" For the first time since I'd arrived home, I saw a small smile steal across Ginny's lips.

"I don't know. Isn't that your job to find out?" It was her way of apologizing for rejecting me and my previously offered help. I was relieved to have my friend back.

"If that's what you want, Ginny. If that's what you want."

Chapter 23

Despite reconciling with Ginny, I was worn out, down, and discouraged by the time I returned to my hotel. Ginny was holding something back. But what? If she knew something about her father's whereabouts or about what's been going on at the school, why wouldn't she tell me? I was relieved that we weren't at odds anymore, but something between us had been lost forever. I didn't quite trust her either.

Good thing I have work to do, I thought, grateful once again to Sir Arthur for the much-needed distraction.

I retrieved my handwritten notes on General Thompson from my room and then the ledger from the desk clerk and took it all with me to the school.

"You're working late, miss," a young girl, wearing an apron, said as she locked the school door behind me.

"Yes, I'm afraid so. Where's Gus?"

"He's around here somewhere. Said you might be coming. I heard you knocking first, though, seeing as I was right here cleaning the floors. Where to, miss?"

"Miss Gilbert's room, please."

"Then follow me."

With her lantern held high, she led me up a flight of stairs and down the hall to the typing instructor's classroom. The maid lifted her ring of keys, holding them in the light of the lantern to find the right one.

"Why don't you turn the lights on?"

"Wish I could." She singled out a particularly thick key from the bunch. "It sure would make mopping easier. But Gus says Mr. Upchurch won't allow it. Says it costs too much to burn the lights at night." She lifted the key toward the door but as she pushed the key in, the door opened slightly.

"It was already unlocked?" The maid sighed as she put her keys away.

"Happens all the time. Getting these teachers to lock their doors is like trying to scrub the black off an iron kettle."

I was surprised to hear this since discipline and orderliness was the foundation of what Mrs. Chaplin's school taught me. I expected Miss Gilbert, of all people, to be more diligent, especially with the vandalism and theft of late. The maid reached into the room and pushed on the electric lights. We both put our hands to our eyes to deflect the brilliance.

"There you go. You know where to find me, and Gus should be around every half hour or so if you need anything."

"Thank you." I set my things down next to the nearest typewriter. "I'll be here." She raised her lantern in response and went back to her bucket and mop.

Having been interrupted the last time, I had plenty of typing to keep me preoccupied. I heard Gus pass by three times before I took a break. I'd been typing details I'd learned about General Thompson's involvement with the Pony Express. The Pony Express lasted only eighteen months, yet the daring overland journey had made the riders famous. I suddenly remembered the ledger I'd brought with me. I still hadn't had time to examine it closely. After finishing the page I was working on, I put my work aside, picked up the ledger, and opened it to the first page. I noticed immediately that there were eraser marks, a great deal of them. I flipped through the pages and realized that almost every page had them. But that could be explained by a distracted or incompetent accountant. Frank Hayward was definitely not the latter, but the former was a real possibility. However, that wasn't what had bothered me earlier. As I'd noticed before on pages entered by someone other than Frank Hayward, several of the figures didn't add up. The cost of a dozen bottles of ink varied over several months with no discernable pattern, as did almost everything from a box of paper clips to typewriter ribbon. And the payment to the electric company was often twice the price of the actual cost.

No wonder Mr. Upchurch thinks the light bill is too high, I thought.

Tap, tick, tap, tick.

I looked up at the sound of footsteps approaching. I'd heard the heavy tread of Gus go by several times, but this wasn't Gus. Nor was it the sound of the maid's light tread. I closed the ledger, stepped hurriedly to the wall, and pushed the lights off. I let my eyes adjust to the darkness as I listened to the footsteps grow louder and louder. Then there was silence. The person had stopped outside the door.

Tap, tick, tap, tick.

I let out a sigh and then peered out the door at the sounds of retreating footsteps. Except for the hand that held the candle, the figure, dressed in black, was almost imperceptible. Had Miss Woodruff come back? What was she looking for this time? She'd already searched Mr. Hayward's office for anything that might impliate him in the so-called incidents that had been occurring at the school. Had she learned of "more evidence," as she put it? But why was she haunting the hallways after hours when she knew Gus was on duty? What she was doing wasn't a secret anymore.

As quietly as I could, I stepped into the hall and followed. However, this time she didn't pass by Mr. Upchurch's office as before but tried the doorknob. It was unlocked.

The maid was right, I thought. Mrs. Chaplin would not be pleased.

I watched her enter the office and close the door behind her. I waited a few minutes before following. I tried the door; it was still unlocked. The smooth porcelain knob slipped under my grasp as I twisted it and eased the door open a few inches. No one was in the outer office, so I inched the door forward enough to allow me through. I gently closed it behind me and stood with my back against the wall. A vague shape loomed out at me from the middle of the room. As I tiptoed past, I discovered it was Miss Clary's desk. Suddenly a light streamed beneath the closed door of Mr. Upchurch's office. The woman had turned on the electric light. I put my eye to the keyhole. All I could see was her figure leaning over the front of Mr. Upchurch's desk, with her back to me. She began wadding up papers and tossing them into a metal wastebasket. Before I realized what she was doing, she picked up her candle, lit the corner edge of a sheet of paper, and tossed it too into the basket. Flames leaped up as the other paper caught fire.

"Stop! What are you doing?" I yelled as I burst into the room, the door smashing against the wall behind it. I rushed to put out the fire.

Startled by my sudden appearance, she screamed. Burning wax, smoke, and Florida water mingled in the air as she dashed past me. For a moment I scoured the room, yanking open drawers, but found nothing, not a half-empty pot of tea, not a watering can, not even a bottle of sarsaparilla, to douse the flames.

Curse Mr. Upchurch's austere principles, I thought.

And then she lunged for the lights on the wall. She hit the brass light plate and plunged us into darkness. The flickering flames burning in the wastebasket reflected on the tin tiles of the ceiling directly above. The silk of a newly formed spider's web sparkled in the fire's light.

"What are you doing?" I asked again. She grunted in response.

I reached out, groping for some hold on her. With some luck, I snatched the sleeve of her gown. She slapped at my hand, but I held tight. She dragged me across the floor toward the open door. With her free hand, she tried to grab hold of the book-case against the wall. My pull on her sleeve unsteadied her grasp and only a book came away in her hand. She flung it at me but missed. It landed on the floor with a thud. She grappled again with the bookcase. Gaining purchase, she yanked on it, pulling it forward. In an instant, I released my grasp and flung my arms up in defense. A dense, leather-bound book smacked the top of my head as someone screamed. And then I was deafened by the sound of hundreds of books crashing about me. Sharp corners stabbed my arms, hard spines smacked my hands, and flat covers pelted my shoulders as I fought to keep my balance. One book, which read *School Management*, its gold leaf title shining in the dying firelight, jabbed me in the middle before bouncing off my stays. And then the heavy, unyielding form of the bookcase struck me. I fell back and crumpled beneath its weight as it collapsed on top of me. A loud whack reverberated in my head as I hit the books on the floor beneath me.

And then there was silence.

Where am I? Are my eyes open? Everywhere about me was impenetrable dark. I tried to move, but I couldn't. Was I back in the asylum tunnel? Had they found me and chained me to the wall? *Help!* I tried to scream, but neither my voice nor any other sound could penetrate the silence. I tugged at my chains, feeling the weight of the restraints about me until I no longer had the strength to fight.

Please, someone, help me.

And then he was there, wearing a brand-new gray fedora. He smiled and laughed as he jiggled the silver ring of keys before him.

Father! My breath was ragged and shallow, but he beamed when he heard me.

In that instant the keys disappeared and he held a golden trombone. A crystal chandelier dangled just above his head. The light reflecting off the crystals danced about my father's jolly face. He waved to me to follow as he drifted down the asylum tunnel, playing "I'll Take You Home Again, Kathleen." I yearned to follow, to be in my father's presence once more. I struggled to move, but my head, my feet, my legs, even my hands refused to budge. And then the ceiling of the tunnel lifted, taking the chandelier and the crushing weight on my chest with it. Above me was nothing but welcoming, dazzling light.

And then there was a deep moan in my ear. My father floated toward the light, beckoning for me to follow. I longed to bask in its brilliance, to embrace its warmth. But where was that moaning coming from? For a moment, I heard heavy footsteps approaching and then glimpsed a man, his faceless head floating above me beneath the pale crown of a Panama hat. Something salty dripped into my mouth. The light flickered, wavered even as my body rose in the air to meet it.

Wait for me, Father, I yelled, but couldn't be heard over the endless moaning. And then he and the light and everything else were gone.

Chapter 24

Father! I thought as I tried to sit up. I immediately regretted it. A sharp pain shot through my head, and every muscle in my shoulders, arms, neck, and back ached.

And then it all came rushing back to me: the burning papers in Mr. Upchurch's office, the struggle, the bookcase, and the visions. I moaned as I slowly eased myself back onto the upholstered armrest of the sofa. Fighting the melancholy threatening to overpower me, I focused on my surroundings. I was in the instructors' parlor, a small, comfortable room filled with thickly upholstered furniture, a couple of bookshelves packed tight with books, heavy velvet curtains, and a side table on which sat a silver tea service. I'd been here once before, when I was a student and sent by Mrs. Chaplin in search of the often tardy dance instructor. It had been over ten years and the room hadn't changed; only the colors had faded some.

If only everything could be as untouched by time as this, I thought.

"Thank heaven, you're awake," a voice boomed. I flinched in pain.

Knowing better than to use any sudden movements, I cast my eyes about until I found the source of the voice. Mrs. Chaplin, spectacles perched near the tip of her nose, sat in an armchair with an issue of *Lippincott's* magazine open on her lap.

"You've had quite the accident, I hear. A fallen bookcase. If you listen to Gus, you'd think he rescued you from an evil black phantom." She chuckled as she closed her magazine and rose from her chair.

So Gus must've caught a glimpse of Miss Woodruff as she made her escape. Maybe he'll be able to get the instructors to lock their doors now.

"I'm sorry for the poor accommodations, but you weren't willing to have us send for a doctor and we were afraid to move you too far."

"It wasn't an accident," I whispered. Mrs. Chaplin, setting her magazine and spectacles down in the chair, spun around to face me.

"What?" Again her loud voice pounded in my head.

"It wasn't an accident. Miss Woodruff pushed the bookcase on top of me."

"What are you talking about, Hattie? Mollie Woodruff wouldn't squash a spider if it were crawling across her bedclothes."

"I'm sorry, Mrs. Chaplin, but I saw it with my own eyes."

"It can't be."

"I caught her burning papers in Mr. Upchurch's

office and then she deliberately pushed the bookcase in my direction. Maybe you think she's not strong enough but—"

"No, I'm afraid you misunderstand me, Hattie. When I say it can't be Mollie, it can't be. Along with several others from the school, Miss Woodruff was playing whist at my house last night. We had quite the lively evening. She was there until well past two."

How can that be? I saw her. Or did I? I replayed the events in my mind and realized I never did see the woman's face. I'd assumed it was Miss Woodruff, but it could've been anyone. But who? And why?

"Why would anyone dress like Miss Woodruff? Is there someone who doesn't like her?"

"No, not that I can think of. She can be a bit scatterbrained, but otherwise she's a gentle girl. I think you should be asking that question of yourself, Hattie. Why would someone want to hurt you?"

"Not hurt me, prevent me from discovering who they were."

"Who would be so desperate?" It was a rhetorical question, but a few names popped into my head. "By the way, what were you doing in Mr. Upchurch's office in the first place?" she asked.

"I was working late in Miss Gilbert's room when I heard footsteps. I followed them to

President Upchurch's office. I thought I'd discovered who was behind all of the unfortunate 'incidents' that have been occurring."

"Maybe you did. It would explain why they reacted so foolishly, not wanting to be exposed as our troublemaker."

"Yes, and as the figure was wearing black I assumed it was Mollie Woodruff. Obviously I was wrong."

"You don't think . . ." Mrs. Chaplin hesitated, not sure whether to voice her suspicion or not. The idea had occurred to me, but I wasn't willing to voice it either. There was one other person who was dressed in mourning, Virginia Hayward. But anyone could dress in mourning, I thought, banishing the thought of Ginny deliberately trying to hurt me.

"I hope not," I said. "I truly, truly hope not."

"My work!" I forced myself up. I was alone. I had drifted into a light slumber when a dream I had, of someone trying to cut keys from my typewriter while I tried in vain to hit them with a ledger, reminded me that I'd left all my work for Sir Arthur and the school's missing ledger in Miss Gilbert's classroom. I struggled to get my feet on the ground, for although the pain in my head had lessened considerably, the stiffness in my back, shoulders, and neck had grown worse.

If only Mrs. Chaplin was still here, I thought.

She'd offered to stay, but I could tell she had obligations she was neglecting while she sat by my side. I couldn't inconvenience her any longer. Disregarding the soreness in my hands, I pushed myself up and took a few tentative steps toward the door. Getting that far without mishap, I took a few more. I could feel the protest in my muscles, but I'd kept my balance so I kept moving. Soon I was at the door and stepping into the hallway. If I remembered correctly, Miss Gilbert's classroom was on the same floor, albeit at the far end of the hall. I'd hoped to find someone to help me but judging by the silence in the halls, everyone was in class. It took me far longer than I'd expected and my patience was wearing thin when I finally arrived at Miss Gilbert's room. As I reached for the doorknob, the door swung open.

"Who's hovering outside my door?" Miss Gilbert blanched when she saw me. "Miss Davish, what . . . how . . . here, let me help you." I must've looked a fright for Miss Gilbert to come to my assistance. She rushed forward, put her arm around my waist, and helped me to the chair behind her desk. The students, released from their instructor's watchful eye, jumped up from their desks and crowded around me.

"Give her air," Miss Gilbert commanded. "Let the poor woman breathe."

"Thank you, Miss Gilbert. I'm feeling much better."

"You don't look much better," one of the girls said. Several giggled.

"Mind your manners," Miss Gilbert said. "I speak for all of us, Miss Davish, when I say that we're relieved you weren't more injured."

"Thank you, Miss Gilbert. That's kind of you to say." The typing instructor nodded curtly.

"Was there something you wanted, Miss Davish?"

"I'm sorry to disrupt your class, but I left some research papers and things in here last night. Have you seen them?"

"No, there was nothing here when I arrived this morning. Girls?" In unison the students all shook their heads. "I'm sorry, Miss Davish. Someone must have taken them."

Probably the same person who tipped a bookcase on top of me, I thought.

"Why would anyone steal Miss Davish's things?" one of the girls asked.

"I'm not surprised," Miss Gilbert said, "what with everything that's been going on. Such thievery wouldn't happen if I were running this school."

"So what are you going to do now, Miss Davish?" another girl asked.

What I was going to do, but couldn't reveal, was find the missing ledger and discover why it had been stolen twice.

"I don't know about Miss Davish, but I do

260

know what you all are going to do," Miss Gilbert said, shooing the girls back toward their desks. "Get back to your lesson."

"Aaahhh," the girls moaned.

"I thought we could help Miss Davish with her mystery," one said.

"Yes, can we? Can we?" several girls pleaded.

Before Miss Gilbert could squash their enthusiasm with her sharp tongue, I said, "Thank you, but I won't be party to your delinquency any longer. You young ladies must learn your lessons and I must find my papers. I'm certain we'll both be successful." I nodded to Miss Gilbert and limped out of the room.

I stood with my back against the closed door, taking deep breaths, willing my body to stay upright. I couldn't believe how that short conversation had sapped my strength. Or was it learning that the ledger had gone missing again and I was no closer to learning its secrets?

Then get to it, I thought as I pushed away from the wall and headed toward Asa Upchurch's office.

"Miss Davish!" Miss Clary leaped up from behind her desk. "Are you all right?"

"I'm fine."

How many times has Walter teased me about using that phrase? I wondered, stifling a smile Miss Clary would misinterpret.

"I'm looking for the research papers I left in Miss Gilbert's classroom last night. You wouldn't happen to know—"

"Oh, yes, they're all right here." She opened a drawer in her desk and pulled out everything, including the ledger. Without hesitating, she handed the stack to me. "They were on my desk when I arrived. I didn't know whom they belonged to. I was going to give them to Mr. Upchurch when he arrived."

Thank goodness I arrived when I did then, I thought. Mr. Upchurch already suspected Frank Hayward of misconduct. If Mr. Upchurch discovered the ledger, there'd be further accusations.

"Gus probably found them," Miss Clary said.

"Yes, probably." I held the pile tightly to my chest.

"When I came in this morning and found the chaos in Mr. Upchurch's office, the books everywhere and the bookcase collapsed on the floor, well, I couldn't imagine what had happened. And then Gus told us. How horrible! I was just saying to Miss Corcoran that I can't believe that you aren't in the hospital. People have died from bookshelves falling on them."

I barely heard her pronouncement of the danger I'd been in. All I could focus on was a set of letters fanned out across the desk.

"Are you a graduate of the school, Miss Clary?"

She tilted her head to one side and frowned at my abrupt change in subject.

"Yes, as a matter of fact, I am."

"I thought so. Your penmanship is excellent." I pointed to the letters on her desk. "May I?" She blushed at the compliment and without thinking handed me the topmost letter.

"Well, I do pride myself on it. I'm not the fastest typist, you see, but . . ." She continued on about her skills or lack thereof, as I studied her handwriting. "And so you see that's why I think I was hired over Miss Dimond."

"Thank you." I handed her back the letter. I'd never seen her handwriting before. She wasn't the embezzler.

Then who is it? I wondered. But before I had time to consider, Mr. Upchurch arrived.

"My dear Miss Davish! I just learned what happened here last night. Are you all right? Shouldn't you be sitting down?"

"I'm fine." He put his arm around my shoulder. I tried hard not to flinch as he squeezed my sore arm.

"If there's anything I or the school can do for you, please don't hesitate to ask."

"Thank you." I wanted to squirm out of his embrace. He released me and strode toward his door.

"My God!" he exclaimed when he saw the disarray of his office. I walked over and looked over his shoulder. No one had moved the bookcase yet or picked up the books. I shuddered, not from considering that I once lay prostrate beneath the chaos, but from having to restrain myself from charging in and tidying it all up.

How can they leave such a mess just lying there? I thought. I was immediately answered by Miss Clary.

"Don't worry, Mr. Upchurch, they're sending one of the men up from downstairs to straighten everything out."

"Good, but what's this?" He had entered the room, avoiding the bookshelf and carefully stepping between books. He had stopped near his desk. He was staring down into the wastebasket. He picked up a blackened fragment of paper.

"The intruder burned some of your papers." I made my way across the floor, picking up books with my free hand and stacking them in piles until the pain grew to be too much. "That's why I tried to stop them."

"But why?"

"That's what I'd like to know. Do you know which papers were burned?"

The school president took a quick inventory of his desk, flipping through piles on the desk, opening drawers and skimming through files. Unfortunately, I'd no chance to see a sample of his handwriting. "It seems that some of the invoices for the lake party are missing."

"Why would anyone want to burn invoices for the lake party?"

"I have no idea." And then his cheeks began to burn red. "I'm getting fed up with these unexplained 'incidents.' "

"Do you think they are related?"

"How could they not be?"

He had a point. It would be too extraordinary of a coincidence for them to be unrelated events. Although most of the incidents seemed relatively harmless yet provocative, they were now becoming more violent. First the fire in the etiquette classroom, and now this. Was someone trying to get the school's attention or was this personal?

"Has anyone contacted the police yet?" I asked.

"No police," President Upchurch snapped. "It would be bad for the school's reputation if the police became involved."

"But—"

"Don't worry, Miss Davish. We'll deal with this. We don't need the police."

"Does Mrs. Chaplin know how you're handling this? When I was a student, Mrs. Chaplin made it quite clear that she expected her students to work with and within the law."

"Mrs. Chaplin has given the grave responsibility of the school's welfare to me. Thank you for your advice, Miss Davish, but I already have it in hand." I refrained from commenting to the contrary.

He glanced about him, his eyes lingering now and then on a particular book or notebook on the floor. "I'm so relieved you were unhurt by all of this." He noticed the stack of papers and ledger I was holding. "Thank you, Miss Davish, but you can leave all that right here on my desk. I'll see they get put away."

"Actually this is my own work." I clutched the pile tighter. "It's what I was working on last night."

"Oh, my mistake." If Mr. Upchurch recognized the ledger, he didn't give any indication. "Again, if there's anything we can do?"

"Thank you, but I'd like to return to my hotel and rest."

"Of course. Miss Clary," he shouted, "can you see that Miss Davish has an escort back to her hotel?"

"No need. I'm fine."

"But—"

Before he could protest further, I navigated between the remaining books on the floor and headed out the door. I couldn't say why, but I had an overwhelming desire to be away from that office and the school. Or was it the need to be alone with the ledger that spurred me on? Either way, before I left the building I heard faint footsteps and sensed that I was being watched again. Weary and annoyed, I barely made an effort to look about me. But when I did, no one was there.

Chapter 25

"Mr. Putney, could I ask you for a favor?" The desk clerk pushed his spectacles farther back up his nose and blinked rapidly for a moment.

"Of course, Miss Davish, what can I do for you?" I handed him the stack of papers I'd been working on for Sir Arthur and the accounting ledger.

"Could you keep all this for me again? I have to go right out again and would like to know that all my hard work is in safe hands."

When I returned to the hotel, I realized that after the previous night's episode, I couldn't face the idea of being closed in by four walls, even those of my hotel room, for any longer than I had to. I needed to clear my head and loosen up my stiffened, aching muscles; I had to hike.

"Of course." Mr. Putney took the material from me reverently. "I'll keep them safe until your return."

"Thank you so much. I knew I could count on you."

"Yes, you can." He proceeded to bring the ledger and my work to a back room while I made my escape outside.

Used to the solitude of my early-morning hikes as I was, I was surprised by how crowded the trolley was all the way to its northern terminus, Krug Park. I'd never been there before. The park, at least twenty acres adjacent to Henry Krug's mansion, the businessman who had given his name and the land to the park, opened to the public less than five years ago. Mrs. Chaplin had spoken of it over dinner, raving about how Superintendent Rudolph Rau, formerly the gardener to Kaiser Wilhelm, had transformed the park into a showcase. Remembering how much I enjoyed hiking, she'd recommended I take the time to visit. And I was glad I had. Although my gait was slowed by my sore, stiff muscles and I had to forgo climbing the seventy-foot observation tower, I enjoyed the novelty and beauty of the park. I strolled around lovely circular gardens and lingered in the gazebo, but I also passed areas that were under construction. Already picturesque with tree-lined paths, expanses of manicured lawn, and an abundance of bright, colorful flowers in bloom—New England Aster, Chrysanthemum, Sedum, and Helenium, to name but a few—I could only imagine what Superintendent Rau had in store.

I wandered about the edges of the garden, hoping to find a weed or native flower for my collection that hadn't been mowed or pulled up, but I found little and that which I did find, I already had. I'd been spoiled in Newport and Eureka Springs, both offering me a plethora of species I'd never heard of or had only read about in books. But here in St. Joseph, I'd already combed the countryside, the cracks in the sidewalks, and the lawns of the largest houses for every species native to my hometown. I'd hoped to add something new but wasn't surprised that I couldn't. Even the garden plants were not exotic enough to add. I had to content myself with the fresh air, the warm sun, and the minimal exercise. In the end they were enough.

I grew tired and sat on a bench under an oak tree with such a wide girth that it must have been here long before the park. I spent several minutes watching the passersby: a dapper gray-haired man wearing a white Mackinaw straw hat and carrying an umbrella, a nursemaid pushing a baby carriage, two little boys, who should've been in school, skipping stones across the pond. When a man in his thirties and his young son, both wearing Chicago-style white with blue striped baseball caps, stopped not far from me and began tossing a ball back and forth, I instantly thought of my father.

"Come on, Hattie, you can do it. Keep your eye on the ball!" Father shouted as Hymie threw the ball at me again.

We'd been playing for what seemed like hours and I'd yet to catch the ball. When Father and I played alone, he'd toss the ball gently and aim it for my glove, but the others felt no compulsion to go easy on me. In fact, all of the boys, except maybe Nate, felt resentful that my father insisted that I join their impromptu game. My father coached the neighborhood boys' team and took time out to practice with them as much as his work would allow. He loved to sneak out in the middle of a beautiful sunny day to play catch in the street and the boys loved him for it.

This was the first time he'd asked me to join them. It was the first time he'd called a team practice since my mother died. I thought, after our picnic and the boys arrived, I'd simply sit on the blanket and watch as I always did. I was nervous and thrilled at the same time. The boys, however, tolerated my presence for his sake.

SMACK! I felt the burn as the ball hit the palm of my gloved hand. I stared at it with disbelief and sheer joy.

"Yeah, Hattie!" Nate shouted. "You did it!"

"That's my girl!" Father said. "Now toss it to Stanley."

My sense of triumph dissipated the minute I threw the ball. It lobbed in a high arc falling several feet short of Stanley and his awaiting glove.

"Ah, Mr. Davish," Stanley whined. "Can't we play by ourselves? She throws like a girl."

"That's because she is a girl, Stanley." Father

winked at me. "It's our job to teach her not to throw like one. Now toss me the ball."

"Okay, Mr. Davish, whatever you say." Stanley threw the ball to my father.

"Now go long." Father pulled back his arm and threw it far over Stanley's head. As Stanley took off after it, Father came to stand next to me.

"I'm not very good at this, Father. Maybe Stanley's right. Maybe I should let you play with the others by yourself."

He put his arm around me. I could feel the strong, taut muscles of his arm and chest on my shoulders as he squeezed me.

"We're not quitters, you and me. We can do anything we set our minds to." I nodded, having heard this speech several times since my mother's death. "So I'll keep teaching you and you'll keep trying, won't you, my girl?" I looked up into my father's bright eyes and matched the smile on his face with one of my own.

"I will, Father. I promise."

"That's my girl!" He kissed the top of my head before releasing me from his embrace and returned to his place in the circle.

I'd known at that moment that I'd promise my father anything he asked. But I'd no idea how hard that would prove to be.

When I returned to the hotel, I was exhausted; hours in the bright sun, exercising my injured body, and my lack of sleep were finally catching up with me. I wanted nothing more than to collect my things from Mr. Putney, return to my room, and sleep. But yet again, things didn't go as planned. I'd collected my work and the ledger, but when I arrived at my room, the door was slightly ajar.

"Not again!" I shouted as I pushed the door wide open. "This is getting ridiculous."

My room, as on previous occasions, had been entered and searched while I was out. The wardrobe door was open. My suitcase had been taken off the shelf and left opened next to the bed. My hat boxes and lids were scattered on the floor. My pillows and bedclothes had been rumpled. The drawers of the dresser were ajar with the contents disheveled.

After straightening up, I hobbled back down to the lobby as fast as I could. Could Mr. Putney have done this? I'd thought Mr. Putney's curiosity was harmless. Had I been wrong? Had he been snooping about my room?

"Someone has been in my room, Mr. Putney."

The clerk's mouth dropped open as he fumbled with his spectacles, which he'd been wiping with a rag. With his eyeglasses once again perched on his nose, he looked up at me. I didn't know his eyes could open so wide.

"Oh no! How could anyone do such a thing? I didn't give out your key, Miss Davish. I swear I didn't."

"Then how did they get in my room?" I said it harsher than I intended.

"I'm so sorry. I did take a break. Maybe Maude let someone in your room or one of the chambermaids. Don't worry, Miss Davish, I'll find out what happened and I promise you, it will never happen again."

"Thank you, Mr. Putney."

The little man leaned a bit on the desk. "Was anything taken?" In my vexation, I hadn't even thought to consider what the perpetrator was searching for.

The ledger, I thought. By happenstance, in a hurry to get outside, I'd left it safe with Mr. Putney.

"No, thank goodness. But I'd still appreciate knowing who might have entered my room." Whoever that was, I thought, was involved in more criminal acts than searching my room. I thanked Mr. Putney once more, headed to my room, and immediately sat down in front of the open ledger.

"Time to find out what this is all about."

I spent the next couple of hours poring over the figures, the tables, and the inventory lists that filled the ledger. I made calculations and checked them over and over again, only to confirm my previous suspicions. I'd thought the mistakes of overpayment and miscalculations of costs I'd seen earlier were accidents, but they weren't. No wonder someone wanted this ledger to disappear; someone was embezzling money from the school.

But who? Who had access to the school's ledgers and could effectively change the figures without others noticing? Who could profit from it without drawing suspicion? Was it the same person who placed the ledger in the coffin, or did he or she have help? I pulled out a blank sheet of stationery and started a list of possible suspects, beginning with those Ginny had mentioned.

1. Asa Upchurch
2. Malinda Gilbert
3. Mollie Woodruff
4. Emily Upchurch
5. Miss Clary
6. Miss McGill
7. Miss Corcoran

I hesitated, holding my pencil above the paper, not wanting to commit myself to the suspicion, but I couldn't exclude them because I wanted to. I continued my list.

8. Mrs. Chaplin
9. Frank Hayward
10. Virginia Hayward

Find the person with the matching hand-writing, find the embezzler, I thought.

As someone other than Frank Hayward had made the majority of the entries, the entries with the discrepancies, I drew a line through his name. As I'd seen samples of several others' writing that hadn't matched, I could eliminate several others as well. With gratification, I drew a line through Ginny's name. More reluctantly I did the same for Miss Gilbert and Miss Clary.

I looked at the names that were left. I couldn't imagine how Miss Corcoran, as the English and penmanship teacher, could have much access to the ledgers, but Miss McGill was the office management instructor. She'd know basic book-keeping and might've found an excuse to see them now and again. But now and again wasn't enough. Did she have almost exclusive access? It didn't seem likely. And then there was Mrs. Chaplin. Could she be embezzling from her own school? She did seem reluctant to retire. She could've demanded access and no one would've questioned her. And why hadn't Frank Hayward continued as bookkeeper in the first place? Had he stepped aside as a favor to Mrs. Chaplin? Had she feigned the need to stay involved all the while planning to steal money from the school? Why would she need to do such a thing? I'd seen no evidence at her home or in her appearance that suggested she was destitute.

I dropped my pencil, exhausted and disgusted with the very thought of suspecting my former mentor. I stuffed the list into the open ledger and slammed the cover down. I staggered over to my bed and fell into a fitful sleep. When I awoke early the next morning, I wasn't any more refreshed. I glanced at my list again after dressing and felt the same revulsion for my situation. So many unanswered questions! And now I'd discovered that there was an embezzler among my friends. Could there be a murderer among my friends as well? The thought horrified me. I snatched up my hat and pinned it hastily to my head.

"Ouch." I'd stuck myself. *That's what you get, Davish, for being so careless.*

"So stop being careless!" I shouted to myself out loud.

What would Sir Arthur think if I treated his research in such a lackadaisical fashion? My friends' futures were far more important. I couldn't afford to get careless now. I grabbed the list from the ledger and slipped it into my bag. I picked up the ledger, planning to have it safely locked up downstairs. I locked my door behind me and with it my cares. I took a deep breath and headed out to find some answers.

Chapter 26

"Hello, Miss Davish."

I'd gone straight to the school and had met Miss Woodruff by coincidence in the hallway. She was carrying a stack of shorthand dictionaries toward her classroom. She was still wearing black.

"I'm surprised to see you. I'd thought you'd headed back home by now."

Her simple statement stung. This had been my home.

"No, actually," I said, "I have a few loose ends I need to tie up before I can leave."

"Oh." Miss Woodruff pushed her way into her classroom. I immediately recognized it as the same room in which I'd taken shorthand during my time here.

"By the way, have you seen the newspaper headlines?"

"No, why?"

"So you haven't heard that another man was found buried in Frank Hayward's coffin?" She turned to look at me.

"I had heard a rumor but . . . Is it true?"

"Yes, I've confirmed it with the police." She turned her face away again.

"And Mr. Hayward?"

"Still missing, but now there's hope he's

alive." Miss Woodruff stopped. Her whole body shuddered as she gasped for a deep breath. "But then there's the possibility he's involved with the other man's death. The police suspect murder."

"No!" Miss Woodruff swung around with such force, the top book on the stack she was holding flew into the air. It dropped with a thud on a nearby desk. "Frank would never hurt anyone!"

"As I said, it's just a possibility."

"You don't suspect him, do you, Miss Davish? Are those the 'loose ends' you're trying to tie up?" Her face grew paler with each word.

"No, actually I'm here because I've discovered that someone has been embezzling money from the school."

Crash! Miss Woodruff dropped the books and covered her face with her hands. "Oh my God!" She dropped to her knees, unaware she knelt on the spine of an overturned book.

"Miss Woodruff, if you know anything about this, I need you to tell me." The young woman shook her head, muttering incoherently. "Miss Woodruff, did you steal the money?"

And then I pictured her at the funeral, after the wreath and flowers had been knocked down, her face as white as the coffin, as white as it was now. I hadn't questioned it then; we were at a funeral. But what had made her go so pale?

"Did you hide the accounting ledger?" She jerked her head up and stared at me.

"The accounting ledger?"

I grabbed her arm and pulled her to her feet. I guided her to the chair behind her desk. "Miss Woodruff, what do you know?"

"I did it." She hid her face in her hands. "I did it."

"What did you do? Did you steal the money, hide the ledger, or both?"

She hesitated. "Both," she said, her voice muffled by her hands.

"Why did you steal from the school?"

"Because . . ." Again she hesitated. "Because . . . I needed the money." Something in her voice didn't ring true.

"Why steal it? Why not ask Mrs. Chaplin for help?"

She shook her head. "I don't know. I didn't think. I was desperate. I thought if I hid the ledger no one would ever know."

"You could go to jail for this."

She nodded, finally taking her hands away and looking at me. "How did you find out?"

"The police found the ledger when they exhumed the coffin and then gave it to me. Miss Woodruff, it's none of my business what you needed the money for." My mind raced considering the possibilities: a brother's gambling debt to pay off, an ill parent's surgery to pay for, a widowed cousin's children to feed. "But you teach shorthand. How did you get access to the books? How did you collect the money? When did you learn bookkeeping?"

"Frank taught—" She stopped mid-sentence, an expression of horror flashing across her face. "I mean, I just did it. All of it."

"Frank Hayward taught you bookkeeping?"

"No, I mean, yes. I mean, no. Frank had absolutely nothing to do with this. I did it. Only me."

"Mr. Hayward was an excellent instructor. He taught me as well."

"He did?" Miss Woodruff's fingers traced the scar on her chin. I nodded as I bent over to pick up the shorthand dictionaries that still lay scattered on the floor. A note stuck partially out of one. I pulled it out and read:

Meet Katrina Olmstead, 3:00 p.m. Bring her graded work.

"Is this your handwriting?" I held up the note. She nodded as she knelt down to help me.

"Poor Katrina, I completely forgot. I was supposed to meet her yesterday."

"But it's in longhand?"

"Yes, oddly enough, I enjoy writing in longhand after spending my day teaching shorthand." The handwriting was vastly different from that in the ledger.

"You didn't embezzle the money, did you?"

She shook her head. "But you, like Mr. Upchurch, think maybe Mr. Hayward did?" She nodded. "But why try to protect him?" She gazed up at me and I had my answer. How had I not seen it before?

"You're in love with Frank Hayward, aren't you?"

She nodded, dropping her head in shame. "Nothing ever happened. He was always a gentleman. It's just that . . . he had a scar. We had something in common, you see." She hesitated, unsure whether to continue. "You must understand, Miss Davish. I've been taunted and teased all my life. But Frank . . . he said it was beautiful, a mark of distinction. So while he taught me bookkeeping, Frank also helped me learn to live with . . . this." She traced the raised, red jagged line across her chin. "And I'll love him forever for it."

"So you were trying to protect him." It wasn't a question. I knew.

She nodded as she held a handkerchief up to her chin. "What else was I to do? I went to his office before the funeral, to be where he used to be, and I found that ledger in the middle of his desk. I didn't mean to pry, but it was open. I saw right away that something was wrong. But I knew he couldn't have done such a thing."

"Because of the handwriting?" She frowned.

"Handwriting? No, because Frank's an excellent bookkeeper. He wouldn't have made so many mistakes. Didn't you notice all the pencil marks? He wouldn't do such a thing."

"Then what did you do?"

"What could I have done? I couldn't have his memory tainted in any way. He deserved better than that. So I had to get rid of it."

"So you put the ledger in Mr. Hayward's coffin?" She nodded.

"It wasn't easy. I tipped over the wreath hoping to distract everyone." She shrugged. "It worked, didn't it?"

"Yes, until the casket was exhumed. But why put it in the casket in the first place? Why not burn it or bury it?"

"I did bury it. It was a secret that needed to go with him to the grave."

"But literally?"

Miss Woodruff shrugged. "I was distressed. I'm still distressed. It was all I could think to do."

"So why did you go to his office after hours that night?"

"People were still insinuating that Frank had done something wrong. Some were even willing to believe he was behind all the bad things that have been happening at the school lately. I had to go back and make sure there weren't any more ledgers or notes or anything."

"So that's what you meant by 'more evidence'?" She nodded. "But you didn't come back the next night and rummage through President Upchurch's office?" I trusted what Mrs. Chaplin had told me about the whist party but couldn't suppress my suspicions.

"Why would I do that?" I had the answer I wanted.

"Why do you think the ledger was in his office, if he wasn't involved?" I asked.

"Someone wants everyone to think he did it, but I know he didn't. I know it!"

But who? I wondered. Instead, I asked, "Do you know why he stopped doing the bookkeeping?"

"I didn't realize he had." She suddenly dropped her head to avoid my gaze.

"Have you had any contact with Frank since the funeral?" She didn't answer, turning her face away. "I want to help, but you have to be honest with me. This isn't embezzlement or vandalism Mr. Hayward's accused of; it may be murder."

"Like I said, Frank wouldn't hurt anyone." That's what Ginny had insisted too, but love often blinded people to the shortcomings of others.

"But have you heard from him?"

She shook her head. "No, Miss Davish, I haven't heard from him. God knows I wish I had, but no. Oh, Frank, where are you?"

That's what I want to know, I thought, as Miss Woodruff buried her head in her arms on her desk.

Chapter 27

After mentally crossing Mollie Woodruff off my list, I sought out my next suspect. Knowing Miss Gilbert had little regard for me and would have no tolerance for my questions, I was almost relieved when I found her door closed. I peered through the window. The classroom was empty; the typing instructor must be on her break. I tried the door. As I suspected, it wasn't locked. I glanced about me, to make certain I wasn't seen, and slipped in. I headed straight for the desk and glanced over the books, papers, and folders lying in neat piles. Everything was typed.

Ever since I'd searched my employer's hotel room in Eureka Springs for any sign of the missing temperance leader, I've found it easier and easier to examine the belongings, both professional and private, of other people. Identifying a murderer justified the invasion of any person's privacy. But what about investigating an embezzler? Did that too legitimize my unauthorized scrutiny?

It's for Ginny's sake, I thought, as I opened a desk drawer.

The top drawers revealed nothing. In a bottom drawer I found a notebook filled with typing drills. I flipped through the notebook, musing on the nonsensical nature of drills when I found a sentence scribbled on the bottom of a page: *Pray the red fox feels free as a duck.* The handwriting was very distinct and not at all like that in the ledger. If this was Miss Gilbert's handwriting, as I assumed it was, she wasn't the embezzler either.

Then whose handwriting is it?

I closed the notebook and a slip of paper fell out. It was a list of all of the "incidents" that had occurred at the school. After each was typed an explanation of how they discredited President Upchurch: *shows lack of leadership, questions management style, demonstrates untrustworthy behavior, indicates lack of loyalty.* It even included the most recent act: the burned invoices. I wasn't surprised that Miss Gilbert would document such things. She, like me, had a mind for organization, and it was well-known how much she disliked and envied Mr. Upchurch. But something struck me as odd about the list. Not all of the items had occurred.

Yet, I thought.

"What are you doing?" Miss Gilbert stormed into her classroom. Her face was red as she stomped across the room and slammed the drawer shut. "How dare you! You have no business being in here, let alone going through my desk." She opened another drawer, grabbed the piles of papers and books on top of her desk, and dropped them in, slamming that drawer harder than the first. Now her whole body was shaking. She lifted her arm up and pointed to the door. "Leave my classroom at once."

"Why, Miss Gilbert? Why did you do it?"

"Get out!"

When I didn't move, she shoved me backward. I stumbled, my back hitting against the black-board. I groaned. The muscles in my upper body hadn't recovered yet. She flinched as if she'd incurred the pain.

"Out! Now or I'll call security!" She stepped aside to let me by, but I didn't move.

"I don't think that would be wise, Miss Gilbert," I gasped, trying to catch my breath, "considering what your desk drawer contains."

"I . . . I . . ." she stammered, her fists clenched. She dropped into her chair and glared at me. "What do you want from me?"

"The truth. Why did you do it? The Malinda Gilbert I knew loved this school and loved Mrs. Chaplin. Why sabotage it? What happened?"

"Asa Upchurch is what happened," she sneered, before chewing on the nail of her left thumb. "I should've been head of this school. I worked here for years and everything I did, I did for this school. But did Mrs. Chaplin recognize my experience? Did she reward my loyalty? No. Instead, Mrs. Chaplin hired Asa Upchurch, who never worked here, or at any school for that matter, a day in his life. What did he know about running a professional school for women? Everyone thinks he's the snake charmer, but trust me, he's the snake."

"So you did it out of spite?"

"No!" She spat the word out like a bad taste in her mouth. "You of all people should know better. Like everything I've done, I did it out of love for this school."

"By setting a classroom on fire? By defacing all the new shorthand dictionaries? I don't see how that helps the school, Miss Gilbert."

"Small distresses for the greater good."

"Which is?"

"To rid us all of Asa Upchurch!"

"You did all this hoping the blame would fall on him?"

"Of course. I'd tried telling Mrs. Chaplin how bad of a manager he was, how poorly he ran the school, but she wouldn't listen. I sent her the missing shorthand pages, trying to get her to notice what was going on. She still didn't do anything about it. She's listening now, isn't she?"

Miss Gilbert had a point. It had been the incidents at the school that had motivated Mrs. Chaplin to entice me to St. Joseph in the first place. It had been her concern over what was going on that had prompted us to look for the stolen ledger. Yet Miss Gilbert, in her desperation to discredit Asa Upchurch, had left herself open to suspicion. And then I realized what all this meant for me.

"You were the one in President Upchurch's office that night. You were the one that toppled that bookcase on me!" She flinched as if I'd struck her.

"Yes, I overheard you talking to Mollie Woodruff about her nighttime foray into Mr. Hayward's office. It gave me the idea to dress in mourning." So Miss Gilbert was whom the elderly couple at the Pacific House had seen. "But I never meant anyone to get hurt. I swear on the future of this school. No one was supposed to be here. Even the fire I set was done when no one else was in the building."

"But I got hurt. You left me under a pile of books and a bookcase."

"No, that's not true. After I left the office, I yelled for Gus. He never saw me, but I waited to make sure he found you. I truly didn't mean for you to get hurt."

I remembered how sincerely sorry Miss Gilbert had been, how uncharacteristically sympathetic toward me, the next morning when I came to her classroom looking for the ledger.

"Then why did you do it?"

"I couldn't let you discover it was me, could I? Then all my plans would be for nothing."

"But your campaign against President Upchurch hasn't worked. I haven't spoken to anyone who thinks these 'incidents' reflect poorly on President Upchurch."

"But how could they not? They happened while he was president. He's responsible."

No, you are, I thought but chose to keep my judgment to myself. Instead, I said, "You did all of this so that you could be president?" Malinda Gilbert started biting her nails again.

"I admit that was my motivation in the beginning, but the more I saw the school decline the more I was convinced that anyone else as president would be better than Asa Upchurch."

"But you did want to be president?"

"Of course, I did. I still do."

"So you could more easily continue embezzling money from the school?" Her face screwed up like she'd bitten into a lemon.

"What are you talking about?" I told her what I knew. "How long has this been going on?" she asked.

"Since Mrs. Chaplin's retirement."

"And you think I did it?" Miss Gilbert's voice was once again filled with disdain.

"As the most senior instructor, you could have access."

"Everyone fawns over you, Miss Davish. 'Helped solve two murders,' they say. Everyone sings your praises. Mrs. Chaplin boasts you're the most successful graduate we've ever had." By her mocking tone I knew she didn't agree with one word of it, yet I couldn't help blush at the compliments.

"What does that have to do with the ledger, Miss Gilbert?"

"Exactly. You do a good job of hiding it, but you're not very bright after all, are you?"

I bristled at her casual insult and was on the brink of losing my patience. Barely civil to me since the day we met, she'd shouted at me, shoved me, mocked me, and even pushed a bookcase on top of me. And she was the one who had been tampering with the school's property and reputation.

I wanted to shout, *What did I ever do to you?* But I knew it to be childish and completely unproductive. Instead, I took a deep breath and counted backward in French to calm myself down.

"*Dix, neuf, huit, sept, six* . . ."

"At least you learned something from this school."

I didn't reply but continued to count. "*Cinq, quatre, trois, deux, un.* If you didn't embezzle the money," I said, slowly, still trying to keep my anger at bay, "then who did?"

She shook her head. "You're an idiot." Before I could lash out like I wanted to, she added, "Asa Upchurch, of course."

"Of course." I didn't attempt to hide the sarcasm in my voice. "I should've known you'd say that." Now it was her turn to bristle at my tone.

"It's true," she seethed. "The school has been in decline since he arrived, which coincides exactly with the time the money was stolen."

"There are other instructors who also arrived around the same time; Miss Woodruff, for one."

"Upchurch is the one with the easiest access."

"With the exception of Frank Hayward."

"Yes, but with all his extra teaching duties, Frank had to hand over the bookkeeping."

What? I thought. This was news to me. No one, not even Ginny, had mentioned an increase in Frank's teaching duties. That's why his handwriting wasn't found past a certain point in the ledger.

"Why was Frank teaching more?"

Miss Gilbert, taken aback by my change in subject, pursed her lips. "Because our good president added bookkeeping as a new focus of the curriculum," she said, snidely.

"And you think Mr. Upchurch added to the curriculum simply to get Frank Hayward away from the books?" I couldn't keep my skepticism out of my voice.

"You should ask Mr. Upchurch. He'll deny it, of course; but if anyone is stealing from the school, it's him."

"And that would be convenient for you, wouldn't it? You would rid yourself of Mr. Upchurch, one way or another."

"What are you implying? That I'm implicating him for embezzlement to get his job?"

"You've already admitted to sabotaging the school to get rid of him. Do you think Mrs. Chaplin is going to think this is any different?"

And with that I turned on my heel, leaving the room and Miss Gilbert, speechless, glaring at my back.

Chapter 28

"Mrs. Upchurch?"

President Upchurch's wife was sitting at her husband's desk, bent over the open ledger before her, chewing on the end of a pencil. She'd removed her gloves and had no less than four gold rings on her fingers—two with diamonds, one with a large emerald, and one etched wedding band. She looked up startled at the sound of her name.

"Hello, Miss Davish. What brings you here?"

I wanted to tell her that I'd come to question her husband about embezzling money from the school, but here she was at ease at his desk going over the accounts. I'd never once suspected Mrs. Upchurch of the crime, until now.

I didn't know what to say except, "What are you doing?"

"Oh, this?" She indicated the ledger with a tap

of her pencil. "Asa has been so distracted since Frank Hayward's death that I've been helping him do his bookkeeping. I briefly worked for Price, Waterhouse & Co., you know." She smiled. "That's where I met Asa."

"Really? I didn't know that."

She was more than capable of forging the figures I'd seen in the ledger found in Frank Hayward's coffin. So too then was her husband. But if she was the embezzler, wouldn't she try to deny her involvement?

"How long have you been helping your husband, Mrs. Upchurch?" I walked toward her, leaned on the desk, and glanced down at the ledger. She frowned and flipped the ledger closed. She was too fast. I couldn't tell if her handwriting matched or not.

"Only since . . ."

"Who are you talking to, Emily?" I straightened up and stepped away from the desk as Mr. Upchurch entered his office. "Ah, Miss Davish. How's our celebrity secretary today?"

"I'm fine, thank you," I said, still uncomfortable with the label of "celebrity."

"Recovered from the incident the other night, I hope?"

"Yes." I wasn't about to tell him how my neck and shoulders still ached or that I'd contemplated resorting to taking a patent medicine from the druggist to manage my headaches.

"Is there something I can help you with?" He walked behind his wife and placed his hands on her shoulders.

"Actually, I was asking your wife how long she's been doing the school's bookkeeping." I glanced back and forth between the couple for signs of guilt. With a quick glance up into her husband's face, Mrs. Upchurch's countenance was cloudy with questions. Mr. Upchurch's gaze was placid and clear.

"Since the funeral," Mr. Upchurch said. "As you know, Frank Hayward was our bookkeeper." He smiled as he gazed into her upturned face. "I don't know what I'd do without her. You organized the lake party as well, didn't you, dear?"

"Yes," Mrs. Upchurch said, looking back at me. "It's a joy to be useful again."

"I wish we could offer you coffee and chat, but we're terribly busy. So, if that's all, Miss Davish—" His wife interrupted him.

"Asa, I'm surprised at you. Of course we can offer Miss Davish a cup of coffee." She stood up, forcing her husband to step to the side. She walked over to the door and poked her head out. "Would you mind bringing in a pot of coffee, Miss Clary?" The secretary's assent was muted through the door.

Mrs. Upchurch closed the door and went to her husband's side. She took his arm. "In fact, I was about to tell Miss Davish how wonderful you are."

"Really, Emily? I don't think that's necessary."

"Of course, it is. You're always the first one to praise others. Now it's your turn." Mr. Upchurch's cheeks reddened.

"Such as?"

"Such as the bookkeeping," she said.

"Emily, that's enough now. Miss Davish doesn't want to hear about the boring work that goes into running the school. She has much more excitement to fill her days."

"No, you're quite wrong, Mr. Upchurch. I admire anyone who can run such an institution as Mrs. Chaplin's school. I'd enjoy learning how you do it."

"Well, did you know, Miss Davish, that this husband of mine has not only been doing his own demanding job, but as a friend to a colleague had taken over the task of bookkeeping from Mr. Hayward? But with Mr. Hayward's death and all the strange incidences occurring in the school, it became too much. He needed to focus on those things. I'm glad he's allowed me to help." She squeezed his arm and gazed lovingly toward her husband. If his wife knew that she'd just implicated her husband in a crime, she wouldn't be smiling at him right now.

"You're mistaken, Emily," Mr. Upchurch said, "I never did the bookkeeping."

"But I thought you did after Frank Hayward started teaching full-time?"

"No, no, I offered to help, but Mr. Hayward insisted he could do both."

"But you were aware that a ledger had gone missing?" I said.

"No, I wasn't," Mr. Upchurch said. "Though I'm not surprised, what with everything else that's been going on around here. How did you come to know this before I did?"

"Because the police gave it to me."

"The police? But I thought," Mr. Upchurch said, furrowing his brow. "Where did the police find it?"

"They discovered it when they exhumed Frank Hayward's casket," I said.

"Oh, how grisly," Mrs. Upchurch said. "Why would anyone want to put a ledger in a casket?"

"To bury the evidence," I said.

"Evidence of what?" Mrs. Upchurch asked.

"Evidence that Frank Hayward had been stealing from this school, my dear," Upchurch said to his wife. "I didn't want to believe the rumors but—"

"Frank Hayward didn't steal anything," I said. "There were two different handwritings in the ledger found in Frank Hayward's coffin."

"Really? How remarkable," President Upchurch said.

"May I see the ledger you were just working on, Mrs. Upchurch?"

"I'm surprised at you, Miss Davish. Surely

you're not accusing my wife of embezzling from this school?" I didn't reply.

"Please, Mrs. Upchurch," I said, pointing to the ledger on the desk.

She nervously glanced at her husband, who nodded before she picked up the ledger and handed it to me. I flipped it open and scanned the entire book before looking back up. Mrs. Upchurch was biting her lip, deepening her dimples. There was only her hand throughout the book. And it didn't match.

"Thank you, Mrs. Upchurch. I just had to be sure."

"I could've told you my wife had nothing to do with it," he said. "Now, if that's all, Miss Davish, I think we've discussed this unpleasantness enough for one day. But be sure to let us know if you do discover the culprit." I nodded.

As I rose, a piece of paper dropped to the floor. As I bent to pick it up, Mr. Upchurch scrabbled around the desk and tried to intercept me.

"I've got that," he said. I reached it first. It had several notes about an upcoming staff meeting scribbled hastily on it. I handed it out to him. "Can't lose this," he said, snatching the paper from my hand. But not before I caught a glimpse of the handwriting.

"Your handwriting, I presume, Mr. Upchurch?"

"Of course, it is," his wife said. "Asa? What's

going on?" The handwriting matched that in the accounting ledger.

"Did you put the ledger on Frank Hayward's desk, hoping to incriminate him, President Upchurch?" I said.

"I don't know what you're talking about. As I said, I didn't even know a ledger was missing."

"Did you kill Levi Yardley?"

"Who? What? No, I don't even know who that is."

"He's the man that you mistook for Frank Hayward. I showed you a picture of him. He wasn't trampled by a horse. The police suspect Mr. Yardley was murdered."

"Murdered? What? I didn't kill anyone. What makes you say that?"

"You were the one who found the body, Mr. Upchurch."

"Asa would never hurt anyone." Mr. Upchurch took his wife's hands in his.

"I swear to you, Emily, I didn't kill anyone. I truly thought the dead man was Frank Hayward. If I was wrong, it was a horrible but honest mistake."

"But you did embezzle from the school," I said. It wasn't a question.

"No, of course not."

"With Frank Hayward dead, no one would be the wiser, would they, Mr. Upchurch?"

"I don't know what you're talking about."

This time his wife didn't defend him. "Asa, you didn't?"

Without waiting for another hollow denial I walked over and opened the door. I nearly jumped to see Miss Clary standing immediately in the doorway holding a silver tray with a coffeepot and three cups. "Miss Clary?"

"Yes?" Her face was pale, except two red spots on her cheeks.

How much had she heard? I wondered.

"Would you please call the police? Ask for Officer Quick if he's available." She nodded as all color drained from her cheeks. "And then notify Mrs. Chaplin that she's needed at the school, immediately." She nodded, set the tray down on the top of a bookshelf inside the door, and returned to her desk. I waited to see her pick up the telephone.

"Miss Davish, what's all this about?" Mr. Upchurch said when I closed the door and locked it.

"Now we wait for the police."

"But I haven't done anything wrong!"

"Oh, Asa!" Mrs. Upchurch cried as she threw herself into his arms. "How could you do it? Stealing from Mrs. Chaplin, after everything she's done for us?" As he comforted his wife, he glared at me.

I avoided his gaze by looking out the window. A butcher in a long white apron, stained with the blood of his trade, leaned in the shadow of his shop doorway across the street. He ran his hand through his hair.

At least Miss Gilbert got what she wanted, I thought, feeling less than satisfied. I still didn't know who killed Levi Yardley or what had become of Frank Hayward. And now there was only one place left I knew to find those answers.

I hope you don't live up to your name, Quick, I thought, none too eager to go back to the asylum.

Chapter 29

"I'm sorry, Miss Davish, but Dr. Hillman is busy with his patients and is unavailable to speak with you right now."

After the police arrived and arrested Asa Upchurch for embezzlement, I'd waited for Mrs. Chaplin. I hadn't waited long. I'd explained everything to her, about Miss Woodruff, Asa Upchurch, and Miss Gilbert. She was astonished at the turn of events but most grateful that I'd uncovered the culprits. After promising to have tea with her before I left town, and before my courage failed me, I'd hailed a cab and headed back to the asylum.

I took a deep breath, uncertain what to say next. I had to see Dr. Hillman.

"You could make an appointment," the nurse suggested.

"Very well," I said. "If that's what it will take." She consulted a small notebook she'd pulled from a drawer.

"Would tomorrow at two o'clock p.m. be satisfactory?"

Tomorrow? I thought. Could I wait that long? Did I have a choice?

"Yes, that would be fine." She jotted my name next to the time in the book and looked up again.

"Is there anything else I can do for you, Miss Davish?"

"Yes, there is." I suddenly had an idea. "Mrs. Yardley, as you can appreciate, was unable to join me today as she's overseeing the reburial of her husband. But she requested that I visit the room where her husband stayed. His last days were spent here and she wants to be reassured he was well-attended and comfortable."

"Oh, I can assure you, Mr. Yardley was treated with all the care and concern we give to all of our patients."

"But you will let me see for myself? I can then report back to Mrs. Yardley and ease her mind."

"It's highly irregular, but it's the least I can do for poor Mrs. Yardley. Please follow me." Not wanting to repeat my misadventure of my last visit, I stayed immediately behind the nurse the entire trip through the hall, up two flights of stairs, down another hall that ended at a set of double doors. I peered into several rooms as we passed. With two to four beds per room, the rooms were impeccably clean and tidy and surprisingly often contained small personal mementos. Most patients I saw lay peacefully in bed sleeping or rocking in a chair, reading a book. After my previous experiences, with my father and then with those unfortunate souls in the tunnel, it was heartening to know that many patients were well-treated.

However, as we neared Mr. Yardley's room, I increasingly found patients restrained, some wearing what the nurse called "camisoles," a heavy cotton shirtwaist with corset-like lacing that restrained the person's arms around their torso, some wearing "mitts" that restrained their hands, while several others were confined to human-sized crates on the floor. The nurse, noticing my repulsion, explained that patients in this area were more violent or easily agitated.

"We restrain them for their own good," she explained. "Otherwise they would harm themselves."

I glanced into an open door. The room contained two large bathtubs; a patient's head was barely visible above the canvas that covered one of the tubs. When I asked, the nurse explained the patient was receiving ice-bath treatments. I remembered my experience with a bath treatment, in Eureka Springs, Arkansas; Walter had prescribed it for my sleeplessness. There the waters were healing, soothing, and warm. I shuddered to think what an ice bath would do to my state of mind, let alone my body. I gratefully passed by as the nurse led me to a set of double doors at the end of the hall. She pushed the door and allowed me to enter first. The hall continued past four sets of patients' rooms on either side with an open examination room at the end. I expected to feel dizzy or nauseous at the sight of the surgical instruments laid out on the table nearest the examination table, but it never came.

It's truly gone, I thought.

I could hear my father's voice saying, "We're not quitters, you and me." Had learning the truth behind my father's death freed me of the panic and dizzy spells? I didn't know. But I took a deep breath in appreciation all the same. I followed the nurse to the third door on the left. It was sparse and simple with bare white walls, three whitewashed wrought-iron beds, three gray enamel chamber pots, a high-backed chair, and a bare linoleum floor. All three beds were empty.

"That was Mr. Yardley's bed," the nurse said, pointing to the bed on the far right, against the wall. How could she have thought this would bring Mrs. Yardley comfort? I could find little to recommend how he was treated except for his basic necessities.

"I noticed as we walked here that all of the asylum's rooms were full of patients and yet this room has three empty beds? Why is that?"

"This area houses the patients that are assigned to the progressive treatment program."

Wasn't that the same phrase that I'd seen in the notes about my father? Didn't that mean my father had been assigned to the same program as Levi Yardley? How long has this program been running? What did "progressive treatment" mean?

The nurse was still talking. "The two patients that shared this room with Mr. Yardley have died recently and we haven't yet assigned new patients to the program. I'm certain if you came here again tomorrow, the room would be full again."

I pictured the bodies I'd seen on two separate occasions being taken out on a stretcher. Could they have been Mr. Yardley's roommates? Or do patients die every day here and it's merely a coincidence? I was never one to believe in such coincidences.

"How did the other patients die?" The nurse shook her head.

"I'm not at liberty to discuss that with you, Miss Davish. I do hope you understand."

"Yes, of course. Could you tell me about the program you mentioned?"

"Oh, yes. It's a new, experimental program that we hope will treat many types of diseases of the mind. Some patients are given a mixture of drugs and shock treatments, while others receive shock treatments and placebos. Mr. Yardley was a new member of the program. He was one of the lucky patients given the actual healing drugs."

"Which drugs?"

"I'm not at liberty to say."

"And these other patients?" I pointed to the empty beds.

"Yes, all the patients receiving the drugs were housed together, as are the patients receiving the placebos." I glanced across the hallway. The door to the room directly across was open and all three men lay peacefully sleeping in their beds. The lucky ones get the drugs? I wondered.

"And who's in charge of this program?"

"Dr. Hillman. I thought you knew that? Isn't that why you wished to speak to him?"

It is now, I thought. To the nurse, I said, "Do you have a telephone that I may use?" I knew someone else who'd also want to speak with him.

"Officer Quick," I said into the receiver, "Miss Davish calling."

"Yes, Miss Davish, how can I help you?"

I still was unnerved by listening to a disembodied voice talk to me through the wire attached to the wood I held next to my ear. Without seeing his face, I had no idea if he was giving me his full attention or whether he was simply humoring me.

"Have you received the results of Mr. Yardley's autopsy?" There was a pause from the other side of the telephone. Whether it was a mechanical hesitation or a human one I couldn't tell.

"Yes, we have. Why would you want to know that, Miss Davish?"

"Did you find any unusual medicines or chemicals in Mr. Yardley's body?" I asked, ignoring his question. This time there was no hesitation.

It wasn't a mechanical error then, I thought.

"Yes, we did. But how did you know that?" His voice had lowered in pitch and came out in clipped phrases. I didn't need to see his face to know what he was thinking.

"I'm at the Lunatic Asylum, Officer Quick," I said, again ignoring his question. "You need to drive out here immediately."

"Why, Miss Davish? What's going on?"

"I believe I've discovered who killed Levi Yardley."

A buzzing noise filled the receiver. I jerked it away from my ear, but not before I heard a distant voice exclaim, "Don't move. I'll be right there!"

Not wanting to spend any more time than necessary in the asylum, I waited for the policeman outside. At first I stood by the steps watching the patients lounge in the sun or dig in the flowerbeds. And then a patient, a young

306

woman with plump cheeks and unkempt curly blond hair, invited me to sit with her on the porch. I'd no intention of rocking as I'd seen many of the patients do, but her hopeful countenance tempered my revulsion and I joined her. After exchanging names, we sat in companionable silence. She rocked in her chair, her eyes closed and her lips curled in a small smile of contentment while I pulled out my notebook and compiled a list of reasons to back up my suspicions of Levi Yardley's killer. When that was done, I tried following my companion's lead: leaning back, closing my eyes, and marking time with the cadenced creak of the wood. But it was no use.

How can they do this? I thought, jerking up and sitting on the edge of the chair.

I took a deep breath of the fresh air, a benefit of being this far from the city, but that didn't help either. Finally I heard the horses and crunch of carriage wheels approaching. I leaped to my feet when I saw Officer Quick at the reins. With a glance at my companion, who had fallen asleep, I stepped swiftly off the porch to meet the approaching wagon.

"So you know who killed Levi Yardley?" Officer Quick asked, alighting from his patrol wagon and looking up at the imposing asylum building.

"Yes, I think so."

"Then who is it?"

"Dr. Hillman."

"And why do you say that?" I glanced down at my list.

1. Was witnessed arguing with victim not long before his death, very near to where the victim was found
2. Lied about Levi Yardley's discharge status
3. Hid or destroyed files on Levi Yardley
4. Included Levi Yardley in an experimental program that included a mixture of drugs and shock treatments
5. At least two other patients in the experiment have died
6. Possibly applied similar treatment to my father, resulting in his death

I ripped the sheet of paper from my notebook and handed it to the policeman. He read through it quickly.

"Most of this is circumstantial, Miss Davish; but if you're right about the drugs we found in the victim's body being connected to the experiment, we might be on to something. He may not have killed the man, but he certainly has some answering to do. Let's go talk to Dr. Hillman, shall we?"

I was thrilled that he didn't even hesitate to include me in his investigation. I'd been worried that once he arrived he'd insist I leave it all to him. But instead, he offered me his arm.

"Would it also be possible to search the asylum for Frank Hayward?" I asked.

"That's a good point. Yes, I'll make sure we make every effort to rule out the possibility he's here," Officer Quick said as he escorted me back through the front door.

"As I told Miss Davish, Dr. Hillman is with a patient," the nurse explained to Officer Quick when he inquired after the doctor. The policeman dropped his arm and I pulled my hand away. He took a step closer to the nurse.

"Unlike Miss Davish, I'm not asking to see Dr. Hillman." He had an edge to his voice I hadn't heard before. "I insist. Now take me to Dr. Hillman or I'll find him myself." The nurse glanced at me with wide eyes and grew pale. I sympathized with her. Like me on many occasions, she was performing the duties of her job, nothing more and nothing less. She didn't deserve to be placed in this position. *This is your fault, Dr. Hillman,* I thought.

"Nurse?" Officer Quick said when she hesitated.

"You won't get into trouble," I said, guessing her concern. "You're complying with the police's request. That's all."

"I won't lose my job?" The nurse looked first at me and then at the policeman.

"I'll see to it personally that nothing you do to assist me will affect your position here." She still seemed hesitant but finally nodded.

"Then follow me."

She led us to Dr. Hillman's office, but again it was unoccupied. She found a cabinet and retrieved a key. Then she led us down a series of stairs and through a tunnel door and I suddenly recognized where we were going. This was where I'd followed Dr. Hillman the day I got lost in the tunnels. I grew anxious, remembering the feeling of being trapped, as if I too were chained to the tunnel wall. I almost grabbed Officer Quick's arm in an attempt not to get separated but stopped myself in time. Instead I focused on keeping the nurse no more than three paces ahead of me as we turned this way and that through the tunnels.

I can see how I got lost, I thought.

Eventually after several turns, we stopped at a plain gray door. The nurse unlocked the door and knocked. The policeman didn't wait for an answer. He pushed past the nurse and opened the door. I hesitated, not sure if I wanted to see what was behind the door. I imagined all kinds of horrors—sharp, shiny metal instruments, metal bowls filled with dark blood, patients strapped to tables as the doctor drilled holes in their heads— but the small room was almost empty. All that was inside the well-lit, whitewashed windowless room was a wooden armchair and a small side table covered with a few glass bottles partially full of liquid. A man sat in the chair, one arm bare up to his shoulder, as Dr. Hillman leaned over him. The doctor looked up with a start. He held a large syringe in his left hand. For all my bravado since I'd learned my father's fate, it took everything I had not to collapse in a heap on the floor. Luckily I was still near the door and grabbed the doorjamb for support as the room spun out of control in front of me.

"What's the meaning of this?" Dr. Hillman demanded. "Nurse, get these people out of here. Can't you see I'm in the middle of a very sensitive procedure?"

"Please stop what you're doing, Dr. Hillman," Officer Quick said.

"Nurse, what's going on?" the doctor asked.

"That's what I want to know," Officer Quick said, before the nurse had a chance to respond.

"And who are you?"

"Police Officer Daniel Quick, and I have some questions I need you to answer."

"Not now, man. Not now."

"Yes, now." The policeman walked over to the doctor and yanked the syringe from his grasp. "Please lead the way back to your office, Doctor."

"Damn it!" Dr. Hillman said under his breath.

"Now, Doctor!"

"Nurse, return this patient to his room and monitor him for the next two hours. Notify me immediately if there's any change in his behavior," Dr. Hillman said as the policeman took hold of him and led him past me and out the door. I glanced back once as the nurse began to unstrap the man in the chair before I pushed myself away from the doorjamb and rushed to catch up to the retreating figures of the policeman and doctor. I wasn't going to be left down there again.

Chapter 30

"What were you administering as part of your experimental treatment, Dr. Hillman?" Officer Quick asked.

"We combine a series of electric therapy treatments with drug therapy, a mixture of compounds I developed myself. Some patients receive a placebo instead of the drugs, but they all receive some level of electric therapy. When I first read the work of Duchenne de Boulogne, I knew he was on to something. What I'm doing is very progressive. Very few asylums give these types of patients such advanced care." The policeman nodded curtly, obviously unimpressed.

"And was Levi Yardley given the experimental drugs or the placebo?"

"The experimental drugs, but—"

"And now the man is dead."

"I don't like what you're implying, Officer. You think there's a connection between Mr. Yardley's death and my therapeutic treatment?"

"Not a connection, Doctor, a cause."

"What? You can't possibly believe it was the treatment that killed him? He was responding quite well, as are many of my patients."

"Until he escaped," I said, unable to remain silent any longer. "Why would he escape if you were truly alleviating his suffering?" The doctor ignored me.

"I believe this treatment is going to revolutionize how we treat patients with nervous disorders," he said.

"Why did you lie about discharging him, if his treatment was going well?"

"I'll ask the questions, if you don't mind, Miss Davish," the policeman said. "I'm not here about a possible breach in asylum rules or misconduct on the part of the doctor. I'm here to determine if the doctor played a role in Levi Yardley's death."

"Of course," I said. "But if I may make a suggestion?"

"What is it?"

"Please ask Dr. Hillman about the other patients assigned to the treatment protocol."

"I've already told you that I've seen vast improvements in most of my patients given the new treatment," Dr. Hillman said.

"What about the patients it didn't help, Dr. Hillman?" I asked. "What about the patients assigned to the experimental treatment that died?"

"Other patients died?" Officer Quick said, glancing at me but addressing his question at Dr. Hillman. "I hadn't heard about these additional deaths." I didn't remind the policeman that the deaths were reason #5 on the list I'd shown him.

Dr. Hillman scowled at me. "Of course whenever there's a new treatment we're not one hundred percent certain how it will affect every individual. Like I said, most of my patients have responded very favorably to the treatment, many of whom I've been able to discharge."

"But not everyone?" the policeman said.

"No, unfortunately, not everyone. I'm still looking into the matter, but I'm not convinced that it was the treatment that precipitated the patients' deaths. Each patient comes to us with a medical history that's fraught with complications."

"How long have you been conducting your experiment, Dr. Hillman?" the policeman asked.

"I've been using this particular mixture of drugs for the past several months."

"You experimented on my father, George Davish, didn't you?" I said, suddenly realizing that I'd been right all along; Dr. Hillman had killed my father.

"I've been conducting progressive treatment experiments for many years now, yes. And I've been successful in curing patients of all types of nervous diseases. Of course, I've varied the composition of the formula many times, trying to improve upon the treatment. When I treated George Davish, if I remember right, we used small doses of calomel in the formula. And I added the electric therapy sessions last year."

"And how many patients have you treated during that time?" Officer Quick asked.

"I've probably treated a thousand patients since I've been at the asylum."

"How many were given this particular concoction?"

"Like I said, we started with this formula a few months ago, so maybe fifty? My nurse can give you the exact number."

"And they all give consent to be in your experiment?" the policeman asked. Dr. Hillman shifted in his chair.

"Well, no. By the very nature of their disease, my patients are unfit to give consent. I'm responsible for their care. I'm the one who decides if they're given the treatment or not."

The policeman nodded and jotted a few notes down in his notepad.

"You don't consult with their families?" I asked. Both men ignored me.

Without looking up, Officer Quick asked, "How many, of the fifty patients you have treated with this new method, have died, Dr. Hillman?" When the doctor didn't answer immediately, the policeman looked up. "How many, Dr. Hillman?"

"I can't say for certain; again, my nurse would

have the records and could tell you a more precise number."

"An approximation will do for now, Doctor," the policeman said.

"I'd say nine."

Nine? I gasped at the pronouncement. I'd no idea there were that many. I'd been shocked by the two patients who shared Levi Yardley's room.

"That's almost twenty percent, Dr. Hillman," Officer Quick said, his voice calm and steady. "Does that seem like a reasonable mortality rate to you?"

"Yes, it does." Dr. Hillman squared his shoulders. "That's what it takes to develop techniques that cure patients." The policeman raised an eyebrow but said nothing to counter his argument. He jotted down a few more notes.

"To be clear, it's your assertion that Levi Yardley was benefiting from the therapeutic treatment he was receiving as a result of being assigned to your experiment?"

"Yes, until like the lady said, he escaped," the doctor conceded. The policeman looked at me as if challenging me to question the doctor's claim. I knew better than to say what I wanted to. Officer Quick directed his attention back to the doctor.

"And that's the last time you saw Mr. Yardley?" the policeman said. Dr. Hillman hesitated.

"Yes," he finally said. "I never saw Mr. Yardley

again." The policeman nodded and started to put his notepad away.

"Thank you for your cooperation, Dr. Hillman. I will contact you if I have any further questions." The doctor nodded, his lips pinched tight, but he said nothing more. "Good day," the policeman said, with a tip of his hat. "Miss Davish, come with me."

"No," I said, pointing to the doctor, who was already reading something on his desk, trying to pretend we'd left. "He's lying." Dr. Hillman looked up at me, his eyes wide with fear.

"What are you talking about, Miss Davish?" Officer Quick said.

"That wasn't the last time Dr. Hillman saw Levi Yardley. The day Levi Yardley died Dr. Hillman confronted Mr. Yardley in town."

"How did you know that?" Dr. Hillman asked before he realized his mistake. "I mean, I don't know what you're talking about."

"Someone recognized you," I said, stretching the truth. Emily Upchurch had recognized Levi Yardley from the photograph, but it was I who had extrapolated her description of the man with him as being Dr. Hillman. I made a guess and I was right.

"Care to explain, Dr. Hillman? And this time give me the truth," Officer Quick said, sternly. Dr. Hillman sighed.

"Everything I said was true, everything except

that I did see Levi Yardley again after he'd left the asylum."

"Tell me about the encounter with Levi Yardley," the policeman said.

Dr. Hillman cast an irritated glance toward me. As I'd done many times with an unpleasant employer, I hid my own feelings behind the blank expression on my face. If he knew what I thought of him, he might never reveal the truth.

"After Yardley left the asylum, the orderlies were having no luck in finding him. Eventually I took it upon myself to track him down. He hadn't completed the treatment and wasn't fit for mixing back into the city's population. I found him wandering down the middle of Charles Street, downtown. I tried to lure the man into my buggy. I explained to him that for his own safety he needed to come back to the asylum. But Yardley was defiant: shouting, picking up stones from the road and throwing them at me, kicking horse dung at me. He was incapable of rational behavior. All the more reason that he should return to the asylum."

"And then what happened, Doctor?" Officer Quick said. Dr. Hillman picked up the photograph of his two sons and studied it. "Doctor?"

The doctor replaced the photograph and looked at the policeman. "It was imperative that he come back, you see. He wasn't finished with his treatment. He wasn't cured."

Dr. Hillman settled himself behind his desk

and began sorting through the papers and files tossed about on top.

"Yes, and then what did you do?"

"I did what anyone in my position would do. I attempted to apprehend him and return him to the asylum. But I failed. Now really, Mr. Quick, I must get back to my patients."

"We're not finished yet. Please tell me exactly what you did after Mr. Yardley resisted your attempts to return him to the asylum."

"Very well." Dr. Hillman glanced at his pocket watch before snapping it closed again. "I watched him and followed him when he wandered down the street, waiting for an opportunity to apprehend him. Finally, my chance came when he found an inactive warehouse, clambered up on the delivery dock, and nodded off to sleep. The man was unwell and exhausted. I left my buggy in the street, approached the dock, and before he could be fully aroused, grabbed him. I pulled his arms behind his back. He attempted to free himself but exhausted and weak as he was, I managed to fit him with a mitt restraint that at first seemed to subdue him. I pulled him down from the dock and directed him by the shoulders into my runabout. After seating him, I retrieved my bag and administered a calming agent to the patient. I then climbed up, took the reins, and cracked the whip. It must've been the sound of the whip, but Mr. Yardley immediately grew agitated and began thrashing his body violently about."

"What do you mean 'thrash about'?" Officer Quick asked.

"Flailing his legs, head, and torso about with abandon. He was having a fit of some sort." The policeman merely nodded. I wanted to shout, "Of course he was having a fit, you've been experimenting on the man," but I remained silent.

"He wasn't simply trying to escape from the runabout?"

"No, he was definitely in the throes of a seizure."

"Have you seen this in any of your other patients?"

"Yes, but it's uncommon." Dr. Hillman furrowed his brow quizzically when he caught me glaring at him. Did he truly have no idea how much I disliked him or did he simply not care?

Officer Quick frowned, and said, "Please continue, Doctor." The doctor purposefully avoided my gaze.

"As I was saying, the patient was thrashing uncontrollably about in his seat. With the reins in one hand, I tried to hold him down with the other. In my haste to get the patient back to the asylum, I urged the horse to a run. But then we took a corner too fast and I needed both of my hands to control the horse. In that instant, Mr. Yardley thrashed sideways and was flung from the runabout. I couldn't stop in time. He flew through the air, and without the use of his hands, smashed face-first on the side of the road. The sickening crack as he hit the edge of the curb was enough to tell me he was dead. I confirmed that that was indeed the case when I examined the body."

"You examined him and then you left him there?" I couldn't stay silent another moment. "And what about the mitt?" Asa Upchurch never mentioned finding him wearing a restraint.

"I removed it. The mitt is property of the asylum."

"But he was under your care at the asylum. How could you leave him there?"

Dr. Hillman ignored me. I suspected that Asa Upchurch interrupted him and he panicked. "If that's all, Officer, I must get back to my patients."

"I think you need to come with me, Dr. Hillman," Officer Quick said.

"But it was an accident. It's a tragedy, but I've done nothing wrong."

"Then why did you lie? Why didn't you inform the police?" I said.

"It will be up to a jury to decide whether it was an accident or manslaughter, Doctor, but either way Miss Davish is right. You should've notified the police immediately."

"I felt it was an internal affair. I don't have time to spend idling about with the police, then or now. My experiment is at a critical stage and I must get back to my patients."

"Not today, Doctor. You're coming with me,"

Officer Quick said, grabbing the doctor's arm and forcing him to his feet.

"This is completely unacceptable," Dr. Hillman shouted. "Let me go. What about my patients? Let me go! Nurse!"

I followed the two into the hallway and down the stairs as they navigated past the many gawking and curious patients, nurses, and doctors who had heard the commotion. Demanding to be released, Dr. Hillman struggled in the strong policeman's grasp until they were out the door. I stopped next to Nurse Simmons.

With no little amount of vindication for my father, and the countless victims like him, I said, "You can close down the progressive treatment ward, Nurse. Dr. Hillman won't be experimenting on anyone again."

Chapter 31

"Oh no." I groaned under my breath when I arrived back at the hotel. First the arrest of Asa Upchurch and Dr. Hillman, and now this.

"Well, there's my girl!" Nate Boone jumped up from the cushioned bench lining the lobby wall.

I was exhausted and I wanted nothing more than to go to my room, consult the train timetables for my departure, and then write Walter and Sir Arthur telling them when to expect me. But despite successfully uncovering the embezzler at school, the truth behind the "incidents," and revealing Levi Yardley's killer, I felt disgruntled. I still didn't know what had happened to Frank Hayward. How could I leave without knowing Mr. Hayward's fate? I hated loose ends.

And here's another one, I thought.

I took a deep breath. "I'm not your girl, Nate." His smile revealed he hadn't noticed the exhaustion in my voice.

"You were once, though, right, Hat?" Hearing him use the nickname immediately brought me back to the days when I would've been delighted by the sight of this man. Not anymore.

"Why are you here, Nate?"

"To take you to dinner, what else? I've sent you invitations every day, but they obviously never reached you." With this comment he glared at Mr. Putney, who was attempting to appear preoccupied at the registration desk. "So I thought I'd invite you in person." He flourished his black derby about. "Where do you want to go? I've never tried the Silver Moon. I hear they do an excellent Welsh rabbit, or there's the Parisian on Francis. It can't compare with what I've dined on in Paris, but I'm sure we can find something tasty."

"I did get your invitations, Nate. I simply didn't want to go to dinner." His face twitched in surprise, an oddly familiar expression.

How swiftly the years melt away, I thought. Could it have been eleven years since I'd last seen him?

"Why ever not?"

I shook my head in disbelief. "How can you even wonder? We didn't part on particularly good terms, you know."

"But, Hattie, that was years ago. I think it's wonderful how well we've both done with our lives. What's the harm in chatting about old times and toasting to the new?"

Same old Nate: charming, cheerful, optimistic, and oblivious.

"It's been a long day, Nate."

"I'll cheer you up. We can dine right here; you don't have to exert yourself a bit. I won't even complain when the roast chicken is tough." He beamed at me and put out his arm. "Come on, Hat, take my arm and let's go. I'm starving." I was too tired to say no.

He led me into the dining room, and on the presumption that I was too tired, ordered for the both of us. Did he think I'd forgotten that he'd always ordered for the two of us? Even when we were young he'd pick out the flavor of stick candy we'd get at his father's grocery store after school. As we waited for our food, he chattered on and on: about where he'd traveled, who he'd met, which palace he'd played, while touring with Sousa's band. After dinner arrived, between popping bites of roast chicken, fried potatoes, and boiled parsnips into his mouth, he gossiped about a suspected affair between one of the vocalists and a clarinet player. He blathered on about how important he was to Sousa and how he'd become assistant conductor last year, while I sat there pushing the food about my plate. After the day I'd had, I wasn't in the least bit hungry. And what a day I'd had! Let alone the adventures and misadventures I'd had since we'd last met. But Nate was too caught up in his own story-telling to ask me anything.

Oh, how I miss you, Walter, I thought. How I longed to see the compassion in his eyes, to feel the warmth of his embrace, to hear him ask, in all sincerity, how I was. From the moment I'd met him, he'd displayed nothing but kindness, interest, and concern for me. He'd always valued my opinions, my feelings, and my affection. Without a word between us, I knew he loved me. And as easy as it was to breathe, I loved him. So why had I agreed to dine with Nate Boone?

Another loose end, I thought, watching the animation in Nate's face as he told of a particular concert they'd given at the World's Fair. As with my father, I'd never gotten a proper good-bye, a proper reason for his departure from my life. I'd been in love with him once. He and I had grown up together. We knew each other like no one else. And now all I could do was politely pick at my peach cobbler, nod my head, and wish the dinner would be over.

"And then do you know what he said?"

"I'm sorry, Nate," I said, setting my napkin on the table. "I'm exhausted. Thank you for dinner, but I'm going to retire to my room now." I pushed back my chair and stood. Instead of standing like any gentleman would, he sat gaping up at me.

"Well, heck, Hat. You haven't even finished your cobbler. You love cobbler." And I'd thought he hadn't remembered anything. I smiled at him for the first time.

"It was nice to see you, Nate. I'm happy that you're doing well. Good night." As I turned to leave, I heard the sudden scraping of his chair as he leaped to his feet. Before I could take another step, he grabbed my arm.

"You still haven't forgiven me, have you?"

"Forgiven you for what?" For breaking our engagement so you could pursue your career, for breaking your promise to me to be by my side at my father's funeral, or for breaking my heart? I thought. But I said none of this. It was a long time ago and I was ready to put it all behind me. Confronting Dr. Hillman had allowed me to do that. "Good-bye, Nate."

"Please don't leave like this." He released my arm, slipping his hand into mine. "I'm sorry I broke your heart," he whispered. "I'm sorry about your father. Truly I am."

"Thank you for saying that." I fought back tears when I saw the remorse that I'd heard in his voice reflected in his eyes.

"You were my girl once, Hat. I've never forgotten that."

"I know. And you'll always have a place in my heart."

"I should've been there for you. I should have never let you go." I merely nodded, not trusting myself to speak. "Good-bye, Hattie," Nate said as he released my hand.

"Good-bye."

And even as I made my way back to the lobby and up the stairs, I could hear him singing, "St. Joe girls won't you come out tonight, won't you come out tonight, won't you come out tonight." For the first time in over a decade, I could think of Nate Boone and smile. But the moment I closed the door behind me, my thoughts weren't of Nate Boone or Asa Upchurch or Dr. Cyrus Hillman. I rushed to the desk, plopped down, pulled out a piece of stationery, and began writing:

My dearest Walter . . .

"Miss Davish?" I looked up from my breakfast to see Miss Woodruff standing a few feet from the doorway. She was no longer wearing black. "I didn't know you were staying here?"

I'd spent the two days since Asa Upchurch's

and Dr. Hillman's arrests quietly: finishing my research on General Thompson for Sir Arthur, detailing the events of that day in a letter to Bertha Yardley now back in Omaha, going to Mass at the cathedral, and preparing for my departure. I bought my train ticket at the depot yesterday; I was packed and ready to leave. All that was left was a tea engagement at Mrs. Chaplin's home this afternoon.

"Yes. Will you join me?" I said, stabbing a piece of pancake on my fork. The waiter had gushed that they were the same local Aunt Jemima pancakes that were being showcased at the World's Fair. That's not why I'd ordered them. Pancakes were one of Walter's favorite foods and merely eating one made me feel one step closer to seeing him again.

"Thank you, I will." Miss Woodruff took the chair opposite and poured herself a cup of coffee. "Will you be heading back soon, now that you've helped Mrs. Chaplin uncover the culprits behind all the troubles at the school?"

"Yes, I'm taking the first train in the morning. My employer is expecting me."

"What about . . . ?" She shook her head but didn't finish her thought. She didn't need to. What about the disappearance of Frank Hayward is what she was going to say. I'd struggled with that too. I wanted to help Ginny discover her father's whereabouts. Wasn't that why I'd come home in the first place, to help Ginny with the loss of her father? But I'd failed. I wasn't any closer to uncovering his fate this morning than I was the moment I realized he wasn't in the casket.

"Good morning, Mollie." A decidedly plump girl, around sixteen, with a quick smile and mischievous eyes, lumbered over to our table.

"Good morning, Mary. Mary, this is Miss Davish, a former pupil of the school. Miss Davish, this is my cousin, Miss Mary Wells." Without being invited, the girl plopped down and thrust her hand across the table at me. I took it and she shook it vigorously.

"So thrilled to meet you, Miss Davish," Mary Wells said. "You'll have to tell me all about working for Mrs. Mayhew and the dead bodies you found."

"Mary!" Miss Woodruff's face flushed red from embarrassment.

"What?" Miss Wells said, obviously confused. "Isn't she the one you told me about?"

"I'm sorry, Miss Davish, my cousin arrived last night from Kansas. She lives on a farm, outside Blue Rapids," Miss Woodruff said, as if that explained her cousin's indelicate manners.

But it still gave you time to tell her about me, I thought. I still didn't know if I should be mortified or flattered.

"My rooms are too small to accommodate visitors so she's staying here," Miss Woodruff explained. "I promised to take her to the Jesse James House this morning. That's why I'm here."

"Yes, I don't think there's been a single person in the past twelve years who hasn't associated Jesse James and his band of desperadoes with St. Joseph," Miss Wells said. "I've wanted to come for years. And then Mollie invited me and Mother said I could visit."

"Mary's a real Jesse James enthusiast and wanted it to be the first thing she did. Of course, I've been there at least a dozen times since everyone from out of town always wants to visit. I dare say it's the one thing worth paying admission to in town."

"Come with us," Miss Wells said. She was brash, but her enthusiasm was infectious.

"I'm sure Miss Davish has other plans, Mary. Besides, I'm sure she's probably been there more than a dozen times. She lived here when it happened too."

"Actually Miss Woodruff, I've never been."

"Really?" Miss Wells and Miss Woodruff said simultaneously.

Miss Wells stared at me, her mouth agape. "You lived here then and you've never been?"

"Everyone's been to the Jesse James House," Miss Woodruff said, surprised.

"Not me," I said, counting out coins to pay the bill. "But as a matter of fact, I'd planned to go today; I promised a friend I'd bring him back a souvenir from the house. I'd love to join you." Miss Wells clapped her hands in excitement. We rose from the table and headed toward the lobby.

"Oh, good. We'll make it a real outing. And you can tell me all about the body you found in the trunk on the way," Miss Wells said.

Mr. Putney's eyes widened as we passed the desk, obviously having overheard the comment.

"Mary!" Miss Woodruff exclaimed.

"What?" her cousin said, pinning on her wide-brimmed fancy braided navy blue straw. "What did I say now?"

This is going to be an interesting outing, I thought, as Miss Wells plodded past me, her hat flopping about as she headed out the door. I had no idea just how interesting.

Chapter 32

"I can't believe I'm really going to the house where Bob Ford killed Jesse James!" Miss Wells clapped her hands like a child as we climbed the hill.

"You never did say how you managed to avoid coming here before, Miss Davish," Miss Woodruff asked. "I thought everyone in St. Joseph had visited at least once. I know my brother, who was fifteen, came that very day. It was quite exciting if you remember and everyone wanted to know if it was true. Had Jesse James really been living in St. Joseph? Was he really lying dead in a house on Lafayette Street?"

"It must've been thrilling," Miss Wells said. "I wish I'd been here then. But then again Mother wouldn't have let me go anyway; I was a small child at the time. At least I get to see it now, though, right?"

"My mother wouldn't let me go to the house either," Miss Woodruff said, "but she, my brother, and I went to Sidenfaden's Funeral Parlor and joined the long procession past the body."

"You never told me you actually saw his body, Mollie," Miss Wells said. "Ooooh, am I jealous."

"Tell her there's nothing to be jealous of, Miss Davish. Miss Davish? Is something wrong?" Miss Woodruff said, when I hadn't answered her question or shared in the women's enthusiasm.

Why did I agree to come here? I wondered as I watched the unremarkable single-story frame house loom larger as we approached. I'm doing this for Walter, I told myself. He wanted a souvenir.

"Miss Davish?" Miss Woodruff touched my arm slightly, breaking my reverie. "There's something wrong, isn't there?"

I sighed. "Yes and no." I tried to sound less distressed than I was feeling. "This house reminds me of my father's death." Miss Wells gasped.

"Was your father shot in the back of the head too?"

"Mary!" Miss Woodruff chided.

"Oh, he was an outlaw then," Miss Wells concluded.

"Mary! Of course Mr. Davish wasn't an outlaw. How could you say such a thing?"

"Miss Davish said the house reminded her of her father's death. What else was I to think?"

"I don't know, but certainly not such outlandish things as that."

"You're right, Miss Woodruff. It's nothing like that," I said, forcing myself to smile. Miss Wells's leap to such a bizarre conclusion made me feel silly for brooding. "My father died on the same day. That's all. Somehow I always connected the two deaths. It's silly really. My father had absolutely no connection to Jesse James except the day he died. But that's why I've never been to the house before."

"I avoid the classroom where Frank taught bookkeeping at school," Miss Woodruff said. "I guess we all do silly things to avoid the pain and the reminder of a person lost to us." She pulled out her handkerchief and used it to cover her scar.

"This is supposed to be an adventure," Miss Wells pleaded, "not a bore. Just think, the same house where the notorious outlaw was shot dead by a member of his own gang. It's thrilling to be here!"

"You're right, Mary." Miss Woodruff stuffed her handkerchief back in her bag. "Besides, he might still be out there somewhere, right, Miss Davish?"

"Who, Jesse James?" Miss Wells asked. "I have heard rumors he's not really dead."

"No, Mary, I meant Frank Hayward."

"Who's Frank Hayward?" Miss Woodruff and I looked at each other, waiting for the other to answer.

Finally, Miss Woodruff said, "Someone who used to work at the school. We hope he'll come back soon."

"I do hope so," I said, wishing I had a more definitive answer for her.

"Well, then," Miss Wells said as she linked one arm in mine and the other in her cousin's, "let's go."

She led us through the gate and toward the front door, to the right of which a sign read:

JESSE JAMES HOUSE
ADMISSION 15 CENTS.

"Get out your money, girls." She dropped her hold on us and fished through her purse for the necessary nickels. "Let the fun begin."

Miss Woodruff and I both laughed as we retrieved our coins for a ticket. Entering the home of a dead man, especially one as notorious as Jesse James, solely to spy the hole in the wall made by the bullet after it passed through his head or to see the floorboards still stained with his blood, was ghoulish. Yet I couldn't help but enjoy Miss Wells's enthusiasm.

At least I won't find the dead man himself, I thought, as I paid my fare and followed my companions into the outlaw's home.

We walked through what would've been the kitchen to the front parlor where the shooting had occurred. The room was completely empty—no furniture, rug, or curtains; most of everything, Miss Wells explained to us, had been auctioned off years ago.

"Don't you remember it, Miss Davish?" Miss Wells said. "It was in the paper. You could've bought anything from a skillet to a chamber pot to the breakfast table. Then you really would've had a souvenir." I didn't remember; my grief had been too deep at the time.

The walls too had been stripped of most of their wallpaper. In its place were names, hundreds of them; men and women who had signed the bare plaster to record their visit. Miss Wells pulled out a pencil and scribbled her name in a blank spot. She held it out to her cousin.

"Your turn." Instead of taking the pencil, Miss Woodruff traced her finger on a nearby section that was black with signatures. She pointed to a name.

"I've already signed. See?"

Miss Wells clapped her hands when she spied Mollie Woodruff's name on the wall. "What fun! I hope to come back someday and see that my name's still here. Miss Davish?" She held the pencil out to me.

"No, thank you," I said, trying to hide my distaste for vandalism, even in an outlaw's house.

"Very well." Miss Wells put away her pencil and then proceeded to a section of wallpaper that was still partially intact and stripped a large piece off. She ripped the piece into threes and held two of the pieces out to Miss Woodruff and me. It had a gold background with lines of black through it that might once have been outlines of flowers. I hesitated.

"You did promise someone a souvenir, didn't you?"

"But the wallpaper?" Miss Woodruff said, slowly taking the offered paper.

"Would you rather have a piece of the floorboards still stained with Jesse James's blood?" Miss Wells walked over to a darkened indentation on the floor. She obviously wouldn't be the first to collect her souvenir from the wooden planks. She knelt down next to it, examining the boards. "If I had a penknife, it would be simple, but I'm not sure if I can pull a piece up. Maybe I could get a sliver . . ."

"No, Mary, stop," Miss Woodruff said, mortified

that her cousin was trying to dig into the floor with a key. She pulled her cousin up, with great effort, from the floor. "The wallpaper will do fine." Her cousin shrugged.

"Or better yet," Miss Wells said, staring at the bullet hole in the wall. She stopped beneath it, stood on her toes, and reached up toward it. The tips of her stubby fingers barely reached.

"Mary! It's a bullet hole," Miss Woodruff said. "Isn't it sacrilegious or something to tamper with it?"

"Only if the police were still investigating the crime," I said. "But I wouldn't recommend it. It will further damage the plaster."

"Yes, it will further damage the plaster, Mary," Miss Woodruff repeated. "Besides, it doesn't even look much like a bullet hole, does it? I hadn't expected it to be that big."

"It wouldn't have been," I said. "But as you know, hundreds, maybe even thousands, of others have come before us over the years. I'm guessing Mary wasn't the first to want a part of the wall."

"Miss Davish is right," Miss Wells said, pulling several yellowed newspaper clippings from her bag. She riffled through them until she found the one she wanted. "See here. They have a picture of the original hole and it was much smaller."

She held it out before her. Miss Woodruff and I looked at the newspaper article over her shoulder. It was an article from *The Manhattan Enterprise* dated April 4, 1882, the day after the shooting. It contained two photographs, one of Jesse James dead in a semi-upright coffin and one of the bullet hole in the wall, which was a great deal smaller.

"Where did you get this?" Miss Woodruff asked.

"I clipped it out of the paper that day and kept it with others as keepsakes. I brought them along knowing I was coming here. If you look closely, you can see the bullet hole in his head." Miss Wells moved the paper closer to Miss Woodruff's face. That lady promptly turned pale and looked away. "See, Miss Davish," Miss Wells said. "Some people don't think it was him, that he's still alive, but look, the dead man looks exactly like the live one."

She riffled through the clippings again and this time pulled out one containing a photograph of Jesse James posing for a portrait with other men. "See." Miss Wells held the pictures, the portrait with Jesse James alive and the other of him in his casket, next to each other. "Of course, he's much younger here. It was supposedly taken during the early days of the James-Younger gang, but still I don't know how anyone could think this wasn't him."

"Wishful thinking, perhaps," Miss Woodruff said flippantly, though not willing to look at the photographs.

Not noting the sarcastic tone of her cousin's voice, Miss Wells said, "Maybe. It is thrilling to think that he might still be alive. What do you think, Miss Davish? Is this really him?"

I looked at the comparison photographs, not to confirm that the outlaw was indeed dead (Hadn't the night policeman confirmed it?) but because something caught my eye in the portrait picture. Agrimony. The flowers on the backdrop behind the men looked like agrimony.

Like the misplaced flowers at Frank Hayward's funeral, I thought.

I studied the portrait, wishing I'd brought my hand lens with me but couldn't determine from the yellowing gray photograph if I was right. But then I saw something that made the identity of the flowers irrelevant.

"Oh my God."

"It's ghoulish, I know," Miss Wells said, mistaking my exclamation for revulsion. "But that's part of the fun, isn't it?"

"I'm sorry, I have to go," I said, heading toward the exit.

"What is it, Miss Davish? Are you all right? Shall we go with you?"

I turned to look at Miss Woodruff. I inwardly cringed at the concern on her face. She didn't deserve to have her heart broken again. But if she knew what I was about to do . . . I couldn't let myself think anymore. I had to go.

"I'm sorry," was all I could muster to say as I ran from the room. "I'm truly sorry."

"Well, that's strange," I heard Mary Wells say behind me. "Did you see the look on her face? I thought she'd swoon right here. I know the dead man's picture is ghastly, but you'd think after finding so many dead bodies, she'd be less squeamish than that."

If she only knew, I thought as I raced out of the house and down the hill. *If she only knew.*

Chapter 33

"Tell me about your father, Ginny." Ginny looked up from pouring the tea.

"What do you mean, Hattie? You knew my father. What do you want to know?"

After leaving a puzzled Miss Woodruff and Miss Wells behind at the Jesse James House, I'd run down to Ninth and Penn streets and caught a streetcar. I hadn't wanted to lose any time in confronting Ginny. What I'd seen in the newspaper photograph had equally exhilarated me and appalled me. I'd finally solved the one piece of the puzzle that had eluded me, but it also meant that my friend had been lying to me from the moment I'd arrived.

"I want to know where he is."

"I told you I don't know."

"Yes, you do." I took a sip from my teacup. "I understand you wanting to protect him, but

I know, Ginny. I know. He can't hide forever."

"If you're talking about the embezzlement, you yourself led the police to Asa Upchurch. My father had nothing to do with that."

"I'm not talking about the money or the incidents at the school, Ginny. I'm talking about your father. I'm talking about Charles Mayfield."

"Who's Charles Mayfield?"

"And I'm talking about Jesse James."

"Hattie, what are you talking about? I have no idea who Charles Mayfield is. And what does Jesse James, a notorious outlaw who's been dead for over a decade, have to do with the whereabouts of my father?"

"Everything and you know it."

"I know nothing of the kind."

"Does the flower agrimony mean anything to you?"

"No. Why?"

"You don't have to pretend anymore, Ginny. I know why your father hasn't been seen since the funeral."

"Maybe he's locked up in the asylum like you said."

"No, the staff there denies ever seeing your father and to be certain, the police searched the entire building after they arrested Dr. Hillman."

"Then maybe my poor father is dead after all." She pouted, but her eyes belied what she said. She didn't believe it any more than I did.

"Your father is alive and well and you know it. What I don't know is where and why you still think you need to lie to me."

"Hattie! How can you say such a thing? I'm not lying to you. I have no idea where my father is and I'm worried sick about it." Her teacup shook in her hand. She watched me over the rim of the cup as she tried to take a drink but couldn't bring it to her lips. She set the cup and saucer on her lap. "You believe me, don't you? We're friends after all."

"I believe that you're worried sick about him. I know what it's like to see your father in peril. But I can't leave this alone, Ginny. Your father has to confess to what he's done."

"No!" Ginny leaped up from her seat, sending the teacup and saucer crashing to the ground. The tea seeped into the Belgian carpet, forming a dark irregular stain at her feet. "You stay out of this, Hattie Davish."

"I'm sorry, Ginny. It's too late for that."

"Don't you dare do anything to hurt my father." Ginny's face was red with fury.

"It may be too late for that too."

"Get out! Mrs. Curbow!" Ginny screamed. The housekeeper, who must have been very close, appeared a moment later. "Get this woman out of my house. She's never to be allowed in again." Mrs. Curbow, staring at me with a gaping mouth, barely nodded. "Now!" Ginny commanded again.

"I'm sorry it had to come to this." I set my teacup down on the table and stood. "I came home to give you comfort and friendship. This is the last thing I would've wanted. I wish I could've helped you and your father. Not this."

"I wish you'd never come at all," Ginny said to my back as I left the room.

So do I, I thought.

"You!"

Maybe it was being turned out of Ginny's house or it was the burden of the truth I now knew, but when I saw the man with the Panama hat lingering behind an ice wagon across the street, I didn't hesitate to confront him. He'd been following me for days and I'd nothing left to lose.

He bolted when he realized I was yelling at him. This time I grabbed ahold of my hat, picked up my skirts, and ran after him. I caught up to him when a passing streetcar momentarily blocked his way. I leaped forward and grabbed ahold of his coattails.

"Why are you following me?"

"Let go of me and I'll tell you." He turned to face me. It was the first time I'd gotten a good look at his face. And I didn't recognize him.

"Who are you?"

"Well, at least I did something right," the man said. Then I recognized his voice.

"Gus?" It was the security man from Mrs. Chaplin's school. He nodded. "What's going on?"

"I'm sorry, Miss Davish. I really am." He pushed his hat back from his forehead and reached into his breast pocket. As his fingers grasped for something hard beneath his jacket, he glanced about to see if anyone was near. Only a long-haired gray cat scratching a nearby tree was close enough to witness. "But I'm just doing my job."

"No!" I cried out in surprise and instinctively threw up my hands in defense. I leaped backward, nearly tripping on my skirt.

"Oh, no, Miss Davish," Gus said, waving his free hand. "It's nothing like that." He pulled out a card case, not a gun, and handed a card to me. I sighed in relief and to cover my embarrassment.

What's wrong with you, Davish? I silently chided myself. I looked down at my hand holding the card. It was shaking.

To avoid his gaze and gather my composure, I focused on his card. It read:

GUS ANDERSON, DETECTIVE.
LOCKE'S WESTERN DETECTIVE AGENCY,
P.T. LOCKE, CHIEF.
CENTRAL OFFICE, COMMERCIAL BANK BLOCK
SIXTH AND EDMOND, ROOM 50,
TELEPHONE 125

I flipped it over. On the back was an image, a single wide-open eye in the middle of a rising sun with the words above it: OUR EYE IS EVER ON YOU. It sent shivers down my spine. Maybe I had cause to be leery after all. I immediately handed it back.

"I was hired by Mr. Upchurch when the incidents at the school started," Gus said.

"So you must know that Miss Gilbert was behind the thefts and the fire and the petty acts of vandalism?"

"Really? No, I hadn't heard that. I had the night off last night and haven't spoken to anyone at the school today. Wow, I never would've suspected Miss Gilbert. Never."

"So you don't know that Mr. Upchurch was arrested for embezzling money from the school either, do you?" Gus blinked several times before a big smirk crossed his face.

"Well, you don't say."

"But why have you been following me?"

"Mr. Upchurch paid me extra to watch you, see what you were up to and report back. I have to say you made my job extremely difficult. I've shadowed a lot of people, but you're one of the most observant I've ever known. You almost caught me several times."

"But why would Mr. Upchurch want me followed?" Gus shrugged his shoulders.

"That was his business, not mine."

"Could he have been concerned I might discover what he was up to?"

"Now that you say that, I do remember him becoming extremely agitated when I told him you were talking with the police. So yeah, you're probably right."

"Then you can stop following me."

"Yeah, of course. I'm glad of it too. I hated following a lady like you. And ah . . . sorry for giving you a fright." He held up the card case for a moment before putting it back into his pocket. I blushed with embarrassment and said nothing. He tipped his Panama hat. "Good day, Miss Davish."

"And to you, Gus." I was relieved to no longer be someone's quarry. Then I turned and headed back to the Hayward house as fast as I could. I had my own quarry to pursue.

Chapter 34

I waited less than five minutes before Ginny emerged from her house. She looked about her furtively as she descended the stairs. Hidden behind a coal wagon parked across the street, she never saw me. To my shame, this wasn't the first time I'd followed someone in an effort to spy upon them. But to my credit, I'd learned to do it very well. I easily kept Ginny in my sights, carefully hiding myself behind hedges, wagons, or among groups of fellow pedestrians heading in the same direction. It was easy until we encountered the Labor Day parade.

As we approached Sixth Street, crowds lined the sidewalks as marching bands in gold tassels and tall red hats, carriage after carriage decorated with rainbow-colored bunting carrying dignitaries who waved out the window, and open wagons of all kinds draped with banners advertising which union or brotherhood the men crowded in the back represented passed down the street. As Pryor's Military Band passed, the cacophony of Sousa's "Across the Danube March" mixing with the cheers and claps of the crowd bounced off the buildings. Distracted by the noise, I caught a glimpse of Nate Boone next to Mr. Pryor leading the band. When I turned my attention back to the crowd, Ginny was gone.

I zigzagged my way, pushing past men with children on their shoulders and groups of girls in identical school uniforms. And then I spotted her. She was trying to dodge a slow-moving confectionary vendor attempting to move his cart through the crowd. And then I lost her again until I reached a congested corner. As I searched the multitude, I caught sight of her heading away from the bustle and toward an awaiting streetcar. I took off running as fast I could, dropping all pretense of concealment. She boarded the streetcar, which continued to wait a minute or two longer. It was enough time for me to grab the back handrail and hop aboard. I ducked down into a seat as the streetcar started down the rails.

Ginny was sitting in the front, her back to me. I caught my breath as I dropped my fare into the box. I watched and waited for her to turn back and see me, but she never did. We passed block after block as I anticipated her sudden departure, which never came. She was taking the car to the end of the line, to Rochester Road, otherwise known as Eugene Field's "Lover's Lane." That's where I'd spied a man bearing a resemblance to Frank Hayward, driving his carriage in a mad dash to leave town the day after his supposed funeral. I'd dismissed the coincidence, thinking it might be the escaped patient from the asylum. I'd had it backward. The escaped patient was dead and buried in Frank Hayward's coffin and Frank Hayward was escaping. I could never have imagined what he was actually escaping from. I'd come to believe it was related to Mrs. Chaplin's school, either the embezzlement or the incidents, both of which were wrong. I even speculated he might have had something to do with Levi Yardley's murder. But again, I would've been wrong. But now I knew. At least that's what I was hoping following Ginny would confirm.

But then what? I wondered.

Before I could ponder over an answer, the street-ar stopped and Ginny got off. A young couple, arms intertwined, rose and proceeded to alight as well. I was the last person on the streetcar.

"End of the line, miss," the driver said. I

approached the front and through the window watched Ginny walk up the lane. "You need to get off here."

"Yes, of course." I descended the stairs slowly.

"I'm running on a timetable, miss," the driver fumed.

"Sorry." I stepped off without taking my eyes off Ginny.

As the streetcar drove away, I sprinted to the nearest tree and hid. I peered around it, watching Ginny's progress. Feeling confident she was far enough away, I stepped back into the lane and followed her, careful to keep close to the tree line. She never turned around but after a quarter of a mile or so, she headed down a smaller lane to the right. The moment she did, I hurried to follow. I caught sight of a hat with a large russet-colored chrysanthemum on the crown lying beside a large oak tree. As I passed, the young couple I'd seen on the streetcar peeked around the tree, surprised to see me dashing past. Their cheeks were red, either from embarrassment or from passion. I'd obviously caught them kissing.

I turned into the secondary lane, a quiet path with a few homes spread out down its length. Except for a farmer and some field hands far out in a pasture with two horses and wagon, no one else was about. I watched Ginny, her black silk dress contrasting against the white picket fence as she entered through a gate. She disappeared into a one-story whitewashed stone farmhouse about an eighth of a mile down the lane. I strolled down the lane, taking my time to figure out what I was going to do next. If I was right, Frank Hayward was inside that farmhouse.

But what if I'm wrong? I wondered, as I approached the gate.

My friendship with Ginny was already in tatters. If I was wrong and I'd followed her on false pretenses, she'd be infuriated with me and I'd look the fool. But if I was right, I'd break her heart.

I'm right, I thought, as shadows crossed the windowsill.

But now what? Do I simply walk up to the door and knock? What then? What do I say? That I knew that Frank Hayward was alive and well and hiding inside? That Frank Hayward must confess to his crimes and accompany me to the police station? I hadn't thought this out very well. If he was guilty of the crimes I suspected him of, would he voluntarily go with me?

As I stood staring at the whitewashed little house debating what to do, the decision was mercifully made for me. The door opened and Frank Hayward stepped outside. I immediately noticed the scar across his eyebrow, his right eyebrow.

"Please come in, Miss Davish," he said. "I've been waiting for you for some time."

• • •

"Oh, Hattie, forgive me. Please forgive me!" Ginny threw her arms around me the moment I stepped into the house. Her porcelain cheeks were blotchy, long strands of her silky yellow hair fell unfettered from one side of her head, and her beautiful emerald eyes were red from crying. Although I'd expected to find him, seeing Frank Hayward standing alive and well before my eyes had unnerved me. And if that hadn't, seeing Ginny completely disheveled would have.

I placed a hand lightly on her back but didn't return the embrace. "I was afraid you'd discover my father was alive. I didn't know what to do."

I pulled myself away and took a step back. "Why not simply confide in me?" I was still hurt from all that had transpired between us.

"Because . . . because . . ."

"Because we can't risk discovery," Frank Hayward said, putting his arm around his distraught daughter.

"So what I suspect is true, isn't it?"

"What is it you suspect, Hattie?"

"That you were a member of the James-Younger gang. That your real name is Charles Mayfield." He closed his eyes and stood silently for several moments before finally nodding. Ginny stifled a cry with her handkerchief.

"But he didn't kill anyone," Ginny declared. "He never hurt anyone."

"Jesse James alone is credited with killing over a dozen men," I said. "Are you saying you weren't involved in any of the violence?"

"It's true. I never killed anyone. I was with them for a short period of time. I knew numbers, I knew banks. I proved useful to them in their planning. I rarely even held a gun." He looked down at his daughter, who stared up at him in complete adoration. "But I helped them steal, Virginia. And that's wrong." He turned to me. "How did you find out?"

"A photograph in a newspaper from the day after the shooting. It was a portrait supposedly taken of some of the members of the James-Younger gang. You stood in the back and to the right of Jesse James."

"Oh God, I'd forgotten about that picture. How young and stupid I was. We thought we were invincible."

"But then why, Hattie, didn't you think it was Levi Yardley in the picture?" Ginny asked. "You yourself said how striking the resemblance was between them. Maybe he was the gang member and not my father."

"Because of the scar," I said, pointing to the scar that crossed Mr. Hayward's eyebrow. "It was what caused me to suspect the truth when I saw the body in the coffin. I didn't see it when I saw you that day on Rochester Road, though. It was you I saw, wasn't it?"

"Yes, it was me. I'd hoped to get out of town unrecognized. I shaved off my beard and mustache and used a pencil to fill in the scar." He ran his fingers over several days' new growth of hair on his chin.

"How did you get the scar, by the way? Was it while you were with the James-Younger gang? I've always wanted to know. Did a bullet graze your face?"

Frank Hayward chuckled but didn't answer my question.

"But I'd told you, you were wrong. I thought that would be enough. Why didn't you trust me?" Ginny said.

"Because of the agrimony," I said.

"Agrimony?" Ginny said.

"It was in the bouquet you sent to the funeral, Mr. Hayward."

"Father? You sent one of the bouquets?" Mr. Hayward nodded.

"Not the most appropriate flowers for a funeral bouquet," I said.

"No, it was an act of a liberated man, Miss Davish. I was given a chance at a new start."

"Another new start," I added.

"Yes, I've been lucky. More than anyone knows. Not too many people get a second, let alone third and fourth chances."

"A fourth chance? What do you mean, Father?"

"Do you remember when we almost left St. Joseph, Virginia?" His daughter nodded.

"Yes, I still don't know why."

"It was because I saw Jesse, after he moved to St. Joe. It was Palm Sunday at the Presbyterian Church near the old World's Hotel. I was terrified he'd recognize me. I had already changed my name and moved to a new city. I couldn't risk being associated with him again. I spent the rest of the day packing and planning to leave town. You and I were waiting for our train at the depot the next morning when we heard the news. Bob Ford had shot and killed Jesse James. I couldn't believe my good fortune." I inwardly cringed thinking about the misery I'd encountered that same day.

"And what happened this time?" I asked. "Jesse James has been dead for years."

"You have to remember whispers had already begun that connected my name with the school's dwindling financial reserves. Who had better access to the school's funds but its bookkeeper? And then the 'incidents' at the school began. I started to panic. I'd absolutely nothing to do with the missing money or the incidents at the school, but it wouldn't matter if my true identity was discovered. I'd no idea what I was going to do. I could leave town for good this time, but the police would pursue me. And of course, there was Ginny's future to think about."

"And then Asa Upchurch appeared on your doorstep with a dead body that could've been your twin," I said.

"Yes, I was upstairs at the time and Asa never saw me. I have to admit I didn't hesitate for a moment to take advantage of the mistaken identification. I told Ginny what she had to do, and the moment it was safe, I disappeared, intending never to return. I wasn't considering the consequences. Now I have to bear the burden of knowing how much pain and distress I've caused." Had Ginny told him about Miss Woodruff? Had she told him about me?

"But what about the agrimony?" Ginny asked, fiddling with her locket.

"You remember our lessons from Mrs. Chaplin on the language of flowers, Ginny. Your father's bouquet had zinnia, mullein, and agrimony. Zinnia means 'I mourn your absence' and mullein means 'take courage.' But agrimony means 'thankfulness or gratitude.' No one would ever place that flower in a funeral bouquet."

"Except for a silly man who couldn't believe his extraordinary good luck," Frank Hayward said.

"Oh, Father!" Ginny hugged him close.

Over his daughter's head, Frank Hayward said, "What now?"

"I have to notify the police."

"Of course."

"Oh, Hattie, must you?" Ginny said, clinging to her father.

"I'm sorry, but I have to. Of course, I'll have to take the streetcar back into town and it will take some time before the police arrive." Ginny suddenly looked at me with wide, comprehending eyes. "What they find when they arrive is up to you."

Ginny hugged her father tightly, gazing lovingly into his face. "Thank you, Hattie," she said, looking back at me. "You're a true friend indeed."

"All I ever wanted to do was help."

But had I? Had I really been helpful or merely the instrument in uncovering lies, secrets, and murder? I was gratified that Ginny had been reunited with her father and that all of the troubles between us had been a product of her fierce protection of him. But no matter how much she apologized and no matter how much I understood, something had died between us.

"Good-bye, Mr. Hayward. Good-bye, Virginia," I said, knowing I'd never see or hear from either of them again. Again I'd lost someone special to me in the place I'd called home.

They walked me as far as the gate and were still watching when I turned to look back before entering the main road. They waved one last time before disappearing into the farmhouse. As I sauntered back toward the streetcar stop, I thought about all that had happened since I'd arrived. I'd found peace with my father's death. I'd uncovered an embezzler and a murderer. I discovered the whereabouts of a wanted outlaw. *How simple my life is when I'm working for Sir Arthur,* I thought. I wanted nothing more than to be at my typewriter again. No, that's not quite true, I thought, imagining myself once again in Walter's embrace.

Maybe I have found a new home. And I couldn't get back there soon enough.

Chapter 35

"But he was gone when the police arrived?" Mrs. Chaplin said.

I was sitting in Mrs. Chaplin's front parlor sipping tea with her, Miss Woodruff, Madame Maisonet, and Mrs. Emily Upchurch. Over a plate of lemon shortbread, wine cake, scotch cake, and a variety of cheese and crackers, I'd told them everything, or at least almost everything, I knew about Frank Hayward's deception and disappearance.

I nodded. "Officer Quick promised they would pursue the outlaw but pressed upon me the possibility that they might never catch him or bring him to justice."

"Well, I don't care what he's done, he'll always be a gentleman to me," Miss Woodruff said, defiantly. Although she'd given up her mourning dress, she still had a small black ribbon tied around her wrist.

"*Ah l'amour*," Madame Maisonet wistfully said. "One can forgive anything, yes?"

"Despite the shocking truth, I for one am not going to judge the man," Mrs. Upchurch said. I'd noticed the moment I arrived that she was no longer wearing her pearls and I could detect only her wedding band beneath her gloves. "Despite his past transgressions, it seems he has led a fault-less life since working for you, Mrs. Chaplin."

Unlike your husband, I thought, knowing from Mrs. Chaplin's raised eyebrow, I wasn't the only one.

"Yes, you're quite right, Mrs. Upchurch," Mrs. Chaplin said, her booming voice filling the room. "This comes as a complete shock to me. I knew Mr. Hayward as an outstanding member of my staff. I was deeply saddened by his supposed death and have no reason to believe he was anything but loyal to me and the school. But a member of the James-Younger gang? Those men were cutthroats, thieves, and murderers. I don't know how to reconcile the Frank Hayward I knew and this . . . what did you say his real name was, Hattie?"

"Charles Mayfield." I'd read it on the news-paper cutout of the James-Younger gang portrait.

"Yes, and this Charles Mayfield fellow," Mrs.

Chaplin said, finishing her thought. "You did say he denied any involvement in violence of any kind?"

"Yes," I said. Yet I wasn't so certain; there was still the scar on his face to explain.

"And he was quite young at the time," Miss Woodruff said, adding to his defense.

"And he showed considerable remorse for putting everyone through such pain," I said, looking directly at Miss Woodruff. She lowered her eyes to the floor as she lifted her handkerchief to her face once more. "He saw the opportunity and took it. He didn't consider the consequences. He didn't know of any other way."

"And if we atone, we all deserve forgiveness for our mistakes," Miss Woodruff said. She lifted her head high. "Isn't that right, Mrs. Upchurch?" Mrs. Upchurch's cheeks burned red. Shamed into silence, she merely nodded.

"*C'est vrai, ma chère*," Madame Maisonet said. "It is true."

We all looked at Mrs. Chaplin, waiting for her verdict.

"Well, then," Mrs. Chaplin said, as if that concluded the discussion.

"Speaking of transgressions," I said, noticing out of the corner of my eye that Mrs. Upchurch blanched in anticipation of my comment. "May I enquire about the fate of Miss Gilbert?" Without looking at her, I heard Mrs. Upchurch sigh with relief. Her husband wasn't going to be the topic of conversation.

"If you're asking in your polite and discreet manner whether I'll be turning her in to the police, Miss Davish, the answer is no," Mrs. Chaplin said. "I have, however, encouraged Miss Gilbert to seek employment elsewhere."

"Then what about the president's position?" Miss Woodruff asked. Mrs. Upchurch blanched again, her dimples nearly disappearing.

The poor woman, I thought. This is torture for her. Why had she even been invited to tea? And then I got my answer.

"Obviously I will come out of retirement and run the school myself until my successor can be properly trained."

"Your successor?" I asked.

"*Oui,* it is a good decision," Madame Maisonet said, nodding her approval. "You choose well, Madame Chaplin."

"Yes, well, I'm undoing a grievous mistake. I obviously hired the wrong Upchurch in the first place," Mrs. Chaplin said, indicating the blushing woman across from her with her hand. Mrs. Upchurch smiled meekly.

Miss Woodruff's hand flew to her chin. "Mrs. Upchurch?"

"Yes," Mrs. Chaplin said. "She's more than competent. She needs some specific guidance from me, of course, but then I'll be able to rest easy knowing Mrs. Chaplin's School for Women is in good hands." I recalled how she'd organized the funeral and the lake party, had done her husband's book work, and was a genuinely amiable person; not a single staff member or student I spoke to had said a bad word about her. I smiled at Mrs. Upchurch. Mrs. Chaplin had made a good choice.

"Congratulations," I said, knowing how difficult it would've been for the wife of an embezzler to succeed anywhere else. If not for this opportunity, Mrs. Upchurch would be at the mercy of any relatives she might have, or worse.

And Mrs. Chaplin has an excuse to come out of retirement, I thought.

"Thank you, Miss Davish. It's an honor and a challenge. To tell you the truth, I'm quite excited to begin. If I've learned nothing else from your visit, it's that we women can overcome our past, face challenges gracefully and succeed."

She learned that from me? I thought, blushing at her compliment.

"Don't be so surprised, Miss Davish," Mrs. Chaplin said, reading my mind. "You know you're quite capable to inspire." Before I'd a chance to refute her comment, Mrs. Chaplin continued. "Speaking of, what are your plans now, Miss Davish? Off on the grand tour with a millionaire writing his memoirs? Taking dictation for a debutante who'd rather flirt than put pen to paper?

Helping some business magnate conquer the world one typewritten memorandum at a time?"

"Or?" Miss Woodruff added, winking at Mrs. Chaplin. "Do you plan to trade your typewriter for an apron and settle down? I've heard you receive daily letters from a beau, a doctor no less!"

"Ah, mademoiselle, you did not tell me!" Madame Maisonet chided.

Even as I blushed again at the mention of Walter and the possibility of a future together, I wondered how Miss Woodruff had learned about my letters from him.

Maybe Mr. Putney at the hotel likes his gossip a bit too much, I thought.

"Miss Mollie Woodruff," Mrs. Chaplin said, "I'm surprised at you. You make it sound as though you'd recommend this outcome."

"Wouldn't you? What woman wouldn't prefer marrying and settling down to having to work every day for a living and worry about her future?"

"A Chaplin girl, that's who. I train my girls to be independent in body, mind, and spirit. Not to pine after any man that will pay the bills. Beau or no beau, our Miss Davish isn't going to put away her typewriter without a fight. She's one of us. She's a Chaplin girl. We make our own way in the world, don't we, Hattie?"

"Yes, we do but . . ." I wasn't sure if I

completely agreed with Mrs. Chaplin. I did draw immense satisfaction from my work, but I loved Walter too.

If only there was a way to have both, I thought, careful to keep the thought to myself.

"But you were married once, Mrs. Chaplin," Miss Woodruff said.

"Yes, Miss Woodruff, I was and can therefore speak from experience. Wouldn't you agree, Madame Maisonet and Mrs. Upchurch?" Madame simply nodded and smiled.

"Yes, I'm afraid I do," Emily Upchurch said. "As you all know, being married didn't stop me worrying about the future. Asa was a good provider and a generous husband, but at what cost? I actually envy you and Miss Davish."

"Why?" Miss Woodruff and I said simultaneously.

"Because you both have your whole lives ahead of you. You don't know what the future holds. It's quite exciting to think about, really."

"It is indeed something to envy," Madame said.

"But the past?" Miss Woodruff said, obviously thinking about Frank. "How do we overcome the past to face an uncertain future?"

I looked to Mrs. Chaplin, who sighed deeply but remained silent, her tea turning cold in her lap. I looked to Mrs. Upchurch who, despite her earlier declaration, seemed hesitant and unsure. She took a bite of the lemon shortbread instead of answering the question. Madame Maisonet stared at me over the rim of her coffee cup. And then I looked at Miss Woodruff who, with her hand covering the scar on her chin, sat tall in her chair, expectant.

I pictured my typewriter, locked in its case and propped against the desk in the library at Lady Philippa's summer home in Newport.

"With diligence, faith, and love," I said, as the other two women nodded. "With those we can accomplish anything."

"*Oh là là là là là là,*" Madame Maisonet said. I glanced at Mrs. Chaplin; she beamed with pride. "You have become quite the philosopher, mademoiselle."

I should've blushed again as the other women laughed, but I didn't. I wasn't embarrassed by what I'd said. I knew I was right.

"There's my girl," my father said the moment I walked in the door. He had left Mr. Van Beek to finish the display they'd been working on. "Come here, Hattie," he said, a broad smile on his face as he waved for me to approach. "Where have you been, my girl? I didn't think I could wait much longer."

"What is it, Father? I came straight home from school."

He wrapped his arm around my shoulder and led me to the counter. "I know, I know. I'm just an impatient man. I couldn't wait to give you this." He danced around the counter and reaching under, lifted out a large square box. It was wrapped in brown paper and embellished with a wide white satin ribbon.

"For me?" I couldn't keep my eyes off of it. I couldn't remember the last time I'd been given such a gift. I'd always received books, dolls, or sweets for my birthday and at Christmas. But this was special. "It's not even my birthday."

"No, I couldn't wait until your birthday."

"Father! What is it?" The anticipation now was unbearable.

Then the shop bell rang and I thought I would cry. My father would have to serve the customer before he'd allow me to open my present. A rotund man in a top hat entered as I flung myself onto a nearby stool.

"Mr. Van Beek, would you be so kind as to help Mr. Hardin find what he needs?"

Mr. Van Beek coughed to cover his astonishment before leading the gentleman to the latest in top hats. I did nothing to hide my surprise and joy.

"Oh, thank you, Father!" I said, leaping from the stool into his arms. He lifted me off the ground and twirled me around, before setting me before the gift. Mr. Van Beek cleared his throat and Mr. Hardin frowned.

"Sorry, gentlemen, I apologize for the

outburst. Not every day you change your daughter's life."

He snatched up the box and headed to the back room. I dashed after him. He set it down on the little table we dined on and we both stared down at it.

"Well, aren't you going to open it?" I tugged on the bow and carefully removed the ribbon, it in itself a gift. And then I peeled back the edge of the brown paper.

"Oh, come on! Put some muscle into it, Hattie," Father said, yanking at the paper. In a frenzy, we both ripped off the wrapping, revealing a shiny black case beneath.

"What is it?"

"Unlatch it and find out."

With my thumb, I pushed open the silver latch and lifted the lid. Beneath was a machine, of shiny metal, glowing white lettered keys and highly polished wood. It was the most beautiful thing I'd ever seen.

"But why, Father?" I asked, running my finger over the words on the typewriter's black paper label. It read, REMINGTON.

"Now that you're about to finish school, I've been thinking about your future."

"But Nate and I—"

"You'll find a good husband, Hattie. I have no doubt about that, but as your father, it's up to me to provide for you now. But men are fallible and I never want a daughter of mine to have to worry about her future. We're not quitters, you and me, but with this, you can do anything."

I was speechless. He was right. In an instant, my father had changed my life.

"I love you, Father," was all I could say as I threw myself into my father's waiting arms, wishing I could stay there forever.

Center Point Large Print
600 Brooks Road / PO Box 1
Thorndike, ME 04986-0001 USA

(207) 568-3717

US & Canada:
1 800 929-9108
www.centerpointlargeprint.com